SAMANTHA

Panting heavily, she made her way to the
window to twitch the curtains across,
shutting out the purity and the intense loneliness
of the country night.

But, her hand on the heavy velvet, she paused
and stared out into the gloom.

Was that a woman running? She could
scarcely see. There was just that dark glimpse
of bundled skirts, hair streaming and two arms
flung wide. Then the form disappeared into the
shrubbery and it was difficult to be sure
whether she had seen it or not. The night was
so still. Now nothing moved at all . . .

Samantha

Dorothy Eden

CORONET BOOKS
Hodder and Stoughton

First published in Great Britain 1960 by
Hodder and Stoughton Limited

Coronet Edition 1964
Sixth impression 1976

Printed in Great Britain for
Hodder and Stoughton Paperbacks, a
division of Hodder and Stoughton Ltd,
Mill Road, Dunton Green, Sevenoaks, Kent
by Richard Clay (The Chaucer Press) Ltd
Bungay, Suffolk

ISBN 0 340 01733 3

SARAH shivered and drew her cloak more closely about her. The summer house had broken panes of glass in the windows, and the wind blew through in a cold stream. It was rapidly growing dark. Because the trees were leafless, it was possible to see the house. Already lights were blooming in the windows. Sarah could identify them as she stood there, shivering and waiting.

There was Lady Malvina's glowing boldly, with no curtains drawn, probably because she had forgotten to ring for Bessie. She would be nodding in front of an enormous fire (her room was always grossly overheated) with her capacious skirts spread about her and her cap askew. But presently, refreshed by her nap, she would wake to renewed vitality, and probably go to the nursery to thoroughly awake and excite Titus with one of her ferocious games. Eliza winced when she heard her approach. She said privately that Lady Malvina would be the death of her, if not of Titus first.

In contrast to Lady Malvina's uninhibited glow of light, Amalie's windows showed a mere chink between the heavy curtains. Amalie, unlike her mother-in-law, seemed nervous of the outside darkness. She was always starting at something, always looking over her shoulder. Her thin bright anxious face was seldom relaxed. She was constantly watching her husband. Because she loved him too much? Because she was afraid he did not feel a similar affection for her? Whatever it was, the next window, Blane's (one wondered if the communicating door was ever opened into Amalie's bedroom) was in darkness, for Blane's restlessness—a restlessness that was curiously different from Amalie's, and was caused, of course, by guilt—kept him constantly on the move, and seldom indoors.

At the far end of the second floor the nursery window was alight, Sarah noticed with relief, for Titus, like his mother, disliked the dark. Eliza must have obeyed instructions and given him his tea and seen that the fire was in. She must go soon, Sarah reflected, for Titus would be waiting for her. He was a nervous highly-strung little boy, who got into fevers of apprehension if things went wrong. There was also that ridiculous fancy he had about the mouse which was lurking in the cupboard in the nursery, ready to spring when the candles were out. Since Sarah had discovered the little boy's private nightmare she had made a point of seeing that he always had a night light.

If James Brodie didn't come soon she couldn't wait. What adequate reason could she produce for prolonging her walk after dark? And Titus would be waiting for her, as well as the household dressing for dinner. She would have to scramble into her dark-blue tarlatan, making an even quicker change than Blane did. For Blane spent little time over his evening toilet, and seemed to look with some derision at Amalie's elaborate appearance. Probably never in his life before had he dressed for dinner, nor been in a position to.

He was an unscrupulous impostor, Sarah thought angrily. Presently, when James Brodie appeared, she would surely be in possession of at least one piece of indisputable proof which would enable her to unmask him.

Dear Miss Mildmay, [Brodie had written]

On instruktions from Mr Ambrose Mallow who I last seed in Trinidad, I have a packet to deliver to you concerning matters you are deeply interested in. If you will communikate with me at the George and tell me where I can safely hand to you the said packet, it not to be trusted to the post, I will do my best to oblige.

Your obed'nt servant,
James Brodie

The wind was rising and rags of thundercloud, blacker than the approaching night, drifted across the sky. Sarah looked apprehensively into the darkness, and at last heard footsteps approaching.

'Mr Brodie?' she called eagerly.

But her voice could not have been heard, for the man who

6

strode forward and seized her roughly, exclaiming, 'Amalie, why do you moon by the lake in midwinter? What are you up to?' was Blane.

Simultaneously, he realised his own mistake.

'You!' he exclaimed, in a voice of deep hostility, and the hard grip of his fingers on her arm held her there.

In a moment James Brodie would arrive with the letter from Ambrose that was too private and important to be entrusted to the post. It was too much to hope that Blane would respect its privacy. Already he was deeply suspicious of her. She had cleverly improvised reasons for other awkward situations, but it seemed as if this one would defeat her. She was lost . . .

It seemed months, now, since that day when she had paced restlessly about Aunt Adelaide's drawing-room, waiting impatiently for news from the court. News that either declared Blane Mallow the impostor they all believed him, or confirmed his story as true.

Aunt Adelaide had lost patience with her.

'For goodness' sake, child, sit down. You're driving me mad. Fiddle, fiddle, fiddle, all the time. Can't you keep still?'

'I'm sorry, Aunt Adelaide. I'm so nervous. The result of the case must surely be known by now.'

'And none of your fidgeting will make any difference to it. Come away from that window and get out your embroidery.'

'There's a cab now.'

Sarah was peering into the street. Already the fog was making it as dark as night, and the lamplighters had begun their rounds. The sound of horses' hooves approached and passed. It was not Ambrose. In any case, why should she think Ambrose would instantly come to her with the news? Indeed, the jury might not come to a decision until the next day, for there had been so much conflicting evidence. Never would Sarah forget Lady Malvina in the box, with her great arrogant nose thrust forward, the cabbage roses on her bonnet nodding to her reiterated affirmatives. Nothing would shake her evidence. The blackbrowed adventurer in the box, whose arrogance matched her own, was her son, her long-lost son Blane Mallow.

Aunt Adelaide clucked impatiently.

'I suppose you're wishing you were in the courtroom again yourself, looking at that scoundrel.'

Sarah gasped.

'How did you know I've been there?'

'I don't *know* anything because I'm not told,' her aunt retorted tartly. 'But your shopping and your supposed teas with your sisters this week have been very prolonged occasions. From which you have returned looking a great deal more animated than conversation with those exceedingly dull creatures would warrant. No, no, child, don't look at me so accusingly. I haven't questioned the coachman.'

'Lady Malvina must have been telling lies,' Sarah burst out. 'She stood in the box and swore that that impostor was her son, although Ambrose says Blane never had features like that, or that impudence. He was a gentleman.'

'And this man is not?'

'Decidedly not. He was laughing all the time. Oh, not openly. But you could see the shine in his eyes. And one dimple would come into his cheek——'

'Dimple?'

'Well, cleft, or whatever one calls it in a man's cheek,' Sarah said impatiently. 'But it was as if he was laughing inside all the time. At his mother—if she *is* his mother—at the judge, at Ambrose, at everybody. He knew he was running circles round them, with his plausibility.'

'All this,' said Aunt Adelaide consideringly, 'doesn't make him not a gentleman. He speaks like one, I take it?'

'That can be learned, surely.'

'By a clever actor, yes. Even a clever actor would give himself away now and then. Did you never detect a slipped "h"?'

Sarah shook her head with more impatience.

'Then he may have been a gentleman of a sort. Perhaps he has constantly been in the company of gentlemen. But Blane Mallow I am sure he is not.'

Aunt Adelaide gave her niece a shrewd, assessing glance.

'Could it be, my dear, that you believe this because you have every reason to be prejudiced against him?'

Sarah gave an alarmed exclamation.

'Aunt! You haven't told anybody about Ambrose and me?'

'Of course I haven't. Though I told you secret engagements aren't to my liking.'

'But it's all because of this wretched Blane Mallow that it has to be a secret,' Sarah burst out. 'You know very well Ambrose can't afford to marry me if he doesn't inherit Mallow Hall. Under any other conditions he must marry an heiress. I love him far too well to stand in his way.'

'Your feelings could be misjudged, my dear.'

The colour rose indignantly in Sarah's cheeks.

'I know that very well. People could say I was very ready to marry the new Lord Mallow, but not Ambrose Mallow without a title who must make his own way. They could say I was marrying him to be the mistress of Mallow Hall. But that isn't true. I just wouldn't encumber him with a penniless wife, if he is poor himself.'

'So all in all,' Aunt Adelaide said reflectively, 'it becomes very important that this man is denounced.'

'I wish I could do it myself!' Sarah declared feelingly.

'I believe you would if you could.' The old lady tapped her fan thoughtfully. 'You at least have plenty of spirit. I shall never cease to wonder how you alone of that clutch of girls your parents produced have any spirit. Or looks, if it comes to that.'

'Thank you, dear Aunt Adelaide,' Sarah said warmly. There was a very deep bond between the two women. The older woman's astringency and humour appealed to Sarah, as Sarah's somewhat daring and rash behaviour did to her aunt. She was born ahead of her time, Aunt Adelaide thought. But little harm that would do, for the present generation of simpering, swooning, meek, timid young women she could not abide. Something seemed to have happened to the good English stock. She never remembered this excess of false modesty in her youth. But things had begun to change when that brash young creature, Victoria, had come to the throne, and even more so when she had married her stiff-necked dreary Albert. Now everything was pretence and disguise. The very table legs were concealed. No one had bodies. Somehow, and prolifically, babies were produced, but apparently in some strange state of amnesia, for every decent woman shut such thoughts out of her mind.

Yet the sly meek creatures, Aunt Adelaide thought, had developed the art of catching a man to an almost sublimated degree. It was done somehow beneath downcast eyes and such a look of innocent virginity that the wonder was every man was not frightened off to the South Pacific or far-off China to look for a warm-blooded uninhibited bride.

Thank heavens Sarah was too honest and spirited for all this posing. She loved and frankly wanted Ambrose Mallow, and made a secret of it only because of this tiresome litigation as to the ownership of Mallow Hall. How extremely inconvenient it had been of Blane Mallow to arrive home just at this moment, after an absence of twenty years. It was so inconvenient as to be highly suspicious.

No one entirely believed he had come because of seeing the advertisements for him which had been printed in almost every paper on the face of the globe. He couldn't have become conscience-stricken about his widowed mother. He was not the man, popular opinion declared, to have a conscience. On the other hand, he was most definitely the type of man to be an adventurer, a seeker after easy reward, title and position. He may also, conceivably, have been born a gentleman, for there was arrogance and confidence in every inch of him.

But Lady Malvina's son? Heads were shaken sceptically. How could that foolish garrulous posturing woman have got a son like this?

The paradox was that she had identified him unhesitatingly, she had swept aside his strange lapses of memory about certain events, and declared only that he was her son. As added and indeed indisputable proof, there was the little boy, the five-year-old child of this assumed impostor. If his father, to all other people, had changed beyond recognition, this child was the living image of the very good portrait painted by Josiah Blake thirty years ago of Blane Mallow at the same age.

In this way the evidence became overwhelming, and it seemed that Ambrose, because of the return of the rightful heir, would lose Mallow Hall. And poor Sarah with her vivid stubborn face would lose Ambrose.

'Did anybody recognise you in court?' Aunt Adelaide went on, eyeing Sarah sharply.

'Oh, good gracious, no! I stayed right at the back. Even Ambrose didn't know I was there.' She began to giggle with reminiscent mirth. 'James was quite horrified when I asked him to wait for me outside a courthouse! But the dear faithful creature obeyed. Oh, no, Aunt Adelaide, no one saw me. I wore my grey cloak with the high collar that I drew right across my face. I expect I was thought to be an unknown admirer of the claimant. Heaven forbid!'

'I believe you enjoyed yourself, you shameless girl!'

'Indeed I should have if it hadn't been a matter touching myself so deeply. It was a most novel experience. And the wife, Aunt Adelaide. I wish you could have seen her. The deceitful thing, with those great eyes opened so wide, so innocently. She must have known the truth, if anyone did.'

'Is she beautiful?' Aunt Adelaide asked interestedly.

'She's thin and sallow, not like English women at all. I suppose it's from living in tropical countries. But she has a queer brilliant look. I don't know how to describe it. Perhaps she is beautiful.'

'They sound a well-matched pair.'

'Oh, indeed. They well look as if they could scheme together. Yet when the judge asked her questions it was all meekness. Yes, my lord. No, my lord. As if lightning would strike her dead if she told a lie.'

'How would she know if her husband were not what he said he was?'

'He may always have deceived her,' Sarah conceded.

'But why? Until this opportunity presented itself, presumably by seeing the newspaper advertisement, would he ever have heard of Blane Mallow and Mallow Hall?'

'No, I suppose he wouldn't. So that means his wife is as guilty as he.'

'If he is guilty.'

'Oh, he is! I know he is! There were so many questions he couldn't answer, obvious ones. They were excused because of this fall he once had from his horse, getting concussion badly. But it was a too convenient excuse. If it were not for his mother, who isn't to be swayed, he would have been in trouble long ago.'

'And the child,' Aunt Adelaide added thoughtfully.

Sarah frowned.

'Yes. There is the child. It's very strange about the child.'

A little later Ambrose arrived. He flung off his cloak, handing it to a maid, and came striding into Aunt Adelaide's drawing-room. One look at his face told Sarah his news.

'He's won!' she whispered.

'Yes, he's won.' Ambrose made belated greetings to Sarah's aunt, then flung himself angrily into a chair. In contrast to his cousin Blane, he was fair, with rather pale thickly-lashed eyes and a slight stature. He was fashionably dressed, and had an elegance that Sarah found intensely pleasing. He belonged at Mallow Hall, there was no doubt of that. He would have been an ideal master, and his life, for the last ten years, when it seemed that Blane was surely dead in some foreign country, had been shaped to that end. True, he had continued his studies and been called to the bar, but only because he was an earnest young man with few frivolities. Indeed, so far, falling in love with Sarah, the third daughter of a destitute gentleman, had been his only frivolity. Now it seemed that if he wished to live in suitable style, with a house in town and his own carriage, he must sacrifice Sarah and find a wife with money.

It was an impossible position, and he was bitterly angry and aggrieved about it. It should not have happened at the last minute like this when his succession to the title had seemed certain. Moreover, it was doubly galling when he was so convinced that this fellow from the West Indies was an impostor.

But how to unmask him?

'It was my aunt, Lady Malvina, who finally swayed the jury,' he said. 'She stuck absolutely to her story that this fellow is her son.'

'She wanted him to be,' Sarah said indignantly.

'Exactly. Now she can live at Mallow Hall, all her debts will be paid, everything is fine. She knows it would have been quite different if I—and you, my dear Sarah—had been the new owners.'

'No one knows about me,' Sarah said quickly. Her eyes rested in anguish on Ambrose's pale angry face. There was no denying it, secretly, as well as being Ambrose's wife, she had longed to be the mistress of Mallow. Why had this wretched thing had to happen?

'You aren't bound to consider me,' she went on, making herself speak the painful words. 'That was always understood. I set you free, if you wish it.'

'But I don't wish it, my love.'

'Tut, tut!' said Aunt Adelaide. 'Sarah has been indiscreet enough already. She should now have her position made clear.'

'You must marry an heiress,' Sarah told Ambrose earnestly. 'It's the only way.'

'If your own father, Sarah, had not been so irresponsible,' put in Aunt Adelaide, 'you, too, could have been an heiress. As well as your stupid sisters who, I might say, need a dowry much more than you do, my dear.'

Sarah was too honest for modesty or shame.

'I've told you that my father was a desperate gambler,' she explained to Ambrose. 'He lost all his fortune and my mother's as well. That's why I've been dependent on dear Aunt Adelaide. But now I must make some sort of a future for myself.'

'With me,' said Ambrose firmly.

Sarah's face began to light. Then sadly she turned away.

'No, that can't be. There's no way.'

'Yes, there's no way,' Aunt Adelaide agreed. 'Unless you're both content to live in obscurity. That, I promise you, neither of you will be. Ambrose has lived for the last twenty years in the belief of inheriting a fortune. And, if Sarah will allow me to say so, I know her better than she does herself. She's not meek or self-sacrificing. She's too strong-willed. Oh, I warn you, Ambrose, even with an estate Sarah would not be an easy wife. But as a contented housewife in poor circumstances—no, a thousand times.'

Sarah's chin went up.

'Be quiet, please, Aunt Adelaide. All she means, Ambrose, is that I, like my father, am a gambler. I do love you, but what might I do to you? Besides, you deserve so much better than struggle and poverty.'

Ambrose had appeared to be detached from the two women's conversation. He was looking into the distance, his eyes narrowed and thoughtful. He was so handsome, Sarah thought with a pang. A little austere, perhaps, but with all the signs of good breeding. So different from the buccaneerish look of that impostor in court.

'You're both wrong,' he was saying in a dry, cool voice. 'There is a way out of this trouble. I'm sure there is. But you, Sarah,' his eyes flew up suddenly, taking her off her guard by their intensity, 'will have to help me.'

'What can I do?'

'You can help prove this man an impostor.'

'Why, I'd like to, Ambrose. Nothing would give me greater satisfaction. But the judge and jury have made their decision. Whoever would believe a British jury at fault?'

'They've made their decision because of the weight of evidence. Evidence this scoundrel has had months, perhaps years, to prepare.'

'But he has a certain look of your cousin Blane, hasn't he?'

'Vaguely, as far as one can remember. But there are too many discrepancies, too many things he forgets and conveniently attributes to his amnesia. My Aunt Malvina, whatever her ulterior motives, helped him over the worst patches. So did the head groom Soames. I never did trust him, and he knows where he would be if I became master of Mallow. Can you explain Blane forgetting the day I locked him in one of the attics? I left him there until long after dark and he came out as white as a sheet. It's the first time I'd seen him frightened.'

'Why was he frightened?' Sarah asked.

'Because that was the room where a maidservant once hanged herself. She was—in trouble. Oh, a long time ago, in my grandfather's time. But they say that room has been haunted since.'

Sarah had a brief recollection of the tall black-haired man standing so straight and arrogant in the courtroom. Had those piercing black eyes ever held fear? She had a moment of complete incredulity that this could have been so.

She did not comment directly on Ambrose's statement. She said in some perplexity, 'Why did you do that to your cousin?'

Ambrose's voice held unrestrained bitterness and dislike.

'Because he deserved it. He was always fooling about with the maids himself.'

'He was only sixteen,' Sarah said involuntarily.

'But a grown man.'

'Tut, tut,' said Aunt Adelaide. 'The question doesn't seem to be why Ambrose did this curious thing to his cousin, but why his cousin shouldn't remember it. Did he flatly deny it had happened, Ambrose?'

'No. He was too clever for that. He said perhaps it had. But that so many extraordinary things had happened to him since, a few hours in a presumably haunted room were merely trifling. Anyway, he said in that mocking way of his, who believes in ghosts in these enlightened times?'

'So the question was cleverly evaded.'

'Yes. But I saw he couldn't remember. Just for a moment he looked quite blank. Then there were the names of servants that he couldn't remember, his classmates, the master who taught him Latin . . .'

'On the other hand,' said Aunt Adelaide drily, 'he could describe Mallow Hall to the last detail.'

'Oh, Lady Malvina could have coached him on that. He must have had other accomplices besides. This is the task ahead of us now, Sarah, to unmask these people.'

'Wasn't it the task of the prosecuting counsel today?'

'No, not at all. That's just a detached courtroom scene. These things can only be done by someone who lives with these people and watches them day by day to catch them out in small things. That's the true way to build up evidence.'

'And who is to carry out this extraordinary task?' enquired Aunt Adelaide. 'Are you going to bribe the butler, or one of the maids?'

'One of the maids, yes. In other words, you, my dear Sarah.'

'Me!' exclaimed Sarah in astonishment.

'Yes, you. For you say you won't marry me if I'm a pauper.'

'You're not a pauper, Ambrose. But no, I won't marry you and ruin your future for lack of money. I'm quite determined about that.'

'Then there's this other thing you can do for me. For us both.'

'Spy!' whispered Sarah.

'It would be very simple. I know already that they want help

16

with the little boy. Blane—I mean the claimant—had the nerve, when the verdict was announced, to invite me to drink with him. To his good fortune, if you please!'

'And you did?'

Ambrose grimaced.

'One has to behave outwardly like a good loser. All the time I was longing to wring his neck. We had a pint of ale at the Three Crowns. I had to listen to his impudent plans for the future. The family intends to move down to Mallow Hall almost immediately. They think the country air will be better for the child, who isn't strong. Since he's too young yet to be sent to school, he's to have a governess. It was then that the idea came to me.'

'That I should go?' Sarah cried. 'But—granted I must now begin to earn my own living—how am I to get the opportunity to find out anything if they know of my connection with you? They'll be doubly on their guard.'

'But they won't know of it. No one will tell them. Fortunately we've kept our attachment a secret. Only you and I and Lady Adelaide know of it.'

'She's been visiting the court every afternoon,' Aunt Adelaide put in. 'If she was noticed, won't she be recognised again?'

'Sarah, you fool!' Ambrose exclaimed.

Sarah's colour rose. She defended herself heatedly.

'But I would never be recognised again. I was right at the back among all those gaping people, and I kept my collar high round my face.'

'But what on earth made you go there?'

'Because it was my future at stake as well as yours.'

Ambrose's voice grew softer.

'It was, of course. Though you could have trusted me to report the proceedings to you.'

'I wanted to watch those people. They fascinated me.'

'Fascinated?' The quick suspicion was in Ambrose's voice.

'In a repellent kind of way. They lied so smoothly, as if it were second nature to them.'

'Then you didn't believe them?'

'Of course I didn't. Not even Lady Malvina. Although she is

your aunt, Ambrose, I couldn't trust her one inch.'

'She prefers a stranger at Mallow,' Ambrose said bitterly. 'She's always disliked me. It wouldn't surprise me if she concocted the whole plot herself, except that she isn't clever enough.'

'She talks a great deal,' Sarah said thoughtfully. 'One could encourage her in that. Sooner or later she must say something significant.'

'That's exactly what I mean. If you were in the house day after day you must discover things.'

'Listen at keyholes?' Sarah said distastefully.

'In what better cause, my love. Don't you care enough for me to want to right this injustice?'

'You know very well that I do.'

'All this plotting,' said Aunt Adelaide disapprovingly, 'isn't quite seemly.'

'Ah, Aunt, hush! I believe Ambrose is right. This is what we must do.' Sarah was growing excited and enthusiastic. Life since her father had died and they had been so poverty-stricken had seemed without zest. Then she had met and fallen in love with Ambrose, only to find that brilliant future also taken from her. The prospect she had faced, if this case were lost, of obtaining a position as companion to some perhaps eccentric and bad-tempered elderly lady, such as her sisters had been forced to do, was bleak in the extreme. But the kind of position Ambrose suggested would be entirely different. It would be stimulating and perhaps a little dangerous. She would be able to pit her wits against that impudent black-browed impostor and his sallow-faced wife, and also against the garrulous Lady Malvina. She would be living in that beautiful old house which should have been her own. And indeed one day would be, if she were skilful enough. Yes, Ambrose's idea was a brilliant one. It appealed to her enormously, even though the thought of it also made her heart flutter nervously. She did not know how good an actress she could be. But she had inherited her father's gambling spirit. She would not be easily deterred.

'Then you've recommended me to the new Lord Mallow?' she asked.

'Oh, no, I've not been as indiscreet as that. You must appear to be a complete stranger. You know of the family only by reading this celebrated case. You have taken a great interest in its outcome and congratulate them on its success. Knowing their child is five years old you are sure they will be requiring a governess. The rest, my dear Sarah, is up to you. I'm sure you're clever enough and charming enough to be successful.'

It was Aunt Adelaide who expressed shocked disapproval.

'And what, Ambrose, may I ask, will you be doing while my niece belittles herself in this way?'

Ambrose smiled faintly.

'I, dear Lady Adelaide, will be on my way to the Caribbean. I intend to arrange a passage at once.'

'To the Caribbean!' Sarah exclaimed. 'You mean to find what evidence you can there? But a deputation has already been.'

'I'm aware of that. And I'm not saying they didn't discover evidence. Superficial evidence. That would have been there by plan. But this investigation requires something more. It requires a dedicated interest. Did it matter to the deputation who eventually owned Mallow Hall, whether it was this stranger or myself? Not in the slightest.'

'None of the cross-examination could shake Thomas White-house's evidence,' Sarah pointed out.

'Exactly. Yet this same Thomas Whitehouse has been remarkably elusive. Each time I've discovered where he's staying he has moved, and today, at last, when I thought I had run him to earth, I found he had just sailed for Trinidad.'

'Already? With the jury not back!'

'His part was done. It was advisable to get him out of the way quickly, no doubt with a fat fee in his pocket.'

'Ambrose, you mean his evidence has been false? That he has not known Blane since he arrived as a boy in the West Indies twenty years ago? But I thought the deputation who went to Trinidad completely verified that.'

'Then why is Mr Whitehouse so elusive? Why have I never been able to talk to him? Because he isn't such a good liar after all? I promise you I'll run him to earth in his own country. And not only that. I'll discover other evidence. There are things I mean to search for. Blane Mallow's tombstone, for instance.'

'Heavens!' gasped Aunt Adelaide. 'Do you think he's dead?'

'He could be. I don't know.'

'Then if that's so, this scoundrel and his wife must be denounced.'

'The little boy's name is Titus,' Sarah said inconsequentially. Ambrose's eyes narrowed angrily.

'It was my grandfather's name. I wonder if he was called it at birth, or only recently.'

'But there's his extraordinary likeness to that portrait. Everyone agreed on that.'

For the first time Ambrose showed uncertainty.

'I admit that. It's the strongest piece of evidence they have. It's difficult to explain. But there must be an explanation,' he added decisively, 'and I intend to find it. With your help, Sarah. You won't refuse to help?'

'Spying!' muttered Aunt Adelaide, with the greatest distaste.

'I have no references,' Sarah said. 'No one is employed by respectable families without reference.'

'I won't comment on that word respectable,' Ambrose said in a scathing voice. 'But I agree that these people will intend to behave in the most correct way. Therefore I'm sure your aunt will be happy to give you a reference, Sarah.'

'A forgery!' exclaimed Aunt Adelaide, scandalised.

'Is it a forgery to say that Miss Mildmay has been with you for the last eighteen months and is of the most pleasant disposition? Of course it isn't. Come, Sarah. Kiss me, and tell me that you're with me. Are you going to be my wife or not?'

Sarah hesitated the merest second. Then she went happily to receive the brush of his lips on her cheeks. It was such a little kiss. And there would be months, and the seas of the Caribbean between them before she could be kissed properly, as a husband kisses his wife.

But she was immeasurably heartened by Ambrose's definite action, and the future was full of excitement. As reckless now as Ambrose, she could pay no attention to Aunt Adelaide's disapproval.

3

OUTSIDE the house in South Kensington, built in the new fashionable area, another carriage drew up. It was dark now, and Lady Malvina, peering through a parting in the heavy curtains, could not see who alighted. But it must be Blane. Blane? She nodded her head slowly, looking sly and satisfied. What a fine figure of a man he had grown. Tall, handsome, a little swashbuckling. Just the type of man she secretly admired. So different from his cousin, that narrow-minded disapproving dandy Ambrose.

She would never forget the moment when the news had been brought up to her that her long-lost son Blane was downstairs waiting to see her. She had gone down in the greatest trepidation. She could not admit to anyone, not even pompous old George Trethewey, her late husband's solicitor, that she was an old woman now, and had almost completely forgotten what her wild young son had looked like twenty years ago, or indeed how he could be expected to look now.

She was in such a state about the unexpected arrival that she would scarcely have had the wit to reject him even had his skin been black! But the moment she set eyes on the little group waiting in the hall, she knew.

For there was the little boy.

The breathless maid, stupid Bessie with never a brain in her head, had omitted to tell her that not only the man claiming to be her son but his wife and child were downstairs.

Lady Malvina had taken a perfunctory look at the dark thin young woman in the unsuitable too-thin travelling cloak and rather shabby bonnet. She had not, at the moment, spared much more than a glance for the tall man at her side. Because the little boy, dark-haired, pale and quiet in his travelling clothes, clutching his mother's hand and looking at her with the blankness of exhaustion, was her baby over again. That much was perfectly clear to her. It was as if, miraculously, the years had rolled back and she was young and gay, as she had loved to be, and the mother of a perverse, high-spirited, difficult but enchanting little boy.

'Oh, my little darling! Come to me!' she exclaimed, reaching out her arms.

The child shrank back. Lady Malvina did not realise what an alarming figure she must have made, swooping down like this in her voluminous dark-purple gown, with her lace cap nodding on an elaborate erection of stiff grey curls. Protuberant pale-blue eyes, a large haughty nose, and a mouth that seemed, when she smiled so welcomingly, overfull of yellowed teeth, were not reassuring to a nervous child.

'His name's Titus,' said the tall man. 'Have you nothing to say to me, Mamma?'

'Titus!' said Lady Malvina happily. 'You named him for his grandfather.'

The little boy cast a swift unhappy glance at his mother. He seemed about to speak, but the young woman quickly drew him to her, partially concealing his face in her skirts.

'My husband decided on his name, ma'am,' she said primly. 'I confess I thought it an odd name for a little boy. But then my husband has talked incessantly about everything English for so long.'

'Mamma,' said the tall dark man, 'this is my wife Amalie. Or should I say'—he hesitated a moment, as if testing the atmosphere—'the new Lady Mallow.'

An expression of triumph passed fleetingly over the young woman's face. Then her eyelids dropped, and she curtseyed demurely.

Lady Malvina decided at once that she did not like her. A sly ambitious miss. What was her background? Where had Blane picked her up?

Blane?

At last, in her state of bemused excitement, she looked fully into the features of the tall man beside her.

Brilliant dark eyes, magnificent black brows, a nose as arrogant as her own, an expression of inscrutability and—could it be amusement? Skin burned dark with seawinds or tropical suns, a spare strong body with, at this moment, a kind of lazy lounging grace.

Was this the hot-tempered boy who had quarrelled so violently with his father and run off to sea, never to be heard of again?

She was too confused to decide, or to care about making a correct decision. She only knew she most urgently wanted her son home. It was a matter of vital importance.

Everyone had said for years that Blane must certainly be dead. His father had reiterated it with gloomy anger until the day of his own death. Admitted, Blane had a violent temper, and as a boy was impulsive and thoughtless. But no grown man would turn away from an inheritance such as his. Had he been alive he would have returned home ten, fifteen years ago, and made his peace.

Now his father had been dead a year, and the legal machinery had been set in motion to have Blane also assumed dead. So that the correct cold ambitious young man, Ambrose Mallow, who would bring neither shame nor glory to the name, should inherit.

Lady Malvina, for various reasons, had stubbornly refused to admit that this must happen.

And now, like an answer from heaven, this handsome black-browed stranger stood in front of her.

Why should she hesitate to acknowledge him?

'Blane! My dearest son! Welcome home!' she cried.

Later, of course, there had to be the endless questions, for the trustees of the estate, pompous intolerably stupid George Trethewey, and Martin Lang, demanded certain proof that this man, arrived as if he had dropped from the sky, was indeed Blane Mallow. The triumphant evidence of the small scar beneath his left ear, acquired after a fall from his horse, was not sufficient. Anyone, they said dourly, could have a scar. And against this were the man's strange lapses of memory. Vital things seemed to be forgotten where quite irrelevant ones were remembered.

When acquiring the scar he had also suffered a fairly severe case of concussion which, several doctors in consultation agreed, could produce amnesia. But it was a curious amnesia, lightened by flashes of complete memory. As an impostor, he could never have seen Mallow Hall. Shown a plan of it, he could identify each room, even to the attic rooms. Yet later in court he had no recollection of being locked in the supposedly haunted room, a terrifying experience for any child. He could name his schoolmasters and several of his school fellows, and described journeys taken to the seaside and with whom. He unhesitatingly identified his old nurse, but this lady was now so old that she herself suffered from an amnesia too great for her evidence to be of any worth.

The trustees considered the estate too valuable for a decision to be lightly given. A claim must be made and heard in a court of law. A deputation must be sent to the West Indies, from which the man claimed to have come, and evidence sought there. For the purposes of the child Titus's succession, proof of the marriage to Amalie must be produced.

It all took an endless time, and Lady Malvina was beside herself with impatience. Why couldn't they all go down to Mallow and live normally? This was her son and her grandson. Surely that she should say so was sufficient. Surely the final unanswerable proof was sufficient—the astonishing likeness the little boy bore to the portrait of Blane at the same age.

No, there didn't seem to be much doubt about the outcome, especially since the claimant had conducted himself with such superb almost impertinent confidence.

The marriage to Amalie had taken place in a small church, started by a quite respectable Anglican missionary, in Trinidad, and this was duly proved. Amalie was the daughter of a sea captain and a young Spanish woman from Teneriffe. Unfortunately she was not all one would have desired, but she had a certain vivid handsomeness, and a wish, so far at least, to be the kind of English wife of whom Lady Malvina would approve. And her crowning achievement, of course, was producing the next heir to Mallow Hall, the little boy who was the image of his father, and bore his grandfather's name. This surely made his father's claim incontestable.

Now, peering out into the foggy gloom, Lady Malvina saw

the tall figure of the man she had, for the past few months, been calling her son. Wheezing a little as her heart palpitated with excitement, she hurried to ring the bell. When Bessie appeared she said eagerly, 'Tell Lord Mallow I would like to see him at once.'

Then she plumped up the cushions in her overheated sitting-room and sat down to wait.

This she had not long to do. Presently the door swung open and the young man strode in.

'Well, Mamma, thanks to you, we won.'

He stood in front of her fireplace, very tall, very confident, full of triumph. If he were not her son, she thought confusedly, she would dearly like to have such a son. He made all his contemporaries look languid and anaemic.

She was equal to the moment. For she, too, had her triumph. Now she could return to Mallow Hall. How soon, she wondered, could she tactfully request her son to pay her debts?

'Blane, my dear, I'm so happy! Not that I doubted for a moment. Truth must be acknowledged.'

'It can also be twisted. My cousin Ambrose would have liked to do that.'

'With his crafty legal mind! And you realise I might have lost my home to him?'

'Yes, we all realise what you haven't lost, Mamma.'

The deep voice, full of amusement and significance, made Lady Malvina lift her head haughtily.

'And you, too, my son.'

Blane began to laugh, his head thrown back, his laughter hearty and uninhibited. Reluctantly, because she was still so unsure of him, she joined in. Then the humour of the situation struck her, and her raucous voice sounded above him.

'What are we laughing at?' she demanded at last.

'The fact that all our differences are over. You've forgotten what an unpleasant child I was, and you're truly happy to have me home.'

Lady Malvina nodded, quiet for a moment.

Then she asked, 'Have you told your wife?'

'Not yet.'

'But you must. She must be even more anxious than I. Bring her up here. We must have a celebration. Ask Tomkins to put some champagne on ice. We might give Titus a glass. It wouldn't hurt the child.'

'Lord, no. It wouldn't hurt him. And he shares the celebration. After all, he's the heir.'

'Yes,' said Lady Malvina with intense satisfaction. 'The heir.'

'You won't have him running off to sea, Mamma.'

'Not if I can help it. Not that it doesn't seem to have done you some good.' She put her head on one side, studying his splendid figure. He wore his black frock coat and striped neckcloth just that much better than any other man she had seen, with a certain casual air that suggested the clothes were important, but subtly less important than the form they covered. He would have all the young women swooning. Did he make his wife swoon? One couldn't tell what went on behind her secretive face. It was a pity she was not some nice English girl to whom one could talk and grow fond of.

'Do you remember Maria?' she asked suddenly, at random.

'Maria?'

'The gamekeeper's daughter. With the fair curls.'

She saw that he did not remember. His eyes had gone blank.

'Although you were only fourteen you wanted to marry her,' she said slowly. 'You loved her deeply, you said.'

'Mamma, if I remembered all the girls I've imagined myself in love with——'

She shook her head stubbornly.

'One usually remembers the first. But it was before your accident, certainly.'

'Then let's not think of Maria when Amalie's waiting impatiently.'

'No, go and get her and Titus. I want to see my grandchild.'

He turned to obey. He had reached the door before she called to him. He paused, standing there in the richly appointed room that had been built exactly to her late husband's requirements, with marble sculptured in Italy for the fireplace, an elaborately carved and gilded ceiling, and woodwork of the finest mahogany. A great deal of money, time and loving care had been put into this house. It would not be pleasant, Lady Malvina was thinking involuntarily, if it were to be occupied by an impostor.

'What is it, Mamma? You wanted to ask me something?'

'Are you——' her voice was thick and uneasy. 'Tell me, are you really my son?'

He came to kneel before her. He offered his face to the full glow of the gaslight. She could look as closely as she wished at the unfamiliar lean brown cheeks, the superb brows, the long high-bridged nose.

The nose was her own, surely ... The boy she remembered had had dark eyes. But had they been of such intense brilliant darkness as these? Had that unformed sixteen-year-old face given promise of this bony splendid structure? The colouring, the scar beneath the left ear, the look of arrogance—that was all. It was absurd that a woman should bear a child in the greatest agony and then live to be unsure of his identity.

But if this was not Blane, who was it? And what did he want?

A shiver of fear went over her. She saw a ruthlessness she hadn't previously noticed in his mouth, a moodiness in his eyes. She spoke sharply to cover her sudden foolish nervousness.

'Order the champagne. We need it. We need gaiety, a celebration. Fetch Amalie and Titus. Titus must come, even if he's been put to bed. His grandmother needs him.'

The man straightened himself slowly. He stooped to print a kiss on Lady Malvina's hot and fretted brow.

'Thank you, Mamma,' he said gently, and left the room.

4

SARAH dressed with the greatest care. She had to look like a gentlewoman, though an impoverished one. There was not too much difficulty about that, for none of her clothes was new. Indeed, she had not had a new gown for two years, just before Papa had died. Then he had come back from St Tropez in fine fettle, an infallible sign that he had been lucky at the tables. All the girls had been permitted to get new gowns, and Mamma had had the drawing-room done out in one of the modern wallpapers, a deep-maroon colour with a rich gilt design. It was a little like one the Queen had chosen for her new country house at Balmoral. One of the Queen's ladies-in-waiting, who was a cousin of Mamma's, had told them so.

But within a month of that apparent beginning of better times Papa was dead of a chill, and they were all in mourning. And there was almost no money.

From that time, the two eldest, Amelia and Charlotte, had positions as companions to rich elderly ladies, and Sarah had been taken under Aunt Adelaide's wing. Aunt Adelaide had thought to find her a husband, but Sarah, after being annoyingly pernickety about several suitable young men, had chosen to fall in love with Ambrose Mallow who was now as impecunious as herself.

It wasn't fair! Sarah told herself. She had scarcely slept for sorrow and indignation, and now the very thought of this turn of luck that had snatched hers and Ambrose's happy future from them made the colour deepen indignantly in her cheeks.

She must remain calm. She could not present herself to the new Lady Mallow looking flushed and irresponsible. She must remember to keep her eyes lowered, and not to answer her ladyship as if she were an equal. Not only an equal, she thought indignantly, but a superior. For who was this woman, straight from the West Indies, as anonymous as someone picked at random from the streets. That was where she would go back,

Sarah told herself vigorously. In a very short time it would be herself interviewing applicants for positions at Mallow Hall. And the first person to be dismissed would be that sly villain Soames, the head groom, who in court had put words into the impostor's mouth.

The impostor—but in the meantime she would have to learn to call him Lord Mallow. She would keep her eyes downcast and murmur meekly, 'Yes, my lord. No, my lord.' Ambrose confidently expected her to act the part, and she would show him she could.

Excitement made her impatient to hurry with her dressing and set out on the way. To make her unbidden visit even more plausible she had the newspaper which had reported the result of the trial very fully, and a gossip columnist had interviewed Lord Mallow himself.

'Lord Mallow,' the infuriating chit-chat informed her, 'intends to travel to Mallow Hall on the Kentish coast early in the week. He is looking forward with the greatest pleasure to displaying his childhood home to his wife, and, of course, to its heir Titus, named after the fourth baron. Lord Mallow has not yet made any plans for his son's education. He is too young, as yet, for Lord Mallow's old preparatory school, and it seems likely a governess will be employed.'

The fact that the columnist was playing into her hands failed to console Sarah for this smug and triumphant statement. But she had enough sense to cut the piece out and slip it into her reticule. It could be produced if the genuineness of her application was doubted.

She had to confess to some perhaps malicious interest in seeing Blane's wife at close quarters, and more than a little interest in the child, with his reputed famous likeness to the portrait in Mallow Hall.

She had brushed her hair smoothly back from her round young forehead, and arranged it in a cluster of curls at the back. She preferred not to wear the demure forward-falling curls that were in fashion, but to display her ears and the clear line of her cheek. This made her look a little older and more responsible, she thought with satisfaction. Her face, looking so serious now in the little upturned mirror on the dressing-table, had no great beauty. Aunt Adelaide had repeatedly told her her charm lay in animation, and then, trying to cope with Sarah's high spirits, had requested a little less animation. But her eyes, wide apart, and of a curious smoky blue, were most distinctive, Aunt Adelaide conceded. A little less colour in her cheeks would have been desirable, but at least she would not have need to resort secretly to the rouge box.

Sarah herself wished she did not look quite so robustly healthy, for all her slim waist and narrow shoulders. It was so much more fashionable to be pale and languid. She could have wished, too, for more regular features and the stateliness that her sisters, Amelia and Charlotte, possessed. However, in spite of all this, Ambrose had fallen in love with her. Dear Ambrose. She would achieve the required stateliness when she became Lady Mallow.

From her modest wardrobe she took her bottle-green merino day dress, and wore over it the grey felt cloak trimmed with black velvet that could not be more suitable and discreet. Her black velvet bonnet with green silk ribbons completed this picture of respectability. She looked at her reflection and sighed. She dearly loved pretty clothes. The prospect of perhaps several months of this drabness was infinitely depressing.

She was putting on her gloves when Aunt Adelaide bustled in to say that Ambrose was downstairs.

'He means to see that you carry out this mad scheme,' she said.

'Did he think I would lose my courage already?'

'I don't know what he thought, but what I think is that you've both lost your senses.'

'You don't really, Aunt Adelaide. You approve of us fighting for our rights.'

'But not in an underhand way.'

'What other way is there? We must use our enemy's own weapons.'

Aunt Adelaide sighed deeply.

'Then here's one of them. The reference I've perjured myself to write for you.'

Ambrose, waiting downstairs, was full of excitement. He had been down to the docks and contacted the captain of a schooner to sail in two days' time for Trinidad and other West Indian ports. He could have a passage if he wished, and the captain promised him a journey that might be completely dull and uneventful, or full of the drama of hurricanes, becalmings or even attack by pirates.

'But, Ambrose!' Sarah cried in alarm, 'is there danger? Then must you go? What use will either Mallow Hall or a title be to you if you lie at the bottom of the Caribbean Sea?'

Ambrose laughed, gratified by her dismay.

'The fellow was only showing off. Of course there's no danger. Or what there is,' his face hardened, 'if Blane could face it at sixteen I can do the same at twenty-six.'

'You're to sail so soon!'

Ambrose tilted her chin.

'In two days you yourself will be on the way to Mallow. Now tell me, are you ready? You haven't lost courage?'

'Only for you, and the thought of those hurricanes.'

Ambrose laughed gently.

'Would you like me to come part of the way with you in the cab? It wouldn't be wise for me to go all the way.'

'No. I shall go alone.'

'Remember, you must succeed.'

Sarah met his gaze levelly. She didn't think she had noticed that stony look in his eyes before. For a moment it almost frightened her. He was so determined. And supposing, at the very outset, she failed.

She straightened her shoulders.

'I won't fail.'

He took her hand and smiled, and the bad moment, the moment of wondering whether Ambrose was not the person she had imagined him, was over.

'The cab's waiting outside. Are you ready?'

The fog had lifted, but only to show a low grey sky and the still shapes of trees to which the tattered leaves still clung. It was very cold for October. It was going to be a hard winter,

Sarah thought, and she wondered how draughty and uncomfortable Mallow Hall might be. Ambrose said his uncle had let the place fall into disrepair. But the new family, coming from the tropics, would surely take precautions against the cold, and see that the Atlantic winds were shut out. Anyway, Sarah herself would not be there long. She would quickly discover incriminating evidence against this man calling himself Blane Mallow. She would have to listen at doors, and perhaps try to read other people's letters. As Aunt Adelaide had said, it would be distinctly unpleasant. But it was in the cause of right and justice, and must be done. For Ambrose's sake much more than for her own, she did not dare to think of failing.

The cab jogged across London, skirting Hyde Park and then proceeding down the Brompton Road. It was a longish journey, and the driver was glad enough to wait outside the house in South Kensington to rest his horse. Sarah said she would not be more than fifteen minutes. Nervousness had brought the colour to her cheeks again. The cabby was quite ready to trust the vivid face lifted to him. Despite her sober clothes, his passenger had the voice of a lady, and she smiled at him. She knew that he had a miserably chilly job in winter, sitting up there in all weathers, and that his bones got aches just as well as finer people's. Her warm smile told him all that. It was nice for once to be treated as a fellow human being.

'I'll wait, miss. God bless yer.'

This comforting voice following her up the steps kept Sarah's courage high. But when the front door swung open in response to her ring, and the solemn-faced butler stood within, panic filled her.

It had been all very well to invent this scheme and talk blithely about it. But now she was faced with reality, and the whole thing seemed completely crazy.

However, here she was, and the butler was asking her her business.

She straightened her shoulders.

'I should like to see Lady Mallow,' she said firmly.

The butler stood aside for her to enter.

'Take a seat, if you please. I will enquire if her ladyship is

32

available. What is the name, please?'

'Miss Sarah Mildmay.'

The butler bowed and withdrew. Sarah had scarcely time to look round the hall with its fine marble staircase, its tapestries and statuary, before there was a commotion. A little boy dressed in outdoor clothes was running down the stairs pursued by a stout untidy old woman with flying grey curls and lace cap askew.

'The great grizzly is catching you! G-r-r-r! G-r-r-r! Run for your life. Or he'll hug and hug you to death.'

The child flung himself into the arms of a nursemaid who had come running down the stairs in their wake, and the old woman collapsed, panting, into the nearest chair.

'Well, Titus! Wasn't that a fine game? Don't you love to play with your Grandmamma? Now off for your walk. Where's his hoop, Annie? Isn't he to take his hoop?'

'We didn't mean to go far today, your ladyship, it being so bleak. His mother said he wasn't to catch cold.'

'Bah! He's got to be made tough. This is England, not the tropics. Little boys here go out in all weathers. I won't have my grandson pampered.'

'No, your ladyship,' said the maid, hastily taking the child's hand and departing to the door.

Lady Malvina fanned her face vigorously, still gasping and panting noisily.

'Pampering him!' she muttered. 'Making him cry at his own shadow. Never knew such a nervous child.' She looked up and suddenly saw Sarah. 'Who are you?'

Sarah bowed.

'I'm waiting to see Lady Mallow.'

The old lady's prominent pale-blue eyes flicked knowledgeably over Sarah's sober and genteel appearance.

'If you're wanting something, I warn you my daughter-in-law has a sharp tongue in the mornings. And she's been besieged by all sorts of people since the case. You know of the case, of course?'

'Yes, my lady.'

Lady Malvina nodded contentedly. She was obviously a

33

garrulous lonely old woman, ready to talk to anyone who would listen.

'It's brought me great happiness. My son and my grandson home again. But they're spoiling the child. Not my son, but my daughter-in-law, Amalie.' She looked at Sarah in a friendly way. The rice powder showed white in the creases of her plump crumpled cheeks. 'Would you like a word of advice, my dear?'

'Thank you, my lady.'

'Flatter her if you want something. That's the only way.'

The butler had returned silently, and stood before them, his controlled face showing no sign of having overheard anything. 'Her ladyship will see you in the morning-room. Come this way, if you please.'

Lady Malvina gave a flippant wave of a fat beringed hand. Sarah resisted an impulse to wave back. She sensed in Lady Malvina an ally, if an irresponsible and unpredictable one. But she would have to check these unruly noisy games that terrified the little boy. Tactfully, that would be her first task.

If she were employed ... 'Flatter her,' the old lady had said. Already prejudiced against the unknown Amalie, this thought filled Sarah with repugnance. The confidence with which she had arrived was rapidly ebbing, and by the time the butler had flung open a door and ushered Sarah in, she was almost tongue-tied.

The woman sitting on the couch beside the fire rose to her feet.

She was, Sarah saw at once, very elegant. Her gown was obviously new and too rich for morning wear, her hair, done in an elaborate arrangement of curls, was uncovered. Although her dress was the height of fashion with the crinoline skirt exaggeratedly wide, she made no concession to the custom of wearing lace caps indoors. Her hair was no doubt her chief pride, for her face and figure were a little too thin, and her skin quite sallow. Her eyes were bright and restless, her nose too sharp.

Sarah decided at once that she would not be an easy person to handle. She was already extremely conscious of her position as Lady Mallow.

In response to Sarah's greeting she said frigidly,

'Yes, Miss Mildmay? You wished to see me? What society is it you represent?'

'None at all, Lady Mallow. I'm sorry if I gave you that impression.'

'Oh, it's only because I've been so bothered by representatives for various charities. As soon as one's name becomes prominent, one seems to represent easy game for all these people. Not that I don't approve of honest and properly sponsored charities,' she added righteously. 'Then what is your business, Miss Mildmay?'

'I'm seeking a position,' Sarah said, trying to sound meek, and to keep the eagerness out of her voice.

'Here? In my house?'

Sarah opened her reticule to take out the newspaper cutting.

'It says here that you will be requiring a governess for your son. I took the liberty of calling in person because I'd so much like the position. I have excellent references——'

The woman cut her short with an angry gesture.

'Really, Miss Mildmay, this is the greatest impertinence. In the first place, why didn't you come to the servants' entrance?'

Sarah flushed.

'In England, Lady Mallow, a governess is considered one of the family.'

Now she had said the wrong thing, she realised. Her quick indignation and lack of meekness were going to be her downfall. (But why should she have to go to the servants' entrance of her own house? Even for Ambrose she would not do this.)

'I don't require to be told what is the custom in England,' Lady Mallow said icily. 'Certainly not by any strange person.'

'I didn't mean to do that, Lady Mallow.'

But the hasty meekness and the downcast eyes were too late.

'Whatever your newspaper correspondent tells you, Miss Mildmay, I am not looking for a governess for my son. He's too young. But even if I were, I assure you that someone who had gained entry by false pretences would have no hope of getting the position.'

35

'Won't you look at my references, Lady Mallow?'

'Importuning me will get you nowhere.' She was pressing the bell. When the tall butler appeared she said, 'Tomkins, show this—lady out.' The deliberate impertinence of her voice made Sarah furious.

Quite apart from having to go home and tell Ambrose she had failed, she would not tolerate being spoken to like that by an upstart from the West Indies who was only learning to be a lady. And making a very bad showing at it, too. She was so conscious of her lack of knowledge that she would grow angry at an imaginary slight, such as an applicant for a position not coming to the servants' entrance. Poor thing, one should be sorry for her.

But Sarah, watching her draw the black Spanish lace shawl over her narrow shoulders as if she were cold, and lifting her thin nose in the air, could feel only fury, and a wild disappointment. She was almost in tears.

Ambrose, she thought as she followed the stately form of Tomkins down the stairs, could still make the voyage to the West Indies and conduct his private investigation. But was she to wait helplessly until he came back, contributing nothing? Oh, it was too infuriating.

As they came into the downstairs hall, however, there was a commotion. The front door had burst open, and the elderly nursemaid with the child had come in. The little boy was not in tears, but his wan white face showed that these were not far off. Indeed, as Lady Malvina, who must have lingered downstairs, pounced forward with loud cries of surprise and greeting, positive panic showed in his face.

'What is it, Annie? What is it? Why are you back so soon? My little love, couldn't you bear to be away from your Grand-mamma?'

'It's not that, my lady. It's too much champagne last night,' Annie said bluntly, her voice full of bold disapproval.

'But that didn't hurt him!'

'He's feeling poorly, my lady. Sick and poorly. I'm taking him right up to bed.'

'Tch! Tch! Tch!' Lady Malvina exclaimed loudly. 'Come to

Grandmamma, then!'

But as she stretched out her arms to engulf the small boy he seemed to panic completely, and making an unexpected dart sideways flung himself against Sarah, clinging to her skirts.

Whether he had intended to do so or not she couldn't tell. But as his large dark eyes were lifted to hers she saw them full of entreaty. She could not help herself. She lifted him into her arms and immediately he clung to her as to a refuge.

'Titus!' exclaimed Annie in a scandalised voice. 'You can't behave like that to a strange lady. Now come to me and we'll go upstairs.'

The child clung harder, resisting her attempt to take him. Lady Malvina came bustling up to wave her fan wildly in his face.

'Titus, you naughty little love, come to Grandmamma.'

Titus buried his face tightly against Sarah's neck, and muttered desperately, 'I won't!'

'I think,' Sarah tried to speak tactfully, 'you frighten him a little.'

'Frighten him! Frighten my own grandson! When I love him with every fragment of my being. What arrant wicked nonsense! Tomkins, who is this young woman?'

Before Tomkins could reply a door at the end of the hall opened, and the tall dark man whom Sarah had last seen in the witness box in court came striding out.

'What's going on here? What's the reason for all this noise? Annie, if you can't manage the child we'll have to find someone who can.'

'Annie has the impertinence to say that too much champagne has made the boy ill,' Lady Malvina said indignantly. 'As if the little he had could have hurt a fly.'

Sarah, feeling the little body clinging to her as if instinct had driven him, interjected clearly and calmly,

'If you have been giving a child of five champagne, I agree entirely with Annie. No wonder he's ill.'

'And what the devil do you think you're doing?'

'I'm comforting your son who seems to need it.'

'Well, I'll be damned! Who are you?'

Sarah did not flinch from his regard. Now at last she was close to this man and could see the face that hitherto had been at the other side of a badly-lit courtroom. In selfishness and conceit it was all she had decided, and more. The haughty black brows, the moody eyes, the thin cheeks scored with lines, showed signs of intolerance and an exceptionally strong will.

But, holding his gaze, something stirred in Sarah, something jubilant and excited. For she recognised an adversary worthy of her. Here was a battle worth fighting. She could despise Amalie with her petulant temper and her fear of not having correct deference paid to her. But this man she could both admire and hate.

She said calmly, 'My name is Sarah Mildmay. I've just been asking your wife, Lord Mallow, if I could be given the position of governess to your son. Unfortunately, she said you didn't intend engaging anyone at present. If I may express my own opinion, your son is at an age where he requires more instruction and guidance than a nursemaid, no matter how capable'— she flashed a placating glance at the indignant Annie—'can give.'

Blane Mallow (as she must call him until she proved once and for all that that was not his name) stepped back a pace to regard her. His eyes were narrowed, their expression unreadable.

'And why, may I ask, have you my son in your arms? Are you attempting to gain his affections?'

'No, he ran to me.'

'Yes, he did that,' Lady Malvina admitted fairly. 'For some reason he flew to this young woman.'

'I've told you to behave more quietly with him, Mamma. He's not a strong child. What do you think?'

Sarah realised that the abrupt question had been directed to her. She felt the little boy's arms tighten round her neck. His heart was beating against her breast like a bird's.

Unconsciously her voice softened.

'Yes, he is too nervous. He needs gentleness. And time to become accustomed to such different surroundings, of course.'

'Ha! You've been reading the case.'

'Who hasn't?' said Sarah calmly. 'Indeed that's what brought me here. I've followed it with such interest. And when the newspaper reported that you would require a governess, I took the liberty of calling.'

'But my wife would have none of you?'

Lord Mallow's mouth seemed to be twitching slightly. Sarah couldn't decide whether it was in amusement or anger.

'I was perhaps too impetuous?'

'You have recommendations?'

'Oh, yes indeed. From Lady Adelaide Fitzsimmons, to begin with, and——'

Her guess that this forthright man would not want to bother with written references, but would make his own decisions as to character, was right. Those brilliant black eyes, without gentleness, but also without hostility, examined her frankly.

'Mamma, Titus seems to like this young woman.'

'Heaven knows why!'

'A child has an instinct to feel protected. Perhaps that quality in Miss Mildmay——'

Before the slightly ironic voice had finished there was a cry from the stairs.

'Blane, what are you all doing down there? Is there something wrong with Titus?'

Blane looked up the curving staircase. He stepped back to give a slight bow.

'Titus, my love, is suffering from too much *joie de vivre* last night. But he seems to have shown some acumen in choosing for himself a governess.'

Amalie came running down the stairs. Sarah could hear her high indignant voice.

'Blane, not that young woman who forced her way in! But I've already dismissed her.'

Blane went forward to meet his wife at the foot of the stairs. He took her hand.

'I think, my love, that perhaps you made a premature decision. Miss Mildmay seems to be an excellent person, and since the newspapers tell us Titus requires a governess, a governess we must have. Public opinion is of a good deal of importance in England.'

'Blane! How ridiculous! You never cared a fig for public opinion.'

'Perhaps not. But for the sake of our son—and of you, my love—In any case, as you see, Titus has made his own decision.'

'You can't tell me you are going to engage a servant'—again the insolent deliberation of Amalie's words made Sarah hot with fury—'on the passing fancy of a child.'

'It's the child who will have to see the most of her,' her husband retorted. 'However, we'll perform the usual conventions. Perhaps, Miss Mildmay, you'd be good enough to step into the library and have a talk with me. Titus, go to your nurse.'

The little boy wept softly into Sarah's neck.

'Titus!'

The stern voice was one he recognised and interpreted correctly. It would tolerate no disobedience.

A small shiver went over his light thin body. Sadly he detached himself from Sarah and held out his arms to Annie. She snatched him into hers and hastened upstairs, muttering inaudibly.

Blane bowed slightly.

'This way, Miss Mildmay.'

In the book-lined room where a fire burnt cosily, repeating its glow in the highly polished furniture and shiny leather-bound books, Blane waved her to a chair.

'The boy's spoilt,' he said abruptly.

'He seems a nervous child.'

'Nervous? Is that what you'd call it? Perhaps. I know nothing about children.'

Sarah bit her tongue, refraining from pointing out that he had had five years in which to learn. But perhaps he had been away at sea too much. Or was not interested in children. Or secretly regretted that his son was not stronger and more manly.

'A tropical climate is not good for a young child,' Sarah said primly. 'Titus will grow much stronger in England.'

'And grow to love the Atlantic winds rather than the Caribbean?'

The man's eyes were ironic. It was almost as if the prospect of turning his son into a hardy English child amused him. Perhaps memories of his own childhood had not been entirely pleasant. Since he had run away at sixteen—No, it was not this man who had run away. This man had had a secret childhood somewhere else, but one that had driven him, also, to become an adventurer. Sarah must keep reminding herself he was not Blane Mallow, otherwise of what help was she going to be to Ambrose?

'I want Titus to form an affection for Mallow Hall,' he went on. 'I've wandered too much to care a great deal for any one place. Besides, my childhood at Mallow, with a father who was a tyrant, doesn't leave me with the happiest memories of the place. But Titus is the heir. It would be a good thing if he came to love the place. I want him to be a greater comfort to his mother than I ever was to mine.'

Was the man a complete hypocrite? It seemed so.

Yet the keen regard he now bent on Sarah seemed to have more than a degree of honesty.

'But we came in here to discuss you, not Titus, Miss Mildmay. We must go through the right motions. I intend you to join our household. You have firmness and initiative. I like that. You will be excellent for Titus. Frankly, although I can see you are of the greatest respectability, I wouldn't care who your family or your last employer was. I decide on character alone.'

'Thank you, sir,' Sarah murmured.

'But for the sake of satisfying my wife's curiosity, tell me something of yourself.'

This was the hardest moment of all, improvising, while the alert regard of those black eyes was bent on her.

'My father is dead, Lord Mallow. He had misfortune in business matters, and left my mother very poorly provided for. Consequently, my sisters and I have had to seek positions.'

She did not mention the amount of the fortune which her charming profligate father had squandered. She thought fleetingly of her mother shutting up the house in Richmond, selling the elaborate furniture that was too large for the country cottage with which she was left, bidding a sad farewell to all the servants but elderly Martha who would stay with her, and shedding tears over the fashionable gowns and furs that had to be discarded with her old way of life. Now Mamma's only prayer was that somehow, by the kindness of heaven, her daughters would make good marriages. She was so eager about this that Sarah had insisted to Aunt Adelaide that her attachment to Ambrose be kept the closest secret. Otherwise Mamma would have the news whispered in every drawing-room in London.

Though not now that Ambrose also was reduced in status to a struggling barrister, Sarah reflected ironically. It was as well, after all, that Mamma's hopes had not been raised.

'I have been with Lady Adelaide Fitzsimmons for the last two years,' Sarah went on, knowing that this man's confidence in his own judgment would prevent him from any desire to take up her references. If he should do so, Aunt Adelaide would be more than equal to the occasion.

The one danger she had foreseen was that, during her employ, some former acquaintance of hers might visit the house and recognise her. But down at Mallow Hall this was not likely. Nor was it likely that her former friends would be on visiting terms with the upstart Lady Mallow and her impostor husband. As far as she knew, with the case pending, they had not been received anywhere, and public opinion had been strongly in favour of Ambrose.

'Do you mind my observing that no one looks less like a governess?'

Sarah had kept her face prim and her lashes lowered. Now her eyelids flew up guiltily to meet again his frank and impudent scrutiny.

'I can't help my appearance, Lord Mallow.'

'Don't apologise for it. It's quite as satisfactory as your references. Can you begin tomorrow? We leave for Mallow the following day, and the journey may be tiresome. It would be better that Titus grows a little used to you in advance. He's not a good traveller.'

There was no doubt that Blane was disappointed in his nervous delicate son. The child, of course, sensed this, and the trouble was heightened. What a selfish insensitive person he was. Couldn't he at least pretend to show affection for the poor baby?

'Yes, I could be ready, sir,' she answered meekly. 'If your wife wishes it, also.'

'The decision, Miss Mildmay, is mine.'

Sarah fought to hide her active resentment and dislike. Amalie had aroused no admiration in her, but did she deserve this contemptuous disregard for her wishes? This man was impertinent, lordly, patronising, selfish and, though perhaps unwittingly, cruel. She would take the utmost pleasure in spying on him and eventually denouncing him.

'I shall be happy to pay you whatever you were receiving in your last position,' he went on.

'Thank you, sir.'

'If that isn't sufficient you have only to tell me.'

'It is quite sufficient, thank you, sir.' She had no intention of letting him throw Ambrose's money about indiscriminately.

'I'd advise plenty of warm clothes. If Mallow is as I remember it, it's devilish cold in winter.'

Sarah stood up to leave.

'Thank you, sir, for trusting me.' The treacherous words escaped her without her realising their import.

He gave a half smile. His eyes remained brooding.

'On the contrary, the boot's on the other foot. Thank you for trusting me. So far, as you must realise, very few people have.'

Sarah's cheeks were still flushed uncomfortably with the knowledge of her deceit as she left the house.

But almost at once triumph at her success filled her. She had done what Ambrose expected of her. He would be delighted.

She found herself nodding conspiratorially to the cabman, and he winked back, grinning broadly, showing his rotting teeth, and the unquenchable merriment of his eyes.

'All safe and snug, miss?'

Amalie, the new Lady Mallow, would have stiffened with indignation and suspicion had a cabby chosen to show any interest in her welfare. Sarah repressed her regrettable tendency to laugh from amusement and sheer light-heartedness.

'All safe and snug, thank you. Now drive me back to

Portman Square, if you please.'

The recounting of her experience to Aunt Adelaide and Ambrose was even more satisfying.

'I am to be ready in two days' time,' she said, 'to go down to Mallow Hall. We are all moving there for the winter.'

'*We!*' Ambrose echoed in the greatest indignation.

'We must face facts, Ambrose. I am to be one of the household now.'

'Not for long, I swear.'

'For just as long as it takes you to return from Trinidad so that we can prepare our separate evidence.'

'Having spoken to him, you still believe this man is not Blane Mallow?' Aunt Adelaide enquired.

'Of course he isn't. He has the look of the complete adventurer. All I wonder is how the jury could have been so misled.'

'A jury has to decide a case on evidence. The evidence in this matter was unassailable.'

'Seemed so,' Sarah corrected. 'There's a simple answer. Lady Malvina is concerned for her own comfort, and ridiculously sentimental about her grandson. Blane—I should say his impersonator—is an ambitious adventurer, and his wife is worse. She has ideas about her social status. She is really, beneath her pretended sophistication, quite ignorant.'

'My darling child!' cried Aunt Adelaide. 'If all this is true, you can't go to live with people like that. Especially not to work for them.'

'Oh, tush!' Sarah exclaimed. 'It will do me no harm, and the little boy needs care and affection. Between them all, they're turning him into a scared little shadow. Champagne at his age, indeed!'

Aunt Adelaide gasped. Ambrose said gloomily, 'It's no more than I expected. Think what people like that will do to Mallow Hall.'

Sarah nodded.

'They must not be allowed to stay there a moment longer than necessary. But I'll soon get into Lady Malvina's confidence, I promise you. Amalie, I'm afraid, is my enemy already.'

44

'And the man?' Ambrose enquired stiffly.

'Oh, he can act the part of gentleman. But we've already crossed swords as to the way he's allowing his son to be brought up.'

'Then why did he allow you to be engaged?'

Sarah gave a small retrospective smile.

'I think I was a challenge to him just as much as he was to me. And there was the little boy clinging to me. Perhaps even he wasn't hard-hearted enough to resist that.'

'Sarah, you almost make me believe you're as innocent as you sound,' Ambrose cried exasperatedly. 'Have you never looked in your mirror?'

Sarah opened her eyes in astonishment.

'You mean he might have admired me? That he might have ideas of—of seduction?'

'He's a blackguard, isn't he?'

'But not in that way. Not as far as we know. After all, he's respectably married. No, Ambrose, we must be fair. And if it should remotely come to that, I can take care of myself. Can't I, Aunt Adelaide?'

'Nothing,' said Aunt Adelaide, 'would surprise me about this man. But I admit if you hadn't the spirit to do something about this miserable affair I'd have been very disappointed in you both. I wish you luck. Though if Sarah has the least trouble with her employer, she is to pack her bags and come home at once.'

'And,' said Ambrose, his eyes as hard as stone, 'I shall kill him.'

5

AMBROSE would not allow Sarah to come to the docks to see him sail. Under the circumstances they must not risk being seen together, even in such an unlikely place.

So they said their farewells in Aunt Adelaide's drawing-room, that lady thoughtfully leaving them alone for a precious twenty minutes.

Ambrose was dressed for travelling. His face was thin and pale and serious, and there was already a dedicated look in his eyes.

'How long shall you be away?' Sarah asked. All her excitement had evaporated, and she was filled with nothing but loneliness and a persistent feeling of apprehension.

'There's no telling. Perhaps three months, perhaps six, or even twelve.'

'And I must stay at Mallow all this time?'

'Unless something happens to make that impossible. If they should discover what you are up to, for instance, or if, for any other reason, their behaviour can't be tolerated.'

'I will tolerate it.'

'No, my love, you mustn't go beyond reasonable bounds. Even for me.'

Ambrose smiled, but Sarah privately wished that his smile had had more warmth and tenderness. Always a serious young man, since the outcome of the case he seemed to have lost his remaining youth. He had now only this look of coldness and determination.

'And remember, I will communicate with you when possible.'

'Telling me everything you discover,' Sarah begged.

'That I could only do by personal messenger. I couldn't risk a letter falling into the wrong hands. Then the fat would be in the fire.'

'But I must hear from you,' Sarah cried. 'Supposing you're

away a whole year!'

'That's unlikely, but if so you must be patient. Think of our reward. Our rights established.'

Sarah smiled at last.

'I shall secretly pretend I'm mistress of Mallow all the time.'

'But with the right master.'

'Ambrose, there's no need to remind me of that!' Nevertheless, a quick picture sprang into her mind of the dark-browed man she had last seen sprawling at his ease with all the confidence of ownership in the firelit library. It would be difficult to oust his memory from any house he lived in, especially after several months of ownership. He was not a nonentity.

'Ambrose,' she cried urgently, 'come back as quickly as you can.'

'I shall surely do that. And I shall send you news when possible.'

He added, 'If anything of importance happens to you, or you discover evidence such as letters or documents which will help our case, communicate with me at once.'

'You mean I'm to steal documents!'

'It isn't likely that our clever opponent will leave anything of any significance lying about, but if he does, yes, you are to steal it. Or let us say, borrow.' Ambrose gave his faint smile that was intended to be reassuring. 'Don't look so alarmed. Would you rather do nothing, accept this injustice?'

'Oh, no! I'm as determined as you,' Sarah declared. But for a moment that queer unreasonable feeling of apprehension had touched her again.

'Although I can't help thinking,' she added, 'that it would be simpler if you were simply to marry an heiress, after all.'

The bitter intolerant look sprang into Ambrose's eyes.

'And let this impostor win! As well as lose you.' (She had only imagined the last part of his sentence was a little belated.) 'I love you Sarah. You must wait for me. I'll be back as soon as possible, and all will be well. Now I must be off. The ship sails at full tide.'

For a moment he clasped her in his arms. His cheek was cool against hers. If it hadn't been for the tightness of his embrace

47

she would have thought him only half with her, even then, the other half already in the hot sunshine of the West Indies, intent on his revenge.

Sarah's only other farewell was to her two sisters, Amelia and Charlotte. They were full of excited chatter about her new position, and also perhaps a little maliciously pleased that Aunt Adelaide, who so unfairly favoured Sarah, had not been able to find her a husband after all. They knew nothing of Ambrose which was just as well, as they might have thought him a too secretive and cautious person. If he had really loved Sarah wouldn't he have wanted to proclaim his feelings at once, not to wait and see to his future. They had no worldly wisdom about these things, Sarah thought. They had romantic dreams that love was all-sufficient, when more sophisticated and intelligent people realised that a marriage under the present conditions must be doomed to fail. For Ambrose would be constantly brooding over his wrongs, and she would blame herself for having accentuated them.

No, apart from the hypothetical heiress, they were doing the only thing possible.

But she did wish Amelia and Charlotte would not think it so daring and exciting, that she was to be in the household of the new Lord Mallow.

'So much more interesting than me with Mrs Throckmorten,' Amelia sighed. 'We go to Bath to take the waters, then we return to London, and that is the entire sum of our excitement. She has few callers and doesn't like ever to be alone. I get so bored with sitting opposite her, looking at her—she is exactly like a pug wrapped in shawls—that I could scream.'

'At least,' said Charlotte, 'she doesn't have a married daughter who constantly calls to criticise the way things are done now she no longer lives in the house.'

'But Lady Wright-Davis is not unkind or exacting.'

'No, but she's feeble. She says yes to everybody and everything. She lets her horrid daughter walk over her. I could shake her myself. And I never—literally never—see a man!'

'Nor me,' echoed Amelia sadly.

'Neither shall I,' Sarah said tartly.

'But there's Lord Mallow himself. They say he's very handsome.'

'So is his wife.'

'Oh, well, of course. We weren't suggesting anything romantic, Sarah. But at least you'll have masculine conversation. And who knows who will come to the house.'

'A governess isn't encouraged to make friends with guests.'

Amelia sighed again.

'Really, how *does* one get married? I can see myself growing just like Mrs Throckmorten, wrapped up in shawls, and constantly expecting draughts to pounce on me, as if they have personal designs on my life. You will do the same, Charlotte.'

'And be pitied all the time by that abominable daughter because I have no husband!'

Sarah looked from one to the other of her sisters. They were both dowdily dressed, as befitted their situations, and both wore lugubrious expressions that she suspected had now become familiar to them. Supposing Ambrose did not come back, supposing they could not succeed in their plan to unmask the false Blane Mallow, supposing indeed he were genuinely Blane, in spite of all the strange discrepancies, then she, too, would be in a similar case to Amelia and Charlotte.

Her back stiffened. She would go through any kind of dubious and rash adventure rather than grow into a dowdy and complaining nonentity. Her last lingering doubts were dispelled. Now she was impatient to begin her task.

It was obvious that Amalie had been compelled to make the best of an infuriating situation.

She welcomed Sarah with chilly courtesy.

'I'm afraid, Miss Mildmay, that until we get to Mallow Hall you will have to take charge of Titus completely. We've had to give Annie notice.'

'I'm sorry about that, Lady Mallow.'

'Servants, I am told, are becoming far too independent. Annie had some idea that her rights were put upon, as she expressed it.'

The implication of Amalie's words were unmistakable. Sarah

met her cool gaze steadily.

'I shall be happy to do all I can, Lady Mallow.'

'My husband insists that you know how to manage children. I warn you that Titus isn't easy. This sudden change in surroundings and climate has been too much for his delicate constitution. And then there's my mother-in-law. I had no idea——' But at that Amalie must have felt she was being too indiscreet, especially to a woman to whom she was already hostile, and stopping speaking rang the bell for a maid to come and show Sarah to her room.

'It is essential that Titus be in bed early,' she said, 'since we begin a long journey in the morning. Don't let him eat anything but bread and milk for his supper, and I'd suggest no noisy games.'

Sarah looked surprised, until she realised that Lady Malvina was the difficulty. No doubt Amalie, in spite of her airs and graces, was already a little afraid of her.

'One more thing, Miss Mildmay. Since this is your first night here perhaps you'd prefer supper on a tray in your room.'

This gesture, Sarah knew, was no mark of thoughtfulness for her comfort. It was merely postponing the time when Sarah would share their table. But she welcomed it with inner excitement. While the family was at dinner she could do a little quiet investigating. It would be her only opportunity in this house.

She bowed her head.

'Thank you, Lady Mallow.'

The maid appeared and the cool unfriendly interview was over. She was in the house, but on sufferance only. Blane was the dominating partner in this marriage and exercised his will, from whim or perhaps genuine concern for his son's welfare. But one must not make the mistake of underestimating Amalie. She would have weapons of her own. She could attempt to make Sarah's position as intolerable as Ambrose had feared it might be.

The little boy stood in the middle of the large nursery in his flannel nightshirt. He looked small and clean and troubled. His grandmother, obviously exhausted from some recent activity, was sunk back in a chair fanning her flushed face. When Sarah came in she said wheezily,

'Ah, here you are at last, Miss Mildmay. I have had the boy on my hands since that stupid Annie departed in a huff. But we've had a tremendous romp. Haven't we, my little love?'

Sarah went to take the child's hand. He didn't resist, but the hot little palm lay limply within her own.

'You remember me, don't you, Titus?'

He nodded. His sober face gave no sign of pleasure, but neither did it show dislike nor distress. It seemed that he had already learnt to accept what was in any way acceptable. Only the worse shocks, such as growing used to his alarming grandmother, or tolerating the unkind Annie who had secretly pinched him, had badly shaken his self-control. He was already deciding, as his instinct had told him when he had clung to her, that this young woman with the gentle eyes would not pinch or bully him.

'We're going to be good friends,' said Sarah quietly. 'I'm to teach you a great many things, like reading and drawing pictures, and where all the countries in the world are. We shall get an atlas and follow your journey in the ship from Trinidad to England. And we'll have walks in the woods, and you'll have a pony ride.'

'That's right,' said Lady Malvina approvingly. 'Teach the lad some spunk. He's the living image of my own son at that age, but he's got no spunk. Do you think you can give it to him, Miss Mildmay? Is the material there? It had better be.'

Sarah looked down at the silent little figure. The boy was so small and frail, and as tense as a wild kitten. All his fears, whatever they were, were knotted up inside him. Loneliness was one of them. Probably he had been left too much in the care of indifferent servants, while his restless mother pursued her own life. Maternity was clearly not one of Amalie's gifts.

'He's scared of his own shadow,' Lady Malvina went on. 'And a boy should make more noise. He's too quiet. What makes him so quiet?' she finished peevishly.

'Some children are naturally shy and quiet,' Sarah said, thinking that neither of these characteristics would have belonged to Lady Malvina's own son. 'But give Titus time. He's still adapting himself to a new environment. Wait until he's used to the country, and rides his own horse.'

'You seem a sensible young woman, I must say. You've no doubt had a good deal of experience with children?'

'Yes, Lady Malvina,' Sarah lied.

'H'mm. Well, my son saw your points before I did, I admit that. I thought you were a most pushing and impertinent young woman. So did my daughter-in-law. She was not at all pleased, I must say.' The old lady paused to give a rich chuckle. 'Not at all pleased. She suspected Blane had spied a new pretty face. He's a great one, my son, for pretty faces. There was that dairymaid Maria when he was only a schoolboy. He's conveniently forgotten that. His amnesia serves him well. But all the same I like a man to be a man, vigorous, lusty if you like. Better than that cold-blooded correct cousin of his.'

Sarah lifted her eyes innocently.

'Is that the person who would have inherited if your son hadn't returned, Lady Malvina?'

'Ambrose? Yes.' Lady Malvina's lips were turned down in eloquent distaste. 'Oh, he's well enough, perhaps. Industrious, righteous, doesn't gamble, has excellent taste. But he's a type I thoroughly dislike. Do you think he'd have paid my debts, taken me into his family, let me enjoy his children—if he ever begets any!' Lady Malvina began to chuckle again at her obviously bawdy thoughts. Some of the thick white powder on her face had sprinkled on to the shoulders of her dress. Her cap was crooked. She was too fat, was no doubt greedy at the table, and on her own admission she was extravagant and foolish with money. She also was indiscreet with servants, as she was being indiscreet now with Sarah, a virtual stranger. The primness and prudishness of the times seemed to have passed her by. But already Sarah was conscious of an untidy warm-heartedness about her that was difficult to dislike. And there was no doubt that, with her careless talk, she was going to be of enormous help.

Privately, Sarah was already resolving to keep a diary, to note down jottings of conversation that her memory might not otherwise retain. Snatches such as 'Do you think he'd have paid my debts?' She burned with indignation, for Lady Malvina's assessment of Ambrose was so mistaken. But she must listen to this, also, without defence.

'How very fortunate for you, Lady Malvina, that your son did come home. It was like a miracle, wasn't it?'

'In a way it was. Though there was no miracle about all those advertisements in papers all over the world. They cost a pretty penny, I can tell you.'

'And was your son the only applicant?'

She must attend to Titus, get him to bed, but this conversation was too valuable to miss.

Lady Malvina's heavy eyelids lifted. She gave Sarah a curious veiled stare that told nothing.

'What exactly do you mean by that, Miss Mildmay?'

'Only that the advertisement might have lured adventurers to try their luck for such an attractive inheritance.'

Lady Malvina stood up, arranging her rustling skirts, haughtily.

'And did you think, if that had happened, I wouldn't have recognised them for what they were? I'm not a fool, Miss Mildmay.'

She sailed out of the room. Sarah was fearful that already she had gone too far. She didn't think so, however. Lady Malvina was garrulous and lonely. She couldn't have much in common with her daughter-in-law. Because of Titus, she would be in the nursery constantly. She would talk again. There would be ample time in which to decide whether her first impression that the old lady was on the defensive and secretly a little nervous was true.

Her spirits lifted. Already this adventure was full of interest and spiced with danger that made it intensely stimulating.

Titus meekly ate his bread and milk, and allowed himself to be put to bed in the firelit nursery. It was a large comfortable room, too ornately decorated for a nursery, for the late elderly Lord Mallow could not have envisaged it would have such a use so soon.

'Have you travelled in a train before?' Sarah asked. She

discovered that Titus spoke only when spoken to, and then in shy monosyllables.

'No.'

'Then that's very exciting, isn't it? Have you any toys you want to take?'

'No.'

'But don't you have toys you like best? Didn't you have any in Trinidad?'

'I had José then.'

'Who was José?'

'He was a black boy.'

The sparse information showed Sarah another side to Titus's quietness. Had his father, in his ambitious gamble, stopped to give one thought to this minor tragedy it entailed? His son had lost a favourite playmate. He had not yet learned to play with an English child's toys. Well, there could be the rocking horse and the toy soldiers, and the pony. At least this part of her job, Sarah promised herself fiercely, she would do honestly.

'Good night, Titus. Sleep well. Shall I leave the candle for a little while?'

The large dark eyes looked up at her beseechingly. She realised that neither Annie nor anyone else had pampered this weakness. The nervous little stranger to English nurseries had been left to go to sleep in the dark.

'All right. I won't blow it out,' she promised. 'Are we going to be friends, Titus?'

'Why don't you call me Georgie?'

Sarah's heart missed a beat.

'Why should I do that? Is that what'—she made a guess—'José used to call you?'

'Yes. And Mamma, too. When I was a baby.'

'But when you came to England she called you Titus?'

'She said Georgie was a baby name.'

'And Papa used to call you Georgie, too?'

The little boy looked puzzled. 'I think he called me Titus. When he came back from the sea.'

'Was he away at the sea a long time?'

'Ever so long. But Mamma says he won't go to sea again.

And I have to be called Titus because that was my grandpapa's name.'

'It's a good name,' Sarah said. (It was the family name that she would inevitably call her own son. In the meantime, she must not grudge it to this innocent little usurper.)

But already she had significant entries to make in her diary.

It seemed that she was not to see Blane Mallow that night. A very young maid brought her her supper tray.

'Thank you,' said Sarah pleasantly. 'Are you to travel with us tomorrow?'

'No, ma'am. I'm to stay here with Mrs Robbins.'

'Who's Mrs Robbins?'

'The housekeeper, ma'am.'

'Oh. And what's your name?'

'Lucy, ma'am.'

'You're very young. Is this your first position?'

'Yes, ma'am. I'm just fourteen.'

'I hope Mrs Robbins is kind to you.'

'Oh, yes, she's all right. And when the master and mistress isn't here——' Lucy clapped her hand to her mouth, aghast at what she had been going to blurt out to a stranger.

'You can tell me, Lucy. I don't mind what Mrs Robbins does when she's alone. After all, she's left in complete charge of the house so she's her own mistress, isn't she?'

'Yes, I suppose she is. Well, it's just that she's easy-going, ma'am. Ever so kind, but'll turn a blind eye if it suits her.'

Lucy was blushing deeply, and Sarah was left to guess what Mrs Robbins's particular easy-going habit was, men or the gin bottle. Like a magpie gathering treasure, she tucked the piece of information away in her mind.

'What time is dinner downstairs, Lucy?'

'Eight o'clock, ma'am.'

'Thank you, Lucy. You may go.'

Lucy, who was too young and inexperienced to be disdainful about having to wait on a mere governess, departed. Sarah set her supper tray on one side and tiptoed to the door of her room to open it a crack and listen. Almost at once she heard the dinner gong, and a few minutes later the heavy tread of Lady

Malvina, followed by the lighter footsteps of Amalie, on the stairs. Blane must have been downstairs already, for although she waited, scarcely breathing, at the door for another ten minutes there was no more sound.

It did not take long to discover which rooms, on the first floor, were Blane's and Amalie's. The door she first opened was obviously Lady Malvina's, for such a fug of coal smoke and scented cologne and woollen garments came from the room that she withdrew quickly.

The next door she tried led to the master bedroom. The gas had been left burning low, and she could see the wide bed with its elaborate headboard, the carved ceiling, the glint of mirrors and shine of Amalie's discarded silk gown. A maid might come at any moment to tidy up, and turn down the bed. Sarah moved swiftly, startled that she possessed such daring. What was she looking for? She didn't know. Just anything significant that caught her eye which she could add to her magpie hoard of information. Strangely enough there was no sign of masculine occupation of this room. The dressing-table held nothing but Amalie's possessions, the wardrobes only women's clothing. But of course here was the communicating door leading to Blane's room.

Dare she open it? Sarah held her breath and turned the knob.

But the door didn't open. It was locked on the other side.

It took only a moment to tiptoe quickly down the passage and open the main door which showed that it certainly was Blane's room. Smaller than the bedroom next door, it yet was a finely proportioned room. The bed was quite narrow, and Blane, at present, obviously occupied it alone.

Her cheeks hot, Sarah silently closed the door and left. She had stumbled on more than she had bargained for. This, at least, was none of her business, and she was ashamed of herself for discovering it.

But she must not let herself be deterred. Her real goal was the library. If there were any papers to be discovered, they would be in the desk behind which Blane had sat the other day. There would be plenty of time to make a search while the family was at dinner, and her chances of being disturbed there were much less. If she were, she could make the excuse that she had come to look for a book to read.

She had to descend the stairs and actually pass the dining-room door. It was almost closed, however, and safely past she could not resist stopping to listen a moment.

The only person talking was Lady Malvina, and she was doing so with her usual garrulity, and obviously with her mouth full.

'Better than that sly Annie, anyway,' she was saying. 'And Titus seems to take to her. She's as prim as they come, of course.'

'I thought she was remarkably forward and impudent for a person in her position,' Amalie said coldly.

'Oh, that was just a pose. She obviously desperately needed this position, poor thing. Governesses are two a penny at present. And what else can an educated young woman do, if she's forced to earn her own living? Anyway, the main thing is, Titus likes her. All that child needs is a little tenderness. You've been too hard on him, Blane.'

'I won't have him spoilt.' The uncompromising tones were already so familiar that they should not have made Sarah start. 'If this girl is going to spoil him she'll have to go, tender heart or not. Pretty face or not.'

'I thought you said you hadn't noticed her face,' Amalie said in her cool voice.

'It was Mamma who told me it was pretty. Wasn't it, Mamma? But naturally it's a point I shall probably check on. After all, it's pleasant to have a pretty face around. I hope we shall have the pleasure of seeing Miss Mildmay at the dining table tomorrow evening. My love, can I help you to some more chicken?'

Sarah, her cheeks now flaming, moved on. It served her right. If she deliberately eavesdropped she must hear things she would rather not hear. She must just dismiss them and remember only the facts that mattered. At the moment the important thing was to take a quick look about the library. Not to stand reflecting on remarks made by a man who locked his door against his wife.

The fire was burning brightly, and the room again had a cosy welcoming appearance. She had to overcome the impulse to stand by the warm fire, and go instead to the desk where writing materials were laid out and a letter begun. There was the address, Thomas Whitehouse Esquire, and then a street name in Trinidad.

My dear Whitehouse,
It is my wish to express my gratitude to you in some more tangible form than already ...

Whitehouse! That was the man whom Ambrose had sought unavailingly, who had always moved on when his lodgings were located, and who now had reputedly sailed for the West Indies. The man who swore he had known Blane since he first arrived in Trinidad, a runaway youth with his first sailing experience behind him.

So he had been bribed! And now was being rewarded again, whether from desire or because already he had discovered it would be easy to try a little blackmail.

Hesitating as to whether she should merely memorise the letter, or take it with her, as evidence even more tangible than the reward Blane was promising the man, Sarah stiffened as she heard approaching footsteps.

In a flash she had crossed the room and concealed herself behind the heavy curtains drawn against the cold foggy night.

It was the butler, Tomkins, who had entered the room. He was merely doing a little tidying, replenishing the fire, and straightening papers on the desk. But he took an unconscionable time about it, and finally lingered to warm himself at the fire. Sarah was rigid with nervousness and impatience. The devil take the man! First he must hold his hands to the flames, then, leisurely, turn his back and part his coat tails, swinging on the balls of his feet with obvious enjoyment.

Ten precious minutes went by. Then Tomkins' head shot up as he listened. Deliberately composing his face he crossed the room with his pompous tread, and held the door open and bowed as Blane came in.

'I'll take my coffee in here tonight, Tomkins. I have some letters to finish.'

'Very well, my lord.'

Sarah was almost in tears. Through the infinitesimal parting in the curtains she saw Blane seat himself at the desk and pick up his pen. His dark head was bent as he began to write. He seemed to be scowling. But he wrote without hesitation. Presently Tomkins returned with the coffee service on a silver tray. He put it down and withdrew.

The tantalising smell of hot coffee reached Sarah's nostrils. She remembered that she had left her own supper tray untouched. If anyone should go into her room and find it, and wonder where she was, she would be in serious trouble. What an impulsive clumsy little fool Ambrose would think her if he were to see her now, with the firelit room on one side of her, and behind her the cold glass of the windows and the foggy night. There were muffled sounds in the street, the crunching of cab wheels, a cockney voice shouting, hurrying footsteps.

If she were not careful she would be out in that cold world, shut completely from this warm room and its dubious welcome. If she were to make a noise so that Blane heard her and discovered her, she would have her bags packed within the hour.

She just must not make a noise. She must stand here until midnight, if need be, scarcely breathing.

It was not pleasant to be an eavesdropper. The adventure was gone. This was the uncomfortable and humiliating reality.

Perhaps half an hour went by, while the little French clock ticked on in its glass case on the mantelpiece, and Blane's pen made a faint scratching. Then abruptly the door burst open.

'Blane! We've been waiting in the drawing-room for you.'

Blane scarcely lifted his head.

'You heard me say I was coming here to work.'

'But not until after your coffee. Oh, you've had it here.'

'I have. And now, my love, if you don't mind I have urgent business to finish.'

'But, darling, I waited. You know I waited.'

Now Amalie was referring to something that had nothing to do with the coffee, for her voice, uncertain, pleading, strangely humble, seemed not to belong to her. Yet in appearance she was her usual confident self, a little over-dressed for a dinner *en famille*, in a buff-coloured silk gown with rose point lace, and long ear-drops glittering from her ears.

Blane looked up then. His brows were drawn together in a look of barely controlled patience.

'Yes, I know, and you know my answer to that. Now please leave me.'

'But we haven't quarrelled.'

'No, we haven't quarrelled. And there are many other compensations, as you know.'

Amalie's voice grew high and edgy.

'Including the pretty governess?'

'Including the pretty governess, if you insist. There, you see, I'm humouring you, agreeing to your foolish remarks. But Titus, if you will remember, didn't have a pretty governess in Trinidad. He only had a small rather odorous black boy.'

'Whom he misses a great deal,' Amalie flashed.

'Does he? Then we must get him another. But please leave me in peace now.'

'Blane! If you only thought a little——' She was in tears, groping for a handkerchief and looking intensely pathetic.

Sarah heard Blane give an impatient exclamation, then saw him spring to his feet and cross over to his wife.

'Oh, lord! I warn you I can't stand this sort of tiresome behaviour. Come then. I'll have coffee with you in the drawing-room and talk to Mamma. And then you shall play and sing to me for half an hour, and we'll be a completely devoted couple. But heaven knows what time I'll get to bed tonight.'

Sarah slumped back wearily. She had been rescued by Amalie's display of temperament. Now she would always remember, when Amalie put on her haughty confident air, that underneath there was this pathetic pleading person, begging something of her husband that he was reluctant to give. Or was that poignant little scene an act? Was she merely a spoilt little creature constantly demanding attention?

Then why the locked bedroom door?

Baffled and more than a little disturbed, Sarah at last ventured forth, and crept upstairs. From the drawing-room Amalie's voice, with the high virginal note of a young girl, sang a popular sentimental ballad. Lady Malvina talked resolutely through it.

And Sarah remembered, as she reached her room, that she had been too distraught to read the remainder of Blane's letter to Mr Whitehouse. But she had memorised the address. She must quickly write a letter to Ambrose so that when he received it he could call on Mr Whitehouse in Trinidad. The opportunity to send the letter may not come for a few days, but eventually it would.

6

THE departure the next morning was complicated by the immense amount of luggage. In addition to her several trunks, Lady Malvina insisted on carrying a canary in a cage. It was a present for Titus, she said, to amuse him on the journey.

It was difficult to say which was the more dejected, Titus in his Norfolk jacket and cap, or the canary, silent on its perch. Certainly neither enjoyed Lady Malvina's gay jocularity.

Titus clung to Sarah's hand. He had as yet talked very little, and his face looked peaked beneath the tweed cap. But at least he seemed to trust her, and did not wince away as he did from his grandmother. Certainly his involuntary shrinking was as polite and unobtrusive as possible. But there was no doubt Lady Malvina in her travelling clothes, a befurred bonnet and voluminous cloak which made her look the width of two people, was quite alarming.

Amalie was elegantly and discreetly dressed in dark-blue, but for all her elegance she looked pinched and cold. She shivered in the morning mist, and hoped there was some sort of heating in the train.

'There'll be nothing but a fug,' Lady Malvina said. 'You'd better take a hot brick for your feet. And when you learn to dress for our climate you'll feel the cold less. I warrant you haven't a single flannel petticoat on.'

Amalie winced, and Lady Malvina went on, 'I have four, no less. And need 'em all.'

At this moment Blane appeared in his travelling cape and top hat. He also looked impatient and irritable, and scarcely greeted anyone. Sarah, he hadn't noticed. She might have been one of the maids.

She quelled her resentment as she told herself that she was virtually one of the maids, and the sooner she remembered it the better.

'Must all this luggage go?' Blane demanded. 'This isn't an

expedition across the Sahara. And what the deuce is that bird for?'

'For your son,' Lady Malvina retorted. 'The journey is slow and tiresome. And it doesn't seem as if you're going to do much about amusing him, with that scowl on your face.'

The early morning start seemed to have everyone in a bad temper. Blane made a belated attempt to be more gracious.

'Sorry, Mamma. That's very kind of you.' The irony which Sarah suspected was never very far away came back into his voice. 'After all, there'll be no bands out for us at Mallow. So perhaps a canary singing will keep up all our spirits.'

'You'll be welcomed,' said Lady Mallow briefly. 'You're my son.'

Was there a touch of defiance in her voice, as if she challenged anyone to disagree with her? No doubt she had been convincing people for so long that now her emphasis was automatic. At least, Blane flashed her a glance that was half grateful, half amused. But his ill-temper vanished, and he got Titus and the ladies into the waiting cab with brisk efficiency. He himself followed with the luggage, and Tomkins and Bessie in a second cab.

They were to be met by Soames with the carriage at Yarby, the nearest railway station to Mallow Hall. After that there was a ten-mile journey across the marshes, but they expected to reach their destination before dusk. It should not have been an arduous journey, and Sarah was a little perplexed at Amalie making it so. They sat in reasonable comfort in the first-class railway carriage, the windows were tightly closed against the smoke and soot, Amalie had her hot brick, and Lady Malvina her voluminous petticoats. Titus was the most unfidgety small boy Sarah had met. In spite of the fact that it was his first journey by railway train, his excitement was shown only by a tighter grip of Sarah's hand and an increased pallor.

It was his father who was restless. He spent the journey strolling up and down the corridor and occasionally opening the window to stick his head out and let in a blast of frozen smoky air.

One would have thought he was nervous. Not of the still

refreshingly new mode of transport, but of his eventual arrival.

The canary in its cage remained silent, but Lady Malvina talked incessantly. After an hour had gone by she produced the hamper Mrs Robbins had packed, and distributed sandwiches and cold chicken. She also, while Amalie was dozing, persuaded Titus to drink a little out of her glass of port.

'It will put some colour in his cheeks,' she said, and Amalie woke up and exclaimed,

'Mamma, how can you be so foolish! Now he'll be ill. Miss Mildmay, couldn't you have had more sense?'

'I'm sorry,' Sarah murmured meekly. How did a servant oppose this preposterous and determined old lady? She felt her first flash of sympathy for the departed Annie.

Sure enough, an hour later Titus was sick, and his father exclaimed in irritation,

'When you know the boy's a bad traveller, why do you give him things to eat?'

'Or drink,' Amalie finished crossly. 'You must blame your mother.'

Lady Malvina, who had eaten well and partaken liberally of the port herself, nodded amiably.

'Oh, yes. I'm a foolish old woman. But the boy's got to grow. He's got to be built up. He's only half the size you were at that age, Blane.'

Titus, shivering a little on Sarah's lap, curled up and presently went to sleep. Sarah was aware, for the first time that day, of Blane's gaze on her. She had said nothing during the whole episode, merely cleaned the child up and comforted him. She had been comforting herself that journeys like this would not be undertaken every day, so surely she could endure this one well enough. Probably at this moment Ambrose was much more uncomfortable tossing on a stormy sea.

'I've told you not to spoil the boy,' Blane said in his abrupt voice.

Sarah wondered indignantly if the poor baby, sick and tired, was expected to sit upright in his corner for the entire journey.

She raised her eyes innocently and said,

'I won't spoil him, Lord Mallow. Indeed, I don't think he's at all spoilt. He's over-excited and bewildered by his new environment.' Her voice was gentle and uncensorious. Was she being a little too rash? 'But I did wonder last night why he asked me to call him Georgie. Is that a pet name?'

Amalie's eyes flickered slightly. But Blane's were level and composed.

'His baby name, yes. But he's old enough to be called Titus now. I hope you will do so, Miss Mildmay. The boy's no longer a baby.'

'You never told me that, Blane,' Lady Malvina said in her rich drowsy voice. 'Had you just that moment begun to call him Titus?'

'*Which* moment, Mamma?'

'Why, when you appeared in my hall that day.'

'Of course not. We'd been doing so for months. Good heavens, what a trifle to argue about. The child's name is Titus Blane George Mallow. And I don't want him pampered.'

For the first time Amalie spoke vaguely in Sarah's defence.

'Being a bad traveller doesn't consist of being pampered. But this settles it. We don't travel any further today. We spend the night at Yarby.'

'Don't be absurd! Soames is meeting us with the carriage.'

'Then he can be put up for the night, or return again in the morning. I, for one, don't intend to arrive at Mallow completely exhausted.'

Blane made an impatient exclamation. His gaze went over the compartment of women with scarcely concealed contempt. He looked as if he would have liked to be rid of them all and travel unshackled.

'Lady Malvina, wouldn't you prefer to spend the night in a comfortable inn?' Amalie appealed. 'You don't want to jolt all those miles in the dark.'

'I certainly don't,' Lady Malvina agreed. 'I want a good fire and a comfortable bed. I'm not as young as I was. And Titus shouldn't be over-taxed. Yes, Blane, I think we'd make a much more impressive arrival fresh and tidy in the morning.'

Blane shrugged.

'Very well. As you wish. I'll arrange for rooms at the George.

If they can accommodate such a large party.'

'Don't be silly, Blane. You must remember Tom Mercer. He'd never turn anyone from Mallow away. And he'll be over-joyed to see you.'

But again Sarah caught the flicker of uncertainty in Lady Malvina's eyes. She wondered how she could be present at Blane's meeting with Tom Mercer, and knew at once that it would be impossible.

When they arrived Soames, a dark little man with a narrow face, was waiting with the carriage, and in this they drove the short distance to the George where the ladies were ordered to wait while arrangements for accommodation were being made.

Whether Tom Mercer had recognised Blane at once, Sarah was not to know. But at least he acknowledged the importance of the arrivals by coming out to greet them with genuine pleasure.

'Well, Tom,' said Lady Malvina in her penetrating voice, 'do you recognise my scallawag son? Do you remember letting him drink too much ale when he was a schoolboy, and him coming home rolling drunk?'

'That I do, my lady,' said Tom. 'But if I may say so, Master Blane was not a lad you could say no to.'

Lady Malvina chuckled reminiscently.

'No, I grant you that.' Strangely enough, there was little mirth in her eyes.

'If you'd gossip a little less, Mamma, and come inside,' Blane said. 'Rooms are being got ready, and there's tea in the parlour.' His voice was calm. He gave no sign of gratitude to Lady Malvina for putting memories into his mind—or were those memories there already? If not, the man was a fine actor.

But then one knew he was. He had fooled a judge and an English jury. It would not be difficult to fool a village inn-keeper.

Early dusk was falling, and it was a relief not to have the long journey to Mallow that evening. Sarah found she was to share a room with Titus, Lady Malvina had the adjoining one, and Amalie and Blane had the large double chamber at the head of the stairs. Bessie was called on to do some quick un-

66

packing and attendance on the ladies, and then was dispatched to her own quarters somewhere downstairs.

Sarah put Titus to bed immediately where, worn out with the day's excitements, he at once fell asleep. Already, in twenty-four hours, she had settled herself into the part she was to play, and was able quite meekly to offer her services to Lady Malvina or Amalie.

Lady Malvina, seated comfortably before a fire, her bonnet replaced by a lace cap, the canary cage at her side, said,

'Thank you, my dear. How kind. But I don't intend to dress this evening. I shall have a tray sent up here. How's the boy?'

'Asleep, Lady Malvina.'

'Good. But he'll have to get more stamina, as my son says. By the way, you didn't notice——' Her cheeks puffed in and out. Then she sank back, changing her mind, deflated.

'Didn't notice what, Lady Malvina?' Sarah asked.

'No matter. I was just over curious. A great many people, I've discovered, have short memories for faces. It's absurd that my son has had to be humiliated like this, establishing his identity.'

'You mean, did the landlord know him?' Sarah said boldly.

'But he must have, because we have all the attention, as usual. And tomorrow we'll be safely at Mallow. Ha-a!' She gave a great sigh. 'I must buy some more jewels. I like jewels. My husband got a little eccentric for some time before his death. He became most parsimonious with money. I had to sell my pearls. Sacrifice them to that hungry man of mine in Bond Street. But now he can get me some more. Yes, pearls. They're the kindest to ageing throats.'

'It has been quite a change of fortune for you, hasn't it, Lady Malvina?'

The old lady shot Sarah a quick suspicious glance. But her love of a sympathetic listener got the better of discretion.

'Yes, it has. Couldn't imagine my nephew Ambrose buying me jewels. He's a cold fish.'

'Cold?'

'You know what I mean. Careful, self-contained, minds about gossip, hates to be embarrassed. Correct. That's the word. I'd have embarrassed him greatly, but Blane's like myself. Doesn't

67

give a brass farthing for what people say. Walks the earth like a lord. That's what I like.'

Sarah bit her lip. She didn't enjoy the old lady's ability to put people into words so effectively, whether the words were true or not. And of course they were not. She had left out all Ambrose's fine points, his honour and courtesy, his cultured mind, his gentleness. Blane would not know what to be gentle was.

'Tell me about your son when he was a boy, Lady Malvina. Was he like Titus?'

'In looks, yes. But that's all. He was twice the boy Titus is, sturdy, not afraid of anything or anybody, rode almost before he walked, did everything. But difficult and hot-tempered. That's how he came to quarrel with his father. It was all or nothing with Blane. He had his own way or walked out.'

'Do you think he's still like that?'

'Oh, no. He's grown up. He's an adult. I'm exceedingly proud of him. Exceedingly. But that was strange, Miss Mildmay, wasn't it? The boy wanting to be called Georgie. But he really is Titus on his birth certificate. I've seen it. It was one of the exhibits at court. So don't get any odd ideas in your head.'

'But why should I, Lady Malvina?' Sarah enquired innocently.

'Yes, why should you? I've been asked so many questions lately, that I've got a phobia about it. I think everybody is suspicious, even harmless old Tom Mercer.'

(And if their suspicions were proved correct you wouldn't get those pearls, Sarah thought. Or have a grandson to pamper, or plenty of servants to bring you your port and your good food.)

'It's been a difficult time for you, Lady Malvina,' she murmured.

'Yes, it has. But now all is well, and I'd like a glass of port before my supper. Would you ring the bell, there's a good girl. I can see I'm going to grow quite fond of you, Miss Mildmay. You're intelligent as well as attractive. But I wouldn't let my daughter-in-law see too much of either of those qualities. She's suspicious, too.'

Sarah left the room to the accompaniment of Lady Malvina's

deep malicious chuckle. So that was another thing. She was not over-fond of her daughter-in-law.

Sarah had scarcely gone back to her room before Amalie tapped at the door and came in.

She had made a complete new *toilette*, and wore one of her taffeta dinner gowns, cut low so that her narrow sloping shoulders were shown off. A Paisley shawl, a mere gesture towards the chilly evening, hung negligently over her arms. The colour in her thin cheeks was high and her eyes brilliant.

'How is my son, Miss Mildmay?'

'He's asleep, Lady Mallow. I scarcely like to wake him for supper.'

'I shouldn't. By the way, my mother-in-law isn't going down, so my husband and I will also dine in our room. Perhaps you'd make what arrangements you care to for yourself. Tomorrow we'll all be settled normally, I hope.'

'Thank you, Lady Mallow.'

'I'd recommend an early night. We'll be starting at the crack of dawn, if I know my husband.'

She went out leaving a trail of scent behind her. She had not smiled, but she had been almost human. Almost, Sarah thought, conspiratorial. As if something she had planned had worked out very well. There had been an excitement about her that had included Sarah in it. She had not been like that this morning, so it could not have been caused by the triumph of going to Mallow Hall as the new mistress.

Surely it was not because tonight there could be no locked door between herself and her husband!

But that must be it. For it was Amalie who had insisted on breaking the journey, knowing that as a matter of course she and Blane would share a room. And she was the only one who had thought it necessary to dress—and to dress as if for a party.

It was the dinner in the privacy of their firelit room that she was thinking of. When the servant would retire, the door would be shut, and there would be the chance of a reconciliation over whatever their quarrel had been.

Sarah would not allow herself to waste time thinking of their two heads close together in the firelight. She spent an unhappy few minutes at the window looking out into the dark night, and remembering Ambrose's face as it had been when she had last seen it, pale and dedicated. That was all that mattered to her. She must not get embroiled emotionally in other people's lives. If Blane chose to quarrel with or be reconciled with his wife, it was nothing to do with her.

She made another note in her diary. *Lady M. extravagant—must have squandered a great amount of money and was embarrassed by debts when husband died. Looks to Blane to buy her the new jewels she loves. Goes on being determined to think Blane her son when all the time she is uncertain and a little frightened. Wondering what situation she has got into. Did Tom Mercer recognise Blane at once?*

Here Sarah paused, then made another cryptic note: *I think Amalie uncertain of her husband's love. Blane obviously has always been and probably still is a philanderer.*

Then she scratched out the last sentence vigorously. For this man was *not* Blane, and no one knew whether he were a philanderer or not. Except, perhaps, Amalie.

Determined to find out something about Tom Mercer at least, Sarah went downstairs. She asked for her supper to be served in the parlour, and sat down to wait. To walk boldly into the bar seeking Tom Mercer would be too odd a thing even for her to do.

Luck was with her, however, for Tom himself carried in the tray.

'We're short of help tonight, with so many unexpected guests. Hope this is to your liking, ma'am.'

'Thank you,' said Sarah. 'I expect it was a great surprise for you to see Lord Mallow.'

'It was that. I'd heard he was coming any day, but I didn't expect him unannounced like this.'

'And would you have known him anywhere?' Sarah asked, her eyes downcast.

'Well, ma'am, speaking fairly, I can't say that I would have. It's twenty years, after all, and him only a lad when he left. But he's got that same proud look about him, if you know what I mean. That lad, he would do what he willed. Only a schoolboy, and he could carry his liquor like an old timer. And as for the ma——' The man stopped in mid-sentence. He had been going to say too much, and something not complimentary. Something about maids? And there was Amalie upstairs, silk-gowned and perfumed, on the ground of Blane's old conquests. If he were Blane . . .

'He went away because he quarrelled so deadly with his father,' Tom Mercer went on. 'The two of them were too much alike, two hotheads. But now all's well, eh? And the little lad's the dead spit of him, only more delicate like. Well, it's a happy day for Mallow Hall. Except that Mr Ambrose can't be too pleased. But I mustn't gossip, ma'am. Anything more you want you just let me know.'

So that was another thing, Sarah reflected. Tom Mercer had not liked young Blane Mallow. He had been an arrogant spoilt lawless young rascal. This, however, did not constitute evidence, merely a point of interest.

She ate and enjoyed her meal, thankful to have a little time alone. The day had been a great strain. But it was not yet quite over, for when she returned upstairs Lady Malvina was standing at her half-open door. She grabbed Sarah's arm and pulled her to her.

'Are those two downstairs or in their room?' she whispered.

'In their room, I imagine.'

For some reason, Lady Malvina gave her deep chuckle. Her cheeks were darkly flushed and she smelled of wine.

'That'll please her ladyship. At last, eh? Don't be shocked, Miss Mildmay. You'll find that's how the Mallows are, and my son the worst of them all. A drunkard and a lecher at sixteen. But he's learned to behave like a gentleman now. Outwardly, at least. So you need have no fears, Miss Mildmay.'

The outrageous old woman pinched Sarah's cheek and retreated into her room. The door banged. Stiff with indignation, Sarah stood controlling her impulse to march in after the old woman and slap her soundly. In that moment the door of the double room at the head of the stairs opened and Blane came out. He was still dressed in his travelling clothes. He began going downstairs with a purposeful air. At the last moment he lifted his head and saw Sarah. She was standing directly beneath the hanging lamp, and he could not fail to notice her hot cheeks and angry eyes.

'What is it, Miss Mildmay? Has my mother been indiscreet, as usual?'

Sarah collected herself.

'Nothing's the matter, thank you.'

He remained staring at her for a long moment. His own eyes were over-bright from some emotion. Then he gave the faintest shrug.

'Women!' he said under his breath, and went on down the stairs.

Titus awoke early in the morning. He said he was hungry, which was not to be wondered at, since he had fallen asleep supperless. It was only six o'clock, but Sarah could hear stirring downstairs. She decided to go down and find someone who would give her some milk and some bread and butter for Titus.

Putting a wrap on and leaving her hair loose, for she would encounter no one but a servant, she slipped quietly down the stairs. The parlour was empty, and so was the dining-room. The clattering came from behind some other door. She tentatively tried one or two, seeking a way to the kitchen. But one led to the bar parlour, and the other to a kind of office. In this was a long leather couch, and stretched out on it, sound asleep, lay the new Lord Mallow.

Was he drunk? Too drunk to have climbed the stairs? Or had Amalie this time been the one who locked the door in revenge?

Sarah closed the door softly and tiptoed away. She was stumbling on the wrong secrets. This was not amusing at all.

7

THE servants were lined up in the hall. Blane with Amalie clinging to his arm acknowledged their bobs and curtseys with an offhand ease. He was the master come home. Standing a little behind them in the arched doorway of the old house Sarah's blood was hot with resentment and indignation.

Ambrose had planned to dedicate himself to Mallow Hall, even at the expense of getting rid of the extravagant town house. She should have arrived here for the first time as his bride. The deferential bobbing of the servants would have been to her, not to that haughty sallow wife of Blane's who looked sulky and tired this morning, as if she hadn't slept well.

Instead she was forced to stand meekly in the background, taking precedence only over the stout elderly Bessie.

'Ah, Betsey!' she suddenly heard Blane exclaiming, and an elderly woman smiled with gratification. 'At last one face I know.'

No one had prompted him. Lady Malvina was a little distance away. Yet it was simple enough, for the woman he had spoken to was definitely the oldest servant present. He had had only to be warned that there was one elderly woman he should recognise.

But when she was inside the hall her cool and calculated reasoning left her. For at the foot of the stairs hung the controversial portrait. It had had a great deal of significance at the hearing of the case, and Sarah's heart sank as she looked at it. It was quite baffling. For the child in the picture was so remarkably similar to Titus that there was no explaining it away. Could such a likeness be a coincidence, one of those strange freaks of nature? And was there anything of that painted face left in the face of the man who was so confidently surveying his surroundings? The set of the eyes, the beginnings of the strong nose, the merry insolent look?

Who could say this child had not been him?

She must have stood too long gazing at the portrait, for she had attracted Blane's attention. He came to stand beside her.

'Is there any hope for Titus, do you think, Miss Mildmay?'

'I don't know what you mean, Lord Mallow.'

'Starting from those beginnings,' he waved towards the painting, 'will he grow up to look like me?'

He was challenging her, she realised. Suddenly contempt filled her and all her confidence came back. Did he feel so guilty that he even had to test the reactions of a servant?

'I am not good at predictions, Lord Mallow.'

'One doesn't wonder without surmising. You, if I'm not mistaken, have been busily surmising ever since you arrived in my house.'

Sarah had a flash of alarm. She must be careful. She couldn't risk being dismissed.

'The case was a *cause célèbre*,' she murmured.

'Yes, it was.' He began to laugh. 'And worth winning, eh?'

Sarah followed his glance round their surroundings. Mallow Hall was not large, but it had been built with taste and discrimination. The proportions of the hall and the curving staircase were perfect. But the furnishings were shabby and it was evident that a great many repairs were needed. This was what Ambrose had been longing to do, and she would have adored helping him. But now everything was spoilt, for she would never be able to come into the house without seeing Amalie wandering about looking at this acquisitively, and hearing Blane's confident voice.

'You will have more knowledge of current taste in England than my wife who comes from a country where something to keep out the sun is the most important furnishing. Perhaps you'll be able to make some suggestions about new colours and designs.'

Had he found out about Cousin Laura at Balmoral with the Queen? Sarah had her second flash of alarm, realising that just as she might succeed in unmasking him, so might he her.

But if he noticed her involuntary look of guilt there was no time to comment on it, for Amalie had come up to say, 'Let's go

74

over the house room by room, my love. I long for you to show it to me.'

'Certainly. Perhaps we could take Titus and Miss Mildmay to the nursery first. On the second floor. That's one direction I couldn't forget. I don't suppose a single thing has been changed in the nursery. Has it, Mamma? Although I remember being rather destructive.'

Lady Malvina came bustling up beaming with happiness. She was letting no private doubts mar her pleasure in coming home to a house which she must have thought she had lost.

'You were very destructive, indeed. We had to have new wall-papers after you went to school. Don't you remember? We put up the new varnished ones.'

'I remember. A beautiful glossy brown. A hotel I stayed at in San Francisco reminded me of my old nursery. I wondered why I felt so depressed!' He laughed and took his mother's arm. 'Don't be hurt, Mamma. I can't pretend I was particularly happy with my father hating me most of the time.'

'Don't be foolish, Blane. He didn't hate you. He only found you disobedient and wilful.'

'We were too much alike. He probably saw all his own faults in me. Of course he hated me. But let's go and look at the brown nursery, and decide what colour Titus shall have instead. It's most important, after all. One day he may have to tell a jury what colour his nursery was.'

'Don't be absurd!' Amalie said sharply.

'Life is full of uncertainties and surprises,' her husband returned airily.

But he had forgotten the new paper in the nursery until Lady Malvina had prompted him. And then common sense had told him that the fashionable and practical colour was brown. It was another lucky guess, as so many of his answers had been.

Amalie insisted on going over the entire house with Blane. Getting Titus settled and settling herself in her own room next door to the nursery, Sarah heard their footsteps and occasionally the loud voice of Lady Malvina as she threw out apparently casual remarks that Blane's crafty brain would seize on as vital information. Amalie had not cared for Blane's suggestion that

75

Sarah might be useful with ideas for redecoration. If anything was done during the duration of their stay at Mallow, it would be done under Amalie's instructions. That was evident at once.

'Ambrose and I can re-do it,' Sarah said aloud, to comfort herself.

Her room looked out over the garden towards the lake. Early in November this view was melancholy, and the sea-wind pressed against the window. Halfway through her unpacking she felt intensely lonely and homesick. Her sisters, Amelia and Charlotte, envied her, thinking she would have some drama with this queer family resurrected from the past. They didn't know she was grieving for Ambrose, already separated by three days' sailing, and wondering how she could endure months of meekness and self-effacement in a house that should be her own.

Ambrose, with his elegant pale good looks, would look so right in this house. She, too, she thought, glimpsing her face in the oval age-dimmed mirror, would not look amiss. Better than Amalie, at least, with her over-dressing and her sulks. What was wrong between Amalie and Blane? Who had started the quarrel and who was continuing it? Though Amalie had too much sense to let the servants notice anything. She was the devoted wife, clinging to her husband's arm, making herself familiar with her new domain. But one would see at dinner that night who was winning the argument.

Thinking of dinner, her first meal to be shared with her employers, Sarah half-heartedly shook out her modest dinner dress, a green taffeta from which she had reluctantly removed the expensive lace trimming. She had to look like a governess, not a fashionable young lady. Her turn would come.

A gauche eager country girl called Eliza Matthews had been employed to help in the nursery. She had just come to work at the Hall and was very nervous. As a source of information she would be useless, but her nervousness proved a good thing for Titus. It gave him confidence. For the first time Sarah heard him laugh.

'Miss Mildmay, Eliza doesn't know how to do anything.

She's funny.'

Eliza blushed and hung her head. She was a plump healthy creature with bright cheeks and chilblains on her fingers. Her mental age was probably not greatly in advance of Titus's, but she was obviously good-natured and eager to learn.

'Have you any brothers and sisters, Eliza?'

'Yes'm. Seven.'

'Then Titus is a child just like them, so don't be afraid.'

'It's the old lady, ma'am,' Eliza confessed in a rush. 'I'm frit of her.'

'That's Grandmamma,' Titus explained. 'But she's only playing games, isn't she, Miss Mildmay? Eliza doesn't need to be afraid.'

Already they were allies, the thin little boy and the awkward country girl. Titus seemed to have grown up several years already. For him, at least, Mallow Hall was going to be good.

Later when Lady Malvina came sweeping in to play her favourite game of grizzly bears it was Eliza who crouched in a corner, all eyes, while Titus shouted hysterically and allowed himself to be hugged to Lady Malvina's vast bosom, and grumbled and growled at.

'Look at that, Miss Mildmay! No tears tonight. He's growing tough already. It's the sea air. He'll soon be strong and bold like his father used to be. What's that girl goggling at?'

'That's Eliza, Grandmamma,' Titus explained. 'She's frightened of you.'

Lady Malvina gave her alarming stare. She must have put on more petticoats against the cold, for she looked enormous. Jewels flashed on her fingers. Her grey hair had been done in an alarming erection of curls that nodded beneath her cap.

'They're all frightened of me. Silly creatures. But you'll have to put up with me, my girl, because I'll be in and out of the nursery a great deal with my grandson. He has to get used to vigorous games. Well, Miss Mildmay, which room have they put you in? May I see it?'

'By all means. It's just next door.'

Sarah took Lady Malvina into her room, and the old lady poked about inquisitively observing everything.

'You haven't got a lot of things, have you? But there's good material in that gown. That didn't cost sixpence. I thought governesses were poor.'

'It was given to me, Lady Malvina.'

'No! By your last employer? Well, I'm afraid you won't be getting presents like that here. Not from the new Lady Mallow.'

Lady Malvina gave a short laugh and went on, 'What do you think of Mallow?'

'It's a beautiful house.'

'Falling to bits. Everything needs repairs, the roof, the drains, the chimneys, the floors. After all, it's a hundred years old, and even if they built well in those days, there's still damp and woodworm. But my daughter-in-law intends to ignore the dull necessities and spend a fortune on furnishings. Carpets, curtains, pictures. All outward show. She'll find the house falls down about her treasures.'

'Does your son agree to this, Lady Malvina?'

'Of course he doesn't. He's thinking quite rightly of Titus's inheritance. There's money, but not that much. His silly wife will ruin him.' Lady Malvina fiddled with the rings on her fingers. 'And she forgets about me. I have requirements also. It's preposterous how little jewellery I have for a woman in my position. Amalie forgets, or chooses to forget, how I had to sacrifice most of it. Well, Miss Mildmay, you'll be dining with us tonight and you'll be treated to an edifying conversation on Italian brocades and carpets from Turkey. I advise you to keep your mouth shut. You may think it wicked to see the Mallow fortune being disposed of like this—what's left of it after my husband's love affair with that house in Kensington—but my daughter-in-law doesn't enjoy either advice or opposition. She wants to cut a dash. Her first opportunity, if you ask me. She can't hold her own without expensive trappings. Strip her and you'd find a straw figure blowing in the wind. Where did she come from anyway? A shack that would collapse in a hurricane, I'll be bound. Ask my son. He won't tell me. He's loyal to his wife. But there's the new Lady Mallow for you. She can scarcely wait to get her hands on everything she can.'

So Blane had his hands full already with two jealous women, one who may have been his mother, and the other who certainly was his wife.

'What time is dinner, Lady Malvina?'

The old lady's eyes met Sarah's suspiciously.

'You think I talk too much. Perhaps I do, but I must talk to someone, and Bessie hasn't a brain in her head.'

'You have your son home now,' Sarah pointed out. Again the suspicious glare was on her. Did it hold a hint of uneasiness?

'My son is a busy man. He has all the estate affairs to manage. I waste as little of his time as possible. However, what am I complaining of?' The irrepressible vitality was back in the pouchy old face. 'I have my grandson now. We shall teach him everything, Miss Mildmay. Riding, shooting, fishing, hunting.'

'And his letters, I hope.'

'Ah, I like you, Miss Mildmay. You're not afraid of me like those silly goggling maids. I hope you'll stay here a long time.'

'I shall stay as long as I need to, Lady Malvina.'

'You mean until you get a husband. Well, you're an attractive young woman. But who are you going to marry, my dear? Governesses fall between two stools, you know, the gentry and the working classes. But don't despair. We may eventually be able to do something for you. I could persuade the vicar who's an old friend of mine to get a young marriageable curate. And if it doesn't work out, then I shall give you a present, at least. Not a gown, but a ring perhaps, or a brooch. But a husband would be the most welcome, eh?'

It was impossible to dislike the old lady who had a streak of earthiness and vulgarity that certainly did not belong to these prim times. Sarah imagined her face when Ambrose came home, and things were as they should be. Would Lady Malvina ever forgive her? It would be sad if she did not.

Nevertheless she dressed for her first dinner with the family with some nervousness. If Lady Malvina was feeling bored, or at odds with Amalie, she was likely to say anything she pleased. The results might be either entertaining or embarrassing.

It was dark now, and lamps had been lit on the stairs, making yellow pools of light and leaving the high ceilings lost in darkness. The house was too far from a town to have had the new gas fittings installed. Now it smelt pleasantly of beeswax and candle-smoke. The heavy curtains, frayed at the edges, had been drawn across the long windows and the sound of the dying wind shut out.

In the drawing-room a fire crackled on the hearth, its flames leaping up the cavernous chimney. Amalie was there already. She stood facing the fire, the light shining on her ice-blue gown. She was a slim graceful figure with her bent head and tiny waist. One would have imagined Blane to be very proud of her, and not seeking reasons to sleep in another room.

But when she turned Sarah saw that the sulkiness was still in her face. Her dark eyes glittered.

'Well, Miss Mildmay, is Titus settled?'

'Very well, Lady Mallow. And he likes the new nursemaid.'

'Splendid. Though what he likes or dislikes is not here or there according to my husband. He must not be spoilt. And he's such a little boy still. I'll go up to him presently. Ugh! What a draughty house this is. I've been shivering ever since we arrived.'

'Then, as my mother recommends, you must wear more petticoats, my love,' came Blane's deep pleasant voice from the doorway. 'Good evening, Miss Mildmay. I'm glad to see you're joining us.'

Sarah dropped her eyes. She would like to have returned his bold stare. She had always known how to deal with men of his kind when Amelia and Charlotte had only blushed and giggled. But now, to play her part, she had to blush, too, and let the wretched man think he was getting away with his impudence.

'And are you settled comfortably, Miss Mildmay? Do you agree with my wife that this is a cold house?'

'Perhaps it hasn't had time to be thoroughly heated yet, Lord Mallow.'

'That's what I say. But my wife insists the furnishings are at fault. We're to import miles of Genoese velvet, and acres of carpet, handpainted wallpapers, new chandeliers, goodness

80

knows what else. What, I ask you, does Titus care for all that?'

'Blane! This isn't only for Titus. We're living here.'

'I came back solely for Titus, as you know. Let's simply preserve this place for him, as was our intention.'

Sarah was suddenly conscious of his black gaze on her.

'Does that seem strange to you, Miss Mildmay? That I should want to preserve an inheritance for my son?'

He was a better actor than she was. He was also a hypocrite. To pretend not to care for Mallow Hall himself, when he had fought for it for months.

'Blane, Miss Mildmay isn't interested in what you're planning to do,' Amalie said sharply.

Blane grinned. The deep crevice showed in his cheek.

'Isn't she? Not even in hearing I've promised to read the lesson in church tomorrow?'

Amalie clapped her hand to her mouth, stifling an exclamation. For the first time she seemed amused.

'You!'

'Yes, I. The vicar called while you were resting. It's the custom to do this. My father always did.'

Amalie was laughing openly.

'Forgive me, my love. But how long is it since you opened a Bible?'

'If you think I'm more at home at sea, then I'm prepared to agree with you. All the same, you'll be at church tomorrow, and you'll take Titus. He might as well know what's in store for him.'

After that, dinner at the candlelit dining-table was an amicable enough meal, even Lady Malvina refraining from making any too outrageous remarks. Afterwards Blane sprawled in a chair in front of the fire, his head tilted back, his long nose pointing to the ceiling, while Lady Malvina dozed noisily, and Amalie played the piano in a desultory way. Amalie was trying hard to be a fashionable lady.

'We must have dinner parties, Blane.'

'We came down here to rest, don't you remember?'

'Oh, nonsense. Nothing makes you tired. And the case was no

strain since you knew you must win it. Besides, there'll be people here who expect to be invited to the Hall. Old friends. Isn't that so, Mamma?'

Lady Malvina woke with a start.

'Oh, yes, there'll be plenty who expect it. But I warn you, everyone in these parts is as dull as ditchwater.'

'Will you make up a list, Mamma? After all, Blane can't be expected to know who lives here, after twenty years away.'

'No,' Lady Malvina muttered. 'But you'd remember the Fortescues, Blane?' Her voice was suddenly uncertain, worried.

'The Colonel? Of course. Is he still alive?'

Lady Malvina relaxed.

'Do you think anything would kill him? And the Veseys and the Blounts. They're all still here.'

'There you are,' said Amalie triumphantly. 'So we'll give a dinner party as soon as we can. After all we must lead some kind of social life in the depths of the country. We'll begin by church in the morning. Blane is to read the lesson, Mamma.'

Blane stretched easily.

'A respectable beginning, you see. But aren't you afraid, my love, you may dig up too much of my past?'

Amalie's eyes glinted.

'I don't think so.'

'No fair Marias? Eh, Mamma? Now Miss Mildmay is shocked.'

Sarah shook her head deprecatingly.

'I'm not shocked, but I am very tired. May I say goodnight?'

Blane sprang to his feet.

'We'll expect to see you at church in the morning.' His gaze lingered quite deliberately on her throat. Then he seemed to collect himself and said lightly, 'You might even rehearse me in my diction. You look sceptical, as if you really think I'm an illiterate sailor.'

Amalie said crisply, 'Blane, Miss Mildmay is tired. Don't keep her standing. Goodnight, Miss Mildmay.'

'Goodnight,' Sarah murmured and hastened up the lamplit stairs.

How could the man be such a hypocrite? She believed he knew how suspicious she was, and was finding the situation amusing.

But he didn't know about Ambrose. She still held the strongest card.

8

But it was extraordinarily difficult to write her diary that night. She wanted to set down Blane's blatant hypocrisy about reading the lesson in church, then against that remembered his determination to preserve the Mallow fortune for his son. No one would have doubted his sincerity when he said that. He behaved, too, as if he were used to being master of a place like this. That was instinctive, and not learned in a few short months.

Yet there was no doubt Lady Malvina was uncertain of him. She was scheming to get all that she could, money or jewels, while it was possible. Again, contrarily, she was genuinely deeply attached to Titus, and certainly believed, or deceived herself, that he was her grandson.

Everything is a complex web, Sarah wrote helplessly by the light of the candle on her bedside table. *So far there is no tangible proof at all. But tomorrow I will observe closely the people at church and the way they greet the new family.*

She closed and locked the little book, and put it back in her reticule, so that it was never out of her possession, then blew out the candle and settled to sleep.

It was in the early hours that Sarah heard Titus crying. She fumbled for matches to light her candle. The whimper coming from the nursery was stifled and forlorn. When she reached Titus she found him only half awake, but obviously frightened. He had heard strange noises, he said. His thin arms clung round Sarah's neck.

'What sort of noises?' she asked. The wind had died and the big house seemed quite still.

'I don't know. From up there.'

He pointed to the ceiling, and Sarah's breath caught involuntarily. The floor above this one comprised the attic rooms. The servants slept up there, and it was in one of those rooms that the unhappy maid, fifty years ago, had hanged herself. Now no one slept in that room if it could be avoided. Betsey had told her and a wide-eyed Eliza the story.

'It was probably a seagull. Or perhaps the canary. Or a mouse behind the wall. You were asleep. You didn't hear properly.'

'Was it a mouse?' Titus asked.

'I expect so. Lie down and go back to sleep. I'll leave the candle.'

The little boy looked up at her with his docile gaze. The room was draughty, for the candle flame flickered constantly. Tomorrow Sarah decided to arrange for a night light, something in a globe that did not flicker, creating shadows. A child's imagination could so easily become distorted.

The house was very still. The uneasiness of the quiet was surely the product of her own distorted imagination.

It was a bright cold morning, and they were all preparing for church. Sarah, going down early with Titus, had an opportunity to talk to Soames who had brought the carriage to the door. This was the man whom Ambrose believed had coached Blane in his knowledge of the past. It could well be, for the man had a narrow face and an air of servility that was displeasing.

'The young master will be wanting a pony,' he said. 'I've just the one, a half brother to the one his father used to ride.'

'Did you teach his father to ride, Soames?'

'Oh, aye. And a desperate rider he was, wanting to jump before he could canter. This wee lad now will be more cautious.'

'You'd notice a great change in the master?'

Sarah disliked having to chat to this man who had begun to look at her with sly interest. He would have to be dismissed when Ambrose came home, if only because of this necessary familiarity now.

'Not that much, miss. He's still the same devil-may-care person. You wouldn't mistake that face in a lifetime. You ask old Betsey. She's the only one of the old staff. She remembers him.' His eyes slid over Sarah's neat figure. 'This is a good day for the old place, miss. Never thought I'd live to see it.'

'Then you wouldn't have cared for the—cousin—to be master here?'

'I've nothing against Mr Ambrose.' The man's voice was unctuous. 'Well, nothing personal like. But if you ask me, he's not the type for Mallow.'

It was time the conversation stopped. Sarah's cheeks were already hot with indignation. Ambrose not the type for Mallow indeed! He certainly wouldn't be the type for this nasty sly creature who knew that dismissal would await him the moment Ambrose arrived. This certainly confirmed Ambrose's opinion that Soames was in the conspiracy. He must have waited all his life for such an opportunity, something that completely suited his foxy talents.

That was two of them, Soames, and the elusive Thomas Whitehouse whom presently Ambrose would track down in Trinidad.

But still where was the tangible proof, the witnesses, the evidence of bribes? Could Ambrose mean her to go to the lengths of striking up a friendship with Soames? Something that would lead to confidences. In this a streak of Lady Malvina's vulgarity would have served her well. Very well then, she thought, if necessary she would cultivate not only the vulgarity but the unlikeable Soames as well. It was for Mallow and Ambrose.

But in church clarity and good sense left her again. She was hypnotised by Blane's voice as he stood, tall and confident in the pulpit, reading the lesson. He did it as if he had been doing a similar thing every Sunday of his adult life. His voice had the right touch of sonority and depth. He neither hurried nor stumbled over the words. He obviously hypnotised the entire congregation, for the church, except for the grave beautiful voice, was utterly still.

The man was a complete actor, Sarah thought angrily. How could he read the Bible so beautifully, and be so false?

Amalie's lips, she noticed, were slightly parted, her whole face eager and queerly hungry. Although she sulked and made extravagant demands and assumed haughtiness, she clearly worshipped her husband. Like this congregation, he had her in his spell. It amused him to play with people, to exert his power. He knew he could twist most of them round his little finger.

86

Even his shrewd old mother who now looked fatuous and doting.

As he slowly closed the Bible on the last words, his curious moody gaze swept the church. It still seemed to hold irony, an almost sad irony, as if even he felt this was going a little too far. But what a victory it was, for when the service was over he was besieged by eager people claiming friendship and recognition. Amalie began to flush and bridle with pleasure. Lady Malvina, for all her air of torpor after a too-long sermon, was always in the right place to say names clearly for the benefit of a possibly lethargic memory.

'Ah, Colonel Fortescue! How nice to see you. Of course my son remembers you. Mrs Blount, Miss Blount. And Sir Geoffrey. And dear Lady Mary. Thank you, my dear, but you can't be as happy as I am. Let me present my daughter-in-law. And my grandson. Where's Titus? Miss Mildmay, bring Titus. I want you to see how extraordinarily he resembles his father as a child. You remember Blane at this age?'

The sea-wind stirred in the long grass about the old grave-stones. Even the stones, tilted with age, seemed to be bowing deferentially. The lord of the manor was home. Everyone, naturally, must be happy.

Everyone except the lord himself. For Blane's expression now held an intense boredom which he didn't attempt to hide, although he made the necessary conversation. Was this expression even more authentic than his moment of self-derision in church? Was it that of the young Blane who had run off to sea because he was so impossibly bored with country life, and wanted adventure?

This same sea-wind, Sarah thought irrelevantly, would be blowing in Ambrose's face. Perhaps it had some of his breath on it, and one of his cautious admonitions, 'Don't be taken in by the fellow's charm. It's only superficial.'

Sarah walked very slowly towards the carriage. Soames was standing at the horses' heads, grinning too familiarly at her. His expression had all the triumph Blane's had lacked.

'Does your heart good, miss, a sight like that. The prodigal son returned.'

The next day, helped by the elderly Betsey and Eliza, Sarah organised the schoolroom. Betsey was full of sentiment about leaving things exactly as they had always been, but Sarah firmly suggested changes that would brighten up the rather gloomy room. Titus was little more than a baby. Why should he have to endure this dreariness just because his father had? Sarah pulled herself up sharply. She was falling into the treacherous habit of accepting what everyone else in the house apparently accepted without question—that Titus's father had spent his childhood there.

'Look, miss,' Betsey exclaimed triumphantly. 'Here's where the master wrote on the window pane. He borrowed his mother's diamond ring. There was such a row because afterwards he hid it.'

The scratching on the lowest pane behind the curtain was perfectly visible. It was a childish scrawl, and the verse was the invention of an irreverent schoolboy.

> *I hate this room,*
> *It's full of gloom.*
> *I'd rather go away than stay.*

'How old was he when he did that?' Sarah asked.

'Old enough to know better, miss. About ten or eleven. His father punished him severe.'

Old enough to remember, Sarah thought privately. Especially after the severe punishment had emphasised his misdoing.

'Look what naughty Papa did,' Sarah said deliberately to Titus. 'He wrote on the window and it will never come out.'

Titus scrambled up to see.

'What does it say?'

'Why don't you ask Papa to tell you?'

Titus's small fingers scratched at the indelible marks.

'Does Papa know what it says?'

'If he wrote it he'll know, won't he?' Betsey had given her a rather odd glance. Sarah smoothly changed the subject.

'It's time for your walk. Go and tell Eliza to put on your outdoor things.'

She had thought she would have had to do a little more discreet coaching before Titus did what she wanted. But Titus, for all his nervousness and timidity, was a sharp little boy. When, following the custom Amalie had established in London, he was taken down to the drawing-room for an hour before his bath and bedtime, he immediately approached his father and said,

'Papa, what did you write on the window?'

Blane looked bewildered.

'On the window? What window?'

'In the schoolroom. Betsey said you wrote with a diamond. How did you write with a diamond?'

Blane grimaced and said easily, 'Looks as if my untidy childhood is catching up on me.'

'But what does the writing say, Papa?' Titus persisted.

Blane looked at Sarah.

'Is it illegible, Miss Mildmay? I know I was an almost illiterate child.'

'No, it isn't illegible, Lord Mallow. It's quite a clever verse for a ten-year-old boy. I gather from Betsey you were punished rather severely, I don't know whether for writing on the window or for having such a thing as a diamond in your possession.'

Amalie sprang to her feet.

'I must go up and see this evidence of your precocious talents, my love.'

Sarah had not missed her uneasiness, and now she didn't miss the significance of her action. Let Blane read the silly verse before he should be challenged again to remember it.

But Blane was not to be challenged. He merely shrugged and said, 'Frankly, I haven't the slightest recollection of it. What does it say, Miss Mildmay?'

Sarah repeated the verse without expression, and Blane burst into a roar of laughter.

'By jove, it's deuced appropriate. It expressed my feelings. But I wonder where I picked up the diamond.'

'Off your mother's dressing-table,' came Lady Malvina's voice from the door. She stood there, flushed and aggressive. 'It was my most valuable ring. Afterwards you hid it in a bird's nest in the guttering, and only confessed when your father had whipped you. Disgusting child that you were.'

Blane shrugged again, unperturbed.

'This shows how fascinating the sub-conscious mind is. It deliberately shuts out unpleasant memories. Isn't that so, Miss Mildmay? You're the highly educated person here.'

He had subtly turned the challenge to her. He was very clever, much more clever than the rebellious little boy who had thought up a schoolboy rhyme. He was trying to discover whether anyone found this little scene significant. Apart from Titus who was too small, and Betsey who was too unsuspecting, she was the only one who might inconveniently at some time have too good a memory.

She answered carefully, 'I believe the sub-conscious can do quite remarkable things, Lord Mallow. Personally I would not have thought a child likely to forget an escapade like that. But there is, of course, the amnesia from which you suffered.'

'I didn't intend to make use of that reason again,' Blane said. 'The jury were beginning to consider it a too-convenient one, and my cousin Ambrose didn't believe a word of it. But it is perfectly true that I have the most extraordinary blanks. Isn't it, Mamma?'

'Perfectly,' Lady Malvina agreed. 'Especially as regards your misdeeds, whether that's due to your sub-conscious mind or not. I don't understand these modern ideas. But I do know that ring was an exceptionally good one, and I'd lost it for weeks. Most upsetting.'

'Poor Mamma. Then I must make belated amends. We shall find you another one.'

Lady Malvina relaxed and glowed with pleasure.

'What a trifling thing to be making a fuss about,' Amalie said pettishly. 'All little boys are mischievous. And that doesn't seem to have been a very heinous crime. Titus, it's your bedtime. Come and kiss Mamma goodnight.'

Lady Malvina looked pointedly at the very fine yellow diamond on Amalie's finger.

'I wonder if you would think it so trifling, my dear, if Titus followed his father's example.'

'Oh, tush! What nonsense! Titus is an obedient child.'

The next day which was wet and stormy, Blane came un-announced into the schoolroom. Sarah was beginning to teach Titus his alphabet with a box of bricks. For convenience she sat on the floor beside him and interspersed the lesson with a little building of houses and bridges. Titus had grown quite noisy, and was announcing with glee that shortly he would demolish the latest erection when the tall figure stood over them.

'I thought the boy was to learn his letters, not architecture.'

Sarah scrambled to her feet, aware that she had been as interested in the game as Titus. It was unexpectedly satisfying to make the little boy laugh.

'Titus is too young, Lord Mallow, to have long hours at lessons. I think a certain amount of teaching disguised as play is good for the very young.'

'Aren't you a little in advance of the times, Miss Mildmay? Is it that you enjoy the games, too?'

He put out his hand and lightly lifted a drifting lock of hair on to the top of Sarah's head. Startled, she drew back smooth-ing her hair. Blane began to laugh in his sudden explosive manner.

'Well, where's this piece of deathless verse on the window?'

'Here, Papa,' said Titus. 'What does it say?'

Blane stood hunched over it thoughtfully.

'Do you know, Miss Mildmay, I really haven't the slightest recollection of doing that. I sometimes wonder whether the toss I took permanently injured my brain.'

Had he come up specially to convince her of his innocence? But why bother? She was only a servant.

His merry irreverent eyes held her.

'The trouble, no doubt, was that I didn't have nearly as charming a governess as my son has. I remember a Miss Ottway, a holy terror.'

'A match for you, Lord Mallow?' Sarah murmured.

'Never! Though after her I got a tutor, just as mean and deceitful, and then thank heaven I was sent to school.'

'Papa, can I have a diamond to write on the window?' Titus was asking.

'No, you cannot! It's more than I can do to keep your mother happy, let alone my own mother. What is this terrible fascination that jewels have? Do you know, Miss Mildmay? I believe women would do murder for them. Or for any possessions.'

'And do you exclude your own sex from this greed, Lord Mallow?'

Blane's eyes narrowed wickedly.

'The devil I don't! My cousin Ambrose, for instance, was as sour as he— I beg your pardon, Miss Mildmay.'

Sarah began to gather up the blocks.

'If you will excuse us, I think the lesson ought to continue.'

'So you're driving me out also?'

'Also?' Sarah asked involuntarily.

Blane returned to the window. He thrust his hands into his pockets gloomily.

'Look at that rain! That's what I remember about this place. Everlastingly wet. No wonder I ran off to the Caribbean. My wife's arranging a lot of social calls. I never thought she'd want to take to conventional English social life. I didn't come here to be a drawing-room dummy, or to be bored to death.'

Sarah, unable to hold the conversation she would so dearly have liked to, said nothing.

'Papa, will you help us build the blocks?' Titus asked.

Blane flung round.

'Is that what I'm to be reduced to? No, I will not build blocks. Oh, the devil take this place! I'll ride over and have a drink with Tom Mercer. I'll leave you to your pursuit of knowledge.'

'Is Papa angry?' Titus asked uncertainly, as his father flung out.

'No, darling.'

'He looked angry.'

'Help me gather up the blocks and come and say your letters again.' (No, your father isn't angry, he's just bored. How does he have the colossal nerve to oust Ambrose from his inheritance, and then be bored with it himself!)

Lady Malvina also was worried about her son's restlessness. He had been in the place three days, after fighting for months to get possession of it, and already he behaved as if he were in prison. The trouble, of course, was his wife, always wanting something, always peevish. Instead of behaving like a happy and satisfied woman who had everything anyone could reasonably expect in life, one would have thought she was being constantly unfairly treated. The danger was that if she kept on like this she might succeed in driving Blane back to sea. Already he was hankering for the freedom of his old life. Lady Malvina had heard them quarrelling the previous evening.

'Look, Amalie, I told you at the start I couldn't be bothered with Colonel this and Lady that. If you must have a dinner party, have it. But let it stop at that. I won't pay endless calls. I've come here to enjoy country life.'

'This is country life. We must do as other people do, or they'll think it odd.'

'What the devil do I care what they think? We're here, and that's the beginning and end of it. And another thing, I'll tell you once more I won't spend thousands on fancy decorations that will be shabby and out of date before Titus grows up.'

'Titus! This is my house, too.'

'I think of it purely as Titus's!'

'Blane!' Lady Malvina heard Amalie's voice quiver. The sly creature was putting that on. She must know better than to think that she could get round Blane with tears. 'Why are you always so unkind to me?'

'Unkind?'

'What word would you use? After I've shown my feelings so plainly.'

'More than plainly.'

'Blane, darling——'

'Look, Amalie, I warn you, if you start that again I'll leave for the Caribbean tomorrow. I can't stand whining.'

'A wife has the right to say what she pleases.'

'Oh, my God!' Blane came striding out of the room so quickly that Lady Malvina hadn't a moment in which to appear to be innocently passing. He actually collided with her, but setting her straight muttered an apology without seeming to notice who she was. After he had gone Lady Malvina heard Amalie weeping. And this time the tears were real, for the woman was alone, with no one to be impressed.

In a way, however, the scene reassured Lady Malvina, for this was exactly the kind of husband she would have expected her son to make, intolerant, impatient and overbearing. Even the threat to leave for the Caribbean was completely typical of Blane. He would not do it, of course. He would not have struggled so hard to obtain Mallow Hall only to immediately leave it. And he had promised her jewels. Amalie would get some, too, but that couldn't be helped. She was his wife, Lady Malvina merely his mother. At least, one was almost certain about that latter fact. One made allowances for those repeated strange lapses of memory. The verse on the schoolroom window, for instance. What a good thing that had not been brought up in court. Ambrose couldn't have known about it. Now these significant trifles were happening too late for anyone to be unduly interested or suspicious. And they were happily established at Mallow. Everything was well.

Lady Malvina sighed with relief and rang for Bessie to come and light the lamps and replenish the fire. Presently she would have Titus in for a game. The boy, under the care of that gentle and pretty Miss Mildmay, was improving enormously. Soon he would be just as his father had been, arrogant and headstrong and handsome. And his grandmother would have her jewels and her comfort for as long as she needed them.

'Stoke up the fire, Bessie,' she said, as Bessie's stout elderly figure appeared. 'Draw the curtains and shut out the dark.'

'It is dark and cold, my lady.'

'Not in here,' Lady Malvina asserted determinedly. 'In here we're safe and warm. Ah, it's good to be home, Bessie. And with my own family around me again.'

'Yes, my lady.' Lady Malvina fancied there was the slightest hesitation in Bessie's voice. Had there been talking among the servants? Were there suspicions?

But nonsense! How could there be? If she heard so much as a word breathed by any of the servants, out they would go.

Didn't they realise how lucky they were? The new master could have been her cold-fish nephew, Ambrose.

The fire leaped up, and the lighted lamps made the room cosy.

'Ha!' said Lady Malvina triumphantly. 'Now pour me a glass of port, Bessie. And send my grandson in. We'll have a fine romp. Ask Miss Mildmay to come, too.'

Miss Mildmay was a nice girl, quiet and sympathetic. Her behaviour was impeccable. She was a lady and to be trusted. One couldn't confide one's doubts to her, but one could at least have the relief of a little gossip.

9

As the days went by Sarah began to grow disheartened. She was making discoveries, but not the kind that were of any use to her. For instance, she knew without Lady Malvina's confidences that Amalie was unhappy. Amalie had at last persuaded Blane to allow her to do a certain amount of refurnishing and there had been a great coming and going of tradesmen, and the place had been littered with expensive materials. She had also had various people to call, and gone calling herself, driven by Soames in the carriage, and too elaborately dressed for the country. But all this merely seemed to tighten her face and make her more moody and sharp in her manner. Something more than a passing quarrel was wrong between her and Blane, but this did not constitute the kind of evidence for which Sarah was looking.

Titus's conversation was of no help. The past, when he had been called Georgie, had rapidly slipped away from him as he became absorbed in his new surroundings. He scarcely remembered the house in London, let alone his home in the West Indies. He was learning to ride the pony Soames had got for him, and overcoming his timidity. This later fact gave Sarah pleasure, for she was fond of the shy little boy. Whatever she felt about his parents' duplicity, Titus was innocent. The nursery days with the little boy and the slow good-tempered Eliza had a peaceful quality that contrasted sharply with her turmoil of mind when in the presence of Blane and Amalie.

As far as Blane was concerned, Sarah felt as if she were up against a brick wall. He blandly swept aside all awkward moments by pleading his stupidity and unreliability as a child, and his loss of memory. At other times his knowledge of Mallow Hall and the past seemed too uncannily accurate to be assumed. The only explanation for this was Soames, who was too familiar altogether, always hanging about, his dark foxy face missing nothing.

But even Soames could not have known some of the things Blane seemed to know.

The mystery was baffling, and Sarah, who was not a patient person, had moments of wondering whether to give the whole thing up. But before very long she should hear from Ambrose who must have arrived in Trinidad by now. She found she could scarcely remember Ambrose's face. Its pale elegance seemed to slip out of her mind each time she thought she had just secured it. This was the most disturbing thing of all.

But after what had seemed an indefinite stalemate, a strange event happened.

It was caused by a letter that arrived for Blane with the post at breakfast. Blane had been grumbling, but only half-heartedly, and he seemed to be in good humour.

'Fifty yards of silk damask, twenty yards of Swiss muslin, ten yards of French grey taffeta, one hundred yards of bottle-green embossed velvet. Are we setting up a drapery business? But let's not worry so long as the local gentry is impressed. I hope you have something more cheerful than bills in your post, Mamma.'

'I have a letter from my jeweller,' Lady Malvina answered. 'He says he still has the pearl necklace I had to sacrifice when your father was being so eccentric about money. I can have it back for the sum he paid me. I must say I think that exceedingly honest of him.'

'How much was the sum?' Amalie asked suspiciously.

'Only five hundred pounds. Only a trifle compared with all those fabulous materials you are getting, my dear. A hundred yards of embossed velvet. Tch, tch!'

'The materials are for the house. Which we all share,' Amalie said pointedly.

'I'm a little sentimental about the old familiar ones which I chose myself. And I'm superstitious about green.'

'Be quiet!' Blane's voice was startling. He had a letter in his hand. He seemed very disturbed. 'All that chitter-chatter about curtains.'

'What is it, Blane? Bad news?' asked his mother apprehensively.

Amalie half stood up.

'Blane——'

Their tension, Sarah realised, was never very far below the surface. One unexpected incident, and they were on their guard. Wasn't that a sign of guilt if anything was?

'Yes, I have some news.' He spoke in an undertone, and did not add whether the news were good or bad. For a crazy moment Sarah wondered if the letter were from Ambrose.

'I'll have to go to London.' He sprang up, as if he were going to call for Soames immediately.

'Not this minute!' Amalie exclaimed.

'Later today. By the afternoon train.'

'Blane, what is this unexpected news?' demanded Lady Malvina testily. 'Aren't we to be permitted to know?'

Blane had recovered his poise. His eyes were sparkling now. He was a man to enjoy a fight.

So there must still be something to fight over, Sarah reflected. Whatever that letter had contained was not yet a defeat.

It was Amalie who could not hide her alarm. She had become very pale, and when Blane left the room she hurried after him to talk to him privately.

Sarah longed to follow.

'Will you excuse me, Lady Malvina? I must go up to the schoolroom.'

But Lady Malvina clutched her hand.

'What was in that letter, do you think? Something's upset my son.'

'I expect some business affair, Lady Malvina.'

Beside herself with frustration, Sarah made another move to go but the old lady gripped hard.

'It was more than business. Because it affected Amalie, too. Didn't you see the way she looked? Oh dear, I hope nothing's gone wrong.'

It was too late now. Amalie and Blane would be shut in the study beyond overhearing. Sarah swallowed her disappointment.

'What do you mean would go wrong, Lady Malvina?'

'Oh, things, things.' Lady Malvina at last released Sarah's

hand, and picking up her cup nervously swallowed all her coffee. She sucked her lips and looked about her with her vague worried gaze. 'I tell you, Miss Mildmay, I'm never easy about my son. He's been so undisciplined and unpredictable. One always lives on tenterhooks with him. Well, can't you see how his wife is?' she added irritably. 'And now I'll be bound he'll go off to London without telling anyone why he's going. That letter may even have been perfectly harmless and he's trumping up an excuse to get away for a while. He's always so restless.'

'If that's the case, he acted very well,' Sarah could not help commenting.

'Oh, acting. He would find that a very trifling difficulty.'

Lady Malvina drummed on the table with her fingers, then, with her usual optimism, suddenly brightened and exclaimed, 'At least there's one good thing. If Blane's in London he can redeem my pearls.'

Amalie had come back quietly into the room and heard the last words. A flash of vicious anger crossed her face.

'There will be no time for that, I'm afraid. Blane has important business.'

Lady Malvina pouted.

'What sort of business?' she asked waspishly.

'I don't know. My husband doesn't worry me with business details.'

'Amalie!' Lady Malvina's voice held apprehension again. 'It isn't anything to do with the case?'

'Of course not. You must realise that's finished and done with. Miss Mildmay, isn't it time for Titus's lesson?'

Sarah had never found it so difficult to reply meekly. Why should she obey this shallow petulant and at this moment very disturbed woman? Indeed, disturbed was too mild a word. Frightened was a more accurate one.

The mysterious thing that Blane, after a startled moment, intended to meet with his familiar confident arrogance had frightened his wife very much. She was not going to have an easy moment while her husband was in London.

If it came to that, neither was Sarah. For already curiosity was bedevilling her. Somehow she had to get her hands on that very interesting letter.

After turning over every method in her mind, she decided quite simply to imitate Blane himself, and behave with his superb confidence. She would go into the study at the time the maids usually cleaned it, and simply say she had been sent by the master to get something out of his desk.

Indeed, the method was successful enough, as Betsey and the other maid took little notice of her. The catch was that the letter did not appear to be there. Blane must be carrying it about in his pocket. It must be as important as her own diary which she never let out of her possession, carrying it in her reticule all the time.

It seemed she was to remain in ignorance. This was intolerable. What would Ambrose have done? He certainly would not have let an opportunity like this slip by. He would have determined to find out who was meeting Blane, and why.

He would have followed Blane to London. . . .

10

IT was late the next day when Sarah rang the bell at the servants' entrance to the house in South Kensington. She had her face well muffled in a woollen scarf. The story of the agonising toothache which required immediate attention by her own dentist in London had to be told convincingly here, also.

Lucy opened the door and gave a little cry.

'Lawks! Is it you, Miss Mildmay?'

'Yes, Lucy. I had to come to London to see the dentist.'

'Oh, miss! Had you the toothache bad?' Lucy peered sympathetically.

'I had, but it's getting better now. I'll be all right after a night's rest.'

'And me keeping you on the doorstep,' Lucy exclaimed. 'Come right in. There's only me and Mrs Robbins here. And such a fuss when the master arrived yesterday. Mrs Robbins had been—you know——' Lucy giggled. 'But she covered it up wonderful. You'd never know she'd had a glass. It was the shock, she said, pulled her together.'

Following Lucy into the warm kitchen, Sarah said, 'Is the master here now?'

'Yes, he's waiting for someone, but no one's come. Right bad-tempered he's been. Saying why should he come to town on a wild goose chase, and things like that. Will you take a cup of something hot, Miss Mildmay? You look fair frozen.'

Sarah let the scarf drop from her face. Presently she would wash off the rouge which gave her the appearance of a high fever. Everyone, she was sure, had been quite taken in with her story of a night of pain and the necessity to see her own dentist in London immediately. They had not even fussed about her travelling alone. Amalie was certainly not going to sacrifice one of her maids to accompany a mere governess, and anyway a lady suffering from severe toothache was not likely to be molested.

She had had a qualm about leaving Titus, however. She had

never meant to allow herself to grow fond of her enemies' child, but the little boy's dependence on her was having an inevitable effect. She was becoming fond of him, and delighted about his growing assurance and happiness. This latter, however, was still only on the surface. Underneath he still had some deep insecurity.

'Are you going for ever, Miss Mildmay?'

'Titus, you silly little creature! Of course not. I'll be back tomorrow or the next day.'

His large eyes were full of uncertainty and distrust. He didn't attempt to embrace her. He merely stood there, a little boy in a red velvet jacket, too old and too wise, looking at her with his distrustful eyes.

'Who will teach me my letters?'

'You can have a holiday until I come back. Eliza will take care of you, and Soames will take you riding.'

'What if the mouse——' He stopped, not meaning to have exposed his private fear.

'What mouse, Titus darling?'

'The one I hear in the night,' he answered in a rush.

'But not every night, Titus. Only once when you called me.'

'It comes out of the fireplace. It's very large. I think it means to eat me.'

'Titus! You're making that up to keep me here.'

The little boy shook his head stubbornly. How did she know what night fears he had? He apparently only called to her in an extremity.

Sarah knelt to put her arms round him.

'I'll tell Eliza to sleep in the nursery with you, and always leave your light burning. Come now. Surely you'll be all right for two nights while I get my tooth fixed.'

'Is it very sore?'

'Indeed it is, or I wouldn't be going.'

He touched her face gently.

'Promise to come back.'

Sarah had left in foolish tears, but this served to give proof of her assumed illness. Even Amalie who looked to be in some kind of secret anguish herself, expressed wishes for Sarah's quick recovery.

Lady Malvina pressed some money into her hand to pay her railway fare, and that was the last straw. Although she suffered no physical pain, Sarah felt that mentally she was a good companion for the sly-faced Soames who drove her to Yarby to catch the train.

'Don't worry, Miss Mildmay. I'll keep an eye on the boy, and other things,' he said insufferably.

What 'other things' did he mean? Was there a veiled threat in that remark? Whatever it might have been, it served to bring back Sarah's resolution, and she didn't weaken again.

She was here in the London house, and in time, for apparently Blane had not yet accomplished the purpose for which he had come to town. He was expecting a caller, the writer of that letter, no doubt. It simply remained now for her to keep her eyes and her ears wide open.

'I'll go straight up to my room, Lucy. Yes, I would like a cup of tea, if you wouldn't mind bringing it up. And Lucy, would you take care not to let the master know I'm here? It's better not. He might think it impertinent, my coming here. Or he might think I expect to come down to dinner.'

'How could you, with that toothache? What you need, miss, is pap. But I'll have to tell Mrs Robbins you're here, miss, if I'm to be carrying things upstairs.'

At that moment from upstairs there came the crash of the front door being banged shut.

'The master's gone out!' Lucy exclaimed. 'He can't be going to wait any longer for that caller.'

'He's gone out, thank goodness,' came Mrs Robbins's voice from the basement stairs. 'Who do I hear you talking to, Lucy? Not that cheeky grocer's boy again?'

'It's Miss Mildmay, ma'am,' Lucy squeaked. 'She's just come with the toothache.'

Sarah pressed her hand to her cheek.

'I'm just going up to my room, Mrs Robbins. I've asked Lucy not to tell the master I'm here. He might worry about Titus. But I really had to see the dentist. I was suffering so.'

'You poor thing!' Mrs Robbins, plump and good-natured, the effects of her inclination for the bottle already showing in her highly-coloured complexion, was full of sympathy. 'You go right up to bed, my lamb. Lucy will bring you a tray.'

Sarah swayed slightly.

'I don't want to worry anybody, particularly the master.'

'Neither you shall. Though why he shouldn't be told we're all human and get our aches and pains, I don't know. Now he's gone out leaving strict instructions if anyone calls I'm to keep them until he returns. He's been expecting someone, but he's got impatient waiting. Look, how'd it be if we all had a little drop of something?'

'No, thank you, Mrs Robbins. I'll go straight upstairs.'

'It'd do the tooth good. Keep the cold out for me and Lucy, too.'

'You and Lucy do what you like, Mrs Robbins, but I really must rest. I've had a long journey.'

It was unbelievable luck that Blane had just gone out. Now she could slip into the study at once.

Not that she expected to find the important letter there. One would have thought he would have been much too careful to leave it lying about. But he must have expected Mrs Robbins to be too uninterested and Lucy too illiterate to notice it.

For there it was lying on the desk, in the envelope which had been re-addressed painstakingly from this address to Mallow Hall.

It said simply,

Dear Blane,

Fancy, I thought you was dead. But I have just heard about you and all that business. You could have knocked me down with a feather. You never told me all that. So I am coming to London to see you. We have a lot to talk about. Expect me Thursday or Friday this week.

Yours faithfully,

Sammie

The postmark, Sarah noticed curiously, was Liverpool. Liverpool could mean someone just arrived on a ship. From the West Indies? Someone who had only just heard of the celebrated case, and was eagerly expecting some share? Moreover someone who seemed to think that Blane was in debt to him. Was he an old shipmate who thought he had stumbled on to a good thing, or a blackmailer?

Sammie. Sarah's heart was beating rapidly. Soon she would discover who he was. And the coming meeting between the two men promised to provide her with the vital evidence for which Ambrose was waiting. For if the writer of the letter thought the man who had received his letter was the true Blane Mallow, and he found him to be an impostor, what would happen?

Sarah sat with the door of her room ajar listening. The chilly day had turned to snow. Already there was a thick coating on roofs and pavements so that the sound of the few cabs and coaches abroad was muffled and almost inaudible. She had to listen for the front door bell, not for the sound of cab wheels.

When the jangling peal did come an hour later she jumped convulsively, then ran softly to the head of the stairs. The hall was still out of sight, but there was no difficulty in hearing Blane's voice. It was loud and jovial.

'Stoke up the fire in the library, Mrs Robbins, and bring in the whisky. It's a deuced cold night, my friend here is almost frozen stiff.'

'Just about, gov'nor,' came the reply.

'We'll soon improve your condition. What are you standing there staring at, Mrs Robbins? Go and do as I say.'

'Yes, my lord.'

Mrs Robbins hurried away and Sarah, in her extreme curiosity, ventured halfway down the curving stairs. She was just in time to see the two men disappear into the library, Blane's companion, a short man in a shabby cloak liberally dusted with snow. His voice was cockney and he must have walked here, judging by the snow he had collected. How could a man like that have legitimate business with Lord Mallow?

They had shut the library door. Sarah waited until Mrs Robbins had bustled in with the tray of drinks, and come out again, then she boldly went up to the door and put her ear to the keyhole.

But the late Lord Mallow had, as his wife complained, spent a great deal of money ensuring that nothing but the best materials and workmanship were put into his house. The handsome doors were inches thick and quite soundproof. Even through the aperture of the keyhole Sarah could hear only a confused murmur of voices. But fortunately for her she detected the sound of glasses put down and chairs moved after a surprisingly short time, as if the business had been very brief indeed. She was just able to fly to the stairs before the door opened.

But her curiosity was her downfall. For still looking round as she climbed the stairs her foot caught in the hem of her skirt. She clutched wildly at the stair-rail, failed to reach it, and tumbled ignominiously to the bottom of the stairs.

For a moment she was conscious of nothing but exquisite pain. The gaslight danced above her head in a luminous haze, then was blotted out by the shape of a head. She began to struggle up.

'Lor lumme! 'as she 'urt 'erself?' she heard the cockney voice saying.

Then she was aware of Blane leaning over her and the cold furious anger in his face. Her heart turned over with its second shock. She had suspected that he could look like this, that his irritations with his wife and other things had been merely superficial in comparison with this deeply roused anger. But to have that black look bent on her was dreadful. Faintness swept over her again.

'Is she 'urt?' the other man repeated.

'I don't think so, cabby.'

Cabby! Was that all the stranger was? She had been brought to this predicament merely by trying to overhear a conversation between Blane and a London cabby! Indignation made her head clear. She heard Blane's tautly controlled voice.

'Not seriously hurt, anyway. I'll see to her. You get on your way.'

'Well, thanks, guv'nor, for the bit of good cheer. Wish all the gentry 'ad your kind 'eart. Sure you don't want me to stop at a doctor's with a message?'

'Good heavens, no! The young woman's only taken a tumble. Haven't you, Miss Mildmay? You're not hurt, are you?'

Sarah at last managed to sit upright.

'N-not at all. I'm p-perfectly all right. Except for'—she gasped—'the toothache.'

The shabby little man went, albeit somewhat reluctantly, and banged the door shut.

'I didn't know,' said Blane, 'that the toothache came on from falling downstairs.'

'I—had to come up to see my dentist. That's why I'm in London. Ask your wife, Lord Mallow.'

'And the dentist has applied a remedy that has made you dizzy? Allow me to assist you to your feet, Miss Mildmay.'

He was too close to her. She wanted to shrink away. But he seemed to have controlled that moment of black anger. He was wearing his more relaxed look of ironic amusement again.

'I can at least look on your pain as a blessing,' he went on. 'Now I'll have someone to eat dinner with me. Why, I believe you are hurt.'

For Sarah, on her feet, found herself quite unable to stand. She had broken several bones in her ankle at the very least! She had to cling desperately to Blane's supporting arm, and just as Mrs Robbins appeared, full of exclamations, felt herself swung into his arms.

'Lor, has the toothache taken her again, my lord?'

'Yes, in a curious place. Her ankle. Bring hot water and bandages, Mrs Robbins.'

She was carried into the library and laid on the leather couch, pleasantly warm from the heat of the fire. The pain was ebbing a little now, although it came back in a fierce spasm as Blane unbuttoned her boot and took it off. His fingers felt the ankle with a searching touch that was almost professional.

'Not too serious, I think. Just a sprain, Miss Mildmay. But I'll warrant it's dispatched your toothache.'

She believed he was laughing at her now. Kneeling beside her, his face was on a level with hers. The blackness of his eyes was full of light. His colour was heightened and there was a faint smell of whisky on his breath. She believed he was a little drunk. Or at least he had been drinking more than he usually did.

'So you fell down the stairs,' he said, and now the amusement was evident in his voice. 'One could enquire what you were doing on the stairs just at that particular moment. Or even indeed why you should be seized with toothache the moment my back is turned.'

Sarah summoned all her dignity.

'If you must know what I was doing on the stairs, I was coming down to ask Mrs Robbins for something soothing for my tooth. It is still very painful.'

'But, my dear young woman, you should have come to me for that remedy. I've just been dispensing it to the cabby who drove me home from my club. He was almost frozen to his seat, poor devil. I brought him in and gave him a hot rum. Now you shall have precisely the same mixture. Ah, Mrs Robbins, bring the things here. Have you had any experience with sprained ankles?'

'I can't really say so, my lord.'

'Bathing isn't difficult. You might do that while I prescribe more effectively. Our poor patient is suffering severely both from her wrenched ankle and from toothache. Do you think we ought to take a look at the errant molar?'

'My lord!' Mrs Robbins murmured, scandalised.

'Very well, we can assume Miss Mildmay's dentist is efficient since she travelled all the way to London to see him.' Blane, a glass of rum in his hand, stood over Sarah. His face was full of impudence. Now he was playing his familiar part, and the glimpse she had caught of his tension and ruthlessness might have been imagined. But she knew it was not. He was thoroughly suspicious about her.

At the moment Sarah found herself quite unable to care about that last possibility. Her pain and her fury with herself for her stupidity, and with Blane for his sudden extraordinarily intimate attitude, were too much.

'If that drink is to make me recover, Lord Mallow, I'd better

108

have it at once.' Then she gasped as Mrs Robbins touched her ankle with a good deal less skill than Blane had showed, and snatched the glass out of his hand. After she had drained the contents, choking a little over the unaccustomed fiery taste, she scarcely cared when Mrs Robbins said primly,

'May I ask you to be so good, my lord, as to leave the room while I remove Miss Mildmay's stocking?'

'Of course. Of course.' The impudent eyebrows were raised high. 'And after that we'll take our dinner in here. It's the only warm room in the house.'

'You will please excuse me, Lord Mallow. I would prefer to retire.'

'The devil you would. But has it occurred to you that you can scarcely get upstairs without being carried. So I fear you will have to wait my pleasure.'

'Lor!' Mrs Robbins murmured, as he went out. 'He is in a playful mood. It's being away from his wife, if you ask me. And a few drinks, o' course. Wonderful how cheering a drink can be.'

'Playful!' echoed Sarah faintly. 'Is that how you would describe it, Mrs Robbins?'

'Well, you wouldn't think it was anything more serious, would you? Not with Lord Mallow!'

How do you know he is Lord Mallow? Sarah wanted to ask. This man might have no standards of behaviour whatever. And here he was enjoying having her practically at his mercy.

As the rum had its effect the pain at last became tolerable. But her ankle seemed to be the size of two, and there was no doubt she was compelled to stay on the couch until she was assisted elsewhere.

Presently Lucy, wide-eyed and scandalised, came in to prepare the table for dinner.

'Lawks, Miss Mildmay, is he making you his prisoner?'

'Don't be foolish, Lucy!'

'But how are you going to eat venison with that toothache?'

'I'm not. I shall simply have a little gruel.'

Lucy scampered out as Blane returned. He had a glass in his hand which he replenished. Then he came over to look down at

Sarah.

'That's better, Miss Mildmay. You have some colour again. Is the ankle easier? Or the toothache, or both?'

'I believe the drink has helped, Lord Mallow.'

Unaccustomed to strong liquor, her head was swimming. She felt strangely carefree.

'Have another.'

'No, thank you.'

'I say yes. It's important on a cold night. Didn't you see how it cheered my friend, the cabby?'

'Is it your habit to bring in strange people for drinks, Lord Mallow?'

'On cold lonely nights, yes. At that time I didn't know I was to have your company. Now, let me take a look at Mrs Robbins's bandage.'

Before Sarah could prevent him, he had twitched off the rug which Mrs Robbins had spread over her, and his searching fingers were feeling the wrappings round her ankle.

'Tch! Tch! It'll have to be redone. Allow me. Now why are you looking so outraged?'

'I believe you're merely enjoying yourself!' Sarah exclaimed. 'The bandage is perfectly all right.'

'On the contrary! It's giving you no support at all. You and it will part company in the night. See, this is how it should be.'

There was no doubt that he was exceedingly skilful.

'May I ask where you gained your experience, Lord Mallow? Are sprained ankles a natural hazard to a sailor's life?'

'Everything from sprained ankles to broken hearts. And an occasional case of bubonic plague or perhaps a murder.'

'In contrast, all this comfort must seem very pleasant.'

He behaved as if he heard no significance in her voice.

'Pleasant but a little monotonous. A sailor's life is a man's life. If you're wondering what I'm doing here it is, as I've already made it clear to everyone, for my son. And my wife.' There was a slight but noticeable pause between the mention of his son and his wife.

'Your wife doesn't hanker for the life of the tropics?'

'There are different kinds of life in the tropics. My wife

wasn't married to the Governor, you understand. She at least deserves this comfort now. And the boy. By the way, is Titus all right while you're away?'

'Perfectly all right, as I imagine he was before I came into his life.'

'He wasn't as well as all that, Miss Mildmay. You mentioned it yourself in no uncertain terms. But I believe he's growing fond of you now.'

Sarah remembered, with a pang, the little boy's clinging arms.

'You particularly said that I was not to spoil him, Lord Mallow.'

'And, by God, you shall not! There, does that feel better?'

Reluctantly Sarah had to admit that it did.

'Then drink up your rum, and we'll have some food.'

Lucy had lit candles on the table. The crocus flames flickered bewilderingly. Sarah felt her face very hot. She *must* go on hating this man. For his present intimate attitude was merely a pose to discover her own game. She must not be taken in for a moment. Neither must she drink any more intoxicating liquor since she was forced to take only gruel as food.

'You accomplished your own business satisfactorily, I hope?' she said politely.

'No. As it happens, I haven't. The person I was to see has let me down. I shall wait only one more day, and then they can go to the devil.'

His glance was completely without evasion.

'We shall probably travel back to Mallow together. You'll have to tolerate my company since you'll need assistance with that foot.'

A convenient way of keeping her under his eye? If so, she deserved it. At least it seemed she was not to be dismissed.

But sitting up at the table facing him over the yellow candle-light was an ordeal, and even more so confining herself to the thin gruel while he ate with the greatest enjoyment the tantalis-ingly savoury venison. She made herself wince now and then. This subtlety was almost overplaying her part, for Blane, with one of his acute glances, observed,

'I believe that dentist of yours hasn't done his job very well. You'd better see mine tomorrow.'

'Oh, no! I shall be quite recovered tomorrow.'

'I hope so. I fear Titus would be upset at your continued absence.'

The remark could be interpreted in two ways. Either that he believed now in her innocent presence here. Or that he disbelieved the whole story, but refrained from dismissing her because of the pain it would cause Titus. Although one would hardly have thought he had that much heart.

He had opened a bottle of Burgundy to drink with the meal. The meagre half glass Sarah permitted herself increased her feeling of unreality. The face opposite her, she thought, fitted these surroundings after all. With its strong lines, its boldness, even the memory of its black anger, it was eminently suitable. This was something she must not write in her notes for Ambrose. It was a discovery she had stumbled on and must forget. Indeed, it was only an illusion. Tomorrow she would see the face for what it was, greedy, selfish and ruthless.

'So unless I carry you upstairs, Miss Mildmay, it will be you for the couch tonight.'

Sarah started as the words penetrated her dulled mind. Blane had definitely drunk too much now. His eyes glinted with a wicked merriment.

The couch! How was he aware that she had known about that night in Tom Mercer's inn?

'And your reason is as legitimate as mine was,' he added smoothly.

'I—I was looking for the kitchen. For milk for Titus. I didn't mean—I thought you were asleep.'

'And I thought you were snooping. You're much too attractive for that, Miss Mildmay. You're exceedingly attractive, do you realise? Wearing the Mallow diamonds, for instance . . .'

Sarah could scarcely speak. Did he *know*?

'What an extraordinary thing to say, Lord Mallow!'

'Merely a fancy. My wife intends to wear them any day now. She's asked me to get them out of the bank. I'm not entirely sure she has quite the type of looks for them. My own opinion is that she requires more colour in her jewels.'

'Lord Mallow, I must demand to know why you said such an extraordinary thing to me.'

He looked at her above the dancing candle flames.

'Just a passing thought, Miss Mildmay. Nothing more, I assure you. Your eyes are as bright as diamonds tonight. Perhaps it's the wine.' He sat back and his voice changed from its lazy quality to curtness. 'You will go back to Mallow, Miss Mildmay. I accept your story that you had severe toothache and that exhaustion after a long painful day caused you to be rather clumsy in climbing the stairs. The outcome of that mishap is going to be of much more inconvenience to yourself than anyone else. So we'll close the subject.'

'Lord Mallow, are you suggesting that you might *doubt* my reason for being here?'

His eyes narrowed. For a moment his expression was unreadable. Then he threw back his head and gave his disconcerting shout of laughter.

'Never trust a pretty woman. I believe my wife was right when she wanted to send you packing. But you'll go back to Mallow because Titus has grown fond of you.'

11

It seemed to grow dark earlier every afternoon. The snow that fell over London did not touch the coast, although heavy clouds and an arctic wind persisted until late the following day. No one knew why Miss Mildmay had not returned as she had promised to. Soames had driven the ten miles to the station only to return reporting that no one at all had got off the train. Amalie had not expected Blane back so soon, but she was furious about Miss Mildmay's failure to return.

She had not a tea party to divert her today, and wandered about the house in what seemed to be a state of acute nervousness. Yesterday she had been the grand lady, dressed in her expensive plum-coloured taffeta, with skirts so exaggeratedly wide that her tiny waist looked like a child's, and diamond eardrops glittering in her ears.

It had been difficult to know what the Blounts and the Fortescues made of such elegance. They had not been used to it at Mallow Hall, Lady Malvina reflected. Her own parties had been haphazard affairs when she was never sure whether or not her husband would remember to be home, or, if he were, whether he would be polite to his guests. And her own appearance had got shabby and old-fashioned, especially since she had been reduced to pawning her jewellery.

She didn't much relish Amalie, that little nobody from the tropics, queening it like this, but it was the inevitable penalty one had to pay for having one's son home again.

At least Lady Malvina was, for a few minutes, able to hold the floor when Amalie was called from the room to see some unexpected and uninvited visitor. Neither did she lose this advantage for when Amalie returned she seemed vague and distrait, and had lost her assurance as an accomplished hostess.

'Just a sewing woman asking for work,' she apologised vaguely. 'The matter could very well have waited. Some more tea, Colonel Fortescue? Oh, I see you have some. Mrs Blount?'

'Did you employ her?' Lady Malvina asked.

'I've asked her to wait. I'll interview her later. Oh, dear!' Amalie had knocked one of the fragile cups on to the carpet, spilling tea. 'How clumsy of me! Mamma, ring for Betsey, please!'

Lady Malvina tugged the bell rope. She looked at her daughter-in-law in surprise. Amalie, for all her look of being strung-up, had usually the most calm and controlled movements.

'On your gown, too. Never mind, if it stains this new woman can take a tuck in the skirt. There's plenty of material. When are you going to have Titus in?' Lady Malvina turned to the company. 'You must all see my grandson, and how the family likeness persists. It's quite remarkable. If anything convinced me I had my son home, that did.'

Colonel Fortescue lifted his head and remarked irrelevantly, 'I hear Ambrose sailed for the West Indies. Is there any particular reason? Unless of course,' he added gallantly, 'he's looking for another such charming lady as Lady Mallow.'

Amalie's knuckles showed white where she gripped the tea table. Then, with a recovery of self-possession that even Lady Malvina had to admire, she said calmly, 'I've scarcely had the opportunity to get acquainted with Ambrose. Understandably he wasn't over-anxious to be friends. But my husband and I hope to remedy that when he returns to England. Don't we, Mamma?'

'You can try,' said Lady Malvina frankly. 'Ambrose isn't a good loser. And what is he doing in the West Indies?'

'A sea voyage is a wonderful antidote for various ills,' said Mrs Blount. For all her frumpy countrified appearance she had exquisite tact. 'I remember when Mr Blount had the gout so badly. We took a cruise to the Mediterranean. So relaxing. Flora dear, we must think of leaving. I shouldn't be surprised if it snows this evening.'

All the company proceeded to take its departure, and when at last they were alone Amalie flung round on Lady Malvina.

'Did you hear that? Ambrose has gone to the West Indies! Why has he? What does he expect to find?'

Lady Malvina's heart was fluttering again with that queer unspoken apprehension.

'That would be for you to know, my dear.'

The lids dropped over Amalie's uneasy eyes. Too late, she was hiding her own apprehension.

'There's nothing to find beyond what has already been aired in court. Blane will tell you so. Ambrose is wasting his time. But I wish he didn't distrust us so. We should all be friends. Well, I suppose I must go and interview this wretched woman.'

'Wretched?'

'Oh, she looks half-starved, poor creature. I expect I must at least give her a trial, since she's come so far.'

But Amalie was not a person to show pity, Lady Malvina had discovered. Was there something particularly pathetic about this waif and stray? Something disturbing enough to make Amalie drop cups and lose her self-control?

Distinctly uneasy herself, especially when she thought of that poky-nosed Ambrose up to such an extraordinary thing, Lady Malvina spent the next hour with Titus who seemed to be missing Miss Mildmay more than was reasonable. Then Amalie came in to give her brisk orders and say goodnight to Titus.

'Is he all right, Eliza? Are you managing quite well?'

'Yes, ma'am. I'm to sleep in the nursery, Miss Mildmay said.'

'Did she? I'm afraid I disagree with that. Titus isn't to be treated like a baby. He's a big boy. Aren't you, my lamb? You will sleep in your own room as usual, Eliza.'

'Yes, ma'am.'

'If the boy calls——' began Lady Malvina, distressed by the look of alarm on Titus's face. Heaven knew, she wanted her grandson to grow strong and fearless, but this, as Miss Mildmay realised, could not be achieved overnight.

'Why should he call?' said Amalie coldly. She bent to kiss her son's forehead. 'Papa would be very angry, Titus, if you weren't a brave boy. You may have a night light, if you wish, but you must learn to sleep alone.'

She was rustling out in her imperious way before Lady Malvina remembered about the sewing woman.

'Oh, yes, I engaged her on a week's trial,' she answered indifferently to Lady Malvina's question. 'I've put her in the room upstairs.'

'Not Bella's room! Not the hau——' Lady Malvina, belatedly thinking of the child, bit off her words.

'Don't be absurd, Mamma. Of course the room isn't haunted. In any case it's the only empty one, and if she doesn't like it she can go. But if she's to stay she must be kept busy. So give her any sewing you have. I won't be down to dinner, Mamma, if you don't mind. I have a headache and shall go to bed early.'

'Are you expecting Blane back tomorrow?'

'If he has his business finished. I hope so.' For a moment the petulant worried look in Amalie's face gave way to one of longing. But that, too, was quickly hidden, and she said, 'I'm not used enough to making all the decisions, even about sewing women. If Blane thinks Mrs Stone an extravagance she must go.'

Mrs Stone seemed harmless enough. Lady Malvina, who was no less inquisitive than her nephew Ambrose, made a point of visiting her in the attic room which, apart from its unfortunate history, really was perfectly comfortable. The woman was below middle-age, probably not much older than Amalie, but she was very poorly dressed and seemed pinched and yellow with cold. She spoke well enough, although with a slight furtiveness that Lady Malvina didn't care for. She was surprised at Amalie being moved by the troubles of such an insignificant creature.

'What brought you to Mallow, Mrs Stone?'

'I'd heard there was a new mistress, ma'am. I thought she might be needing help. Good situations are hard to come by nowadays.'

'Where's your husband?'

'I'm a widow, my lady.'

'Oh! Well, that's a pity, I suppose.' Lady Malvina's glance took leave to doubt the late Mr Stone's ability as a provider. 'Any family?'

Mrs Stone shook her head.

'That's something to be thankful for, eh? Well, I hope you'll be comfortable here. I'll find you plenty of work to do. Can you unpick and put together again?'

'Unpick?' The woman's pale eyes seemed to be gleaming with some kind of amusement. She behaved as if she were about to burst into laughter. 'Oh, yes, I can unpick very well, my lady.'

Simple in the head, thought Lady Malvina. Better keep Titus away from her. What had come over Amalie employing such a person? It couldn't have been her kind heart.

'I've been putting on some weight. My gowns need easing. None of this tight lacing for me. I'll send some up. Well, goodnight, Mrs Stone.'

'Goodnight, my lady.'

The meek voice still held that queer note of suppressed laughter.

The next day, when neither Blane nor Miss Mildmay turned up, seemed very long and full of tension. For Titus had lost his new confidence and had reverted to his pale-faced timidity, shrinking away from Lady Malvina's boisterous embraces and on the verge of tears. And Amalie couldn't sit still a minute, but walked up and down in her rustling gown dressed as if for another tea party. She was very pale and confessed that her headache still troubled her. She had dressed well, either because she expected her husband at any moment or because the expensive clothes gave her confidence. But something was on her mind. She was worrying about Blane's mysterious business in London. And she was very angry with Miss Mildmay for overstaying in London.

'She was to get her tooth attended to and come back at once,' Amalie stormed. 'I almost believe she didn't have toothache at all.'

'But she was in tears of pain.' Lady Malvina liked and trusted Sarah Mildmay, and intended to defend her. After all, who but she had injected some spirit into Titus?

'Then why is the business taking so long? Even if the tooth had to be extracted it would be done in a few minutes.'

'There may have been after-effects. The poor girl may be ill. Visits to the dentist are not usually noted for their pleasantness. Or do you think, my dear,' Lady Malvina was suddenly malicious, 'that my son finds her company agreeable? He always had a weakness for a pretty girl. He's no saint, you know.'

'You don't need to acquaint me with my own husband,' Amalie snapped. 'I trust him, but I don't trust that sly creature. Look at the way she inveigled herself into this household. Just arriving from nowhere. I always thought it odd.'

'Mrs Stone came the same way and you had no objection to her. But then she's deplorably plain, isn't she?'

Amalie's face was icy.

'I'm afraid my head is too bad for conversation. I shall have to spend the rest of the afternoon in my room.'

So after that there was no one to talk to. Lady Malvina took a gown up to Mrs Stone for alteration. Then sewing materials had to be found for her, since she had arrived with none of her own, not even a thimble. But the woman was disinclined to talk, and when she was set to work Lady Malvina left her, thinking her intolerably dull. She didn't even show signs of that touched simpleness today, but kept her eyes lowered over her work. She was as bony as a starved sparrow and not much bigger. Lady Malvina felt her own ample bosom to be almost indecent and panted away down the stairs in petulant boredom. She would ask Bessie to bring her tea to her room, and then doze by the fire. She might even have her dinner there, since Amalie, even if she decided to appear, was such poor company. She needed a new bottle of port, she discovered. She must have finished the last one the previous evening, although she didn't remember doing so. Bessie must see to that, too. She didn't usually drink in the afternoon, but today was so dark and melancholy, one required a little comfort.

The result of all this was that Lady Malvina fell asleep over the fire, and woke with a start much later to find the fire almost out, the curtains undrawn, and the room filled with the pallid light of twilight.

She shivered violently, hating both the eerie light and the chill. Couldn't Bessie ever come without being rung for? Ugh, that pale wintry sky and the forlorn tree branches gave her the creeps.

Panting heavily, she made her way to the window to twitch the curtains across, shutting out the purity and the intense loneliness of the country night.

But, her hand on the heavy velvet, she paused and stared out into the gloom.

Was that a woman running? She could scarcely see. There was just that dark glimpse of bundled skirts, hair streaming and two arms flung wide. Then the form disappeared into the shrubbery and it was difficult to be sure whether she had seen it or not. The night was so still. Now nothing moved at all.

12

BLANE came into the firelit room with his confident stride. Sarah, lying on the couch with her foot up, made to rise, but he tossed her a package and with a grin said,

'Put that on.'

'Put what on, Lord Mallow?'

'Open it and see. Lord, it's devilish cold out tonight. And we have to be up at the crack of dawn to catch the first train.'

'You have accomplished your business?' Sarah asked.

'No, I haven't. But the post brought a note from my wife. We're to return at once.'

The black brows were up mockingly. The situation which Blane had decided to treat as a joke perpetrated entirely for his amusement Sarah found intolerable.

'I hope you will explain to Lady Mallow that I would have returned this morning.'

'My dear Miss Mildmay. I could have lifted you on to the train at Victoria, but could Soames have lifted you off? Now tomorrow I'll accompany you all the way, and there'll be no difficulty.'

(Beyond Amalie watching our arrival, Sarah thought grimly. And that would probably be the end of her employment at Mallow Hall.)

She still couldn't decide whether Blane was determined to keep her constantly under his eye, using her incapacity as an excuse, or whether he was genuinely concerned for her welfare. He alternated so frequently between this attitude of laughing at her, and what seemed a kindly sympathy that could have been sincere. The day had been a torment. She longed for him to be out of the house, and then found herself constantly listening for his return.

But now he was here she was once more full of indignation. And what had happened to the mysterious Sammie, and why had Amalie peremptorily asked him to come home?

'Do as I told you, Miss Mildmay,' Blane was saying impatiently. 'Open that and put it on. Or shall I do it for you?'

Was this another joke? With a quite unreasonable feeling of apprehension, Sarah undid the wrappings, disclosing a long slim jeweller's box. Her fingers were trembling as she undid the clasp.

The diamond necklace lay shimmering in the lamplight.

She stared at it for so long that Blane snatched the box from her, took out the necklace, and unceremoniously fastened it round her neck himself.

Then he stepped back to admire it.

'It almost is worth perjuring oneself for, isn't it?'

Sarah had at last overcome her speechlessness. Her face flaming, she fumbled for the clasp of the necklace.

'How dare you put them on me! How dare you?'

'My dear young lady, they won't contaminate you.'

But he was a little startled at her reaction, for he added placatingly,

'I merely wanted to see them worn. By a beautiful woman. Diamonds should always be worn, and not hidden in a safety vault.'

'Then find some other beautiful woman!' Sarah snapped.

She was almost in tears. She couldn't understand the violence of her feelings. The Mallow diamonds, her rightful possession, put round her neck by this bragging impostor. Now they were spoilt for her forever. She would always remember this humiliating scene, him treating her as a model, expecting her to swoon with admiration and longing.

And now their destination was Amalie's skinny neck. When she and Ambrose got them back she would never wear them. Never!

'I'll undo it. Don't pull it to pieces.'

'Please keep your hands off me, Lord Mallow.'

Blane straightened himself to give his hearty roar of laughter.

'What an unpredictable creature you are. I thought any woman would enjoy wearing a necklace like this, even only for a few minutes.'

'Your joke is in execrable taste.'

'I believe you think so. Then I must ask you to forgive me. But what with my cousin Ambrose having gone out ferreting to the West Indies'—Sarah's fingers were momentarily still—'and other difficulties, I begin to wonder just how long I'll be in possession of the Mallow diamonds.'

'You have—reason to be anxious, Lord Mallow?'

'Anxious? No, that isn't the word.' His eyes hadn't lost a whit of their superb confidence. 'Amused is a better one. Especially when I think of Ambrose in Trinidad. Poor fellow, it isn't exactly his element. And such an appalling waste of time for him. He'd be much better advised to get on with his profession.'

'You wouldn't think it more becoming to give him a little sympathy than to laugh at him?' Sarah's voice was as impersonal as she could make it.

'Did he give me any sympathy?'

'I believe he thought you an impostor scarcely deserving sympathy.'

'It suited him to think so. I thought he'd finally agreed to gracefully admit his error, but now I see he hasn't. Well, good luck to him. If he ferrets as well into his clients' affairs as into mine he'll make a successful barrister.'

'How did you hear of this journey he has made?' Sarah asked carefully.

'Rumour has it. My wife tells me she heard it from Colonel Fortescue who no doubt is correctly informed. Well, well, poor Ambrose. I hope he made a good sailor. And now, perhaps you'll allow me to unclasp that necklace, Miss Mildmay. I'm afraid the catch is too complicated for you to do it yourself. After all, if my cousin Ambrose were to walk in here now, he'd hardly appreciate this scene. Or I wonder, would he?'

It was impossible to prevent the colour deepening in her cheeks again. Sarah felt the probing eyes on her and for the first time could not meet them. Had this been a trick to catch her out? Did he know about Ambrose and her?

But how could he, for no one in the world except Aunt Adelaide knew?

No, he was merely teasing her cruelly, taking advantage of

her helplessness to amuse himself.

'If I were not Lord Mallow——' she heard him saying slowly.

But he did not finish the remark. Abruptly he swung the necklace away from her, saying with his undertone of irony,

'Don't fret, Miss Mildmay. They looked very beautiful, but they're not your stone. I assure you.'

'Fret!' echoed Sarah.

He looked at her. 'Perhaps some day you'll tell me why you have this aversion to diamonds. To all diamonds, I wonder, or just these?'

Her eyes fell. 'I told you the joke was a poor one.'

'Then I apologise again.' He tossed the necklace into the velvet-lined box. 'I expect these will please my wife. And I have my mother's pearls redeemed. And a present for Titus. So think of the welcome awaiting us tomorrow.'

On their arrival, the first thing Sarah noticed was the way Amalie's face seemed to have grown even more thin and drawn. She was at the door before Blane had helped Sarah from the carriage, as if she had spent the day watching for their arrival. She came running down the steps crying,

'What's the matter with Miss Mildmay? Has she had an accident?'

Blane left Sarah to go and greet his wife.

'How are you, my love? Is everything well?'

'Well enough.'

'Miss Mildmay had the bad luck to sprain her ankle rather severely. She was quite unable to travel yesterday, although she wanted to.'

It was impossible not to notice the quick suspicion in Amalie's face as she glanced at Sarah's feet. Sarah obligingly lifted her skirt a few inches to show the bandages, and the clumsy slipper she was forced to wear.

Amalie flushed a dull colour.

'I don't disbelieve you, Miss Mildmay, though I don't see how a visit to the dentist involves you in this kind of accident. You'd better go up to Titus at once. I warn you he's in one of his difficult states.'

Leaning on the stick Blane had acquired for her, Sarah began to climb the stairs. She was not acting now, for her ankle was still very painful and swollen and it was impossible to move quickly. But she was very conscious of Amalie's and Blane's eyes on her, and would have given a great deal to overhear their ensuing conversation. Would Amalie explain why she looked as if she hadn't eaten or slept since he had been away?

Blane's voice did follow her. He was saying, 'I have Mamma's pearls. And the diamonds for you. Does that please you? We might even invent an opportunity for you to wear them. You were talking of giving a ball, weren't you?'

'But not now!'

'Why not?' As Sarah reached the curve of the stairs she turned to see that Amalie had seized both of Blane's arms and was about to tell him something, or to embrace him. At that moment Blane chanced to look up and saw her pause. With what seemed undue deliberation he bent his head and kissed his wife, on the forehead, and then, more slowly, on the lips. Sarah didn't know whether he looked up again at her, for she hurried on, ignoring the pain in her ankle. At least Amalie must be happy now, and would lose her drawn look. For she had not only her husband to kiss her lovingly, but the diamonds. Sarah wondered vindictively which mattered the most.

But she forgot about Blane and Amalie when she was in the nursery. For Titus had completely lost the endearing gaiety and liveliness which she had encouraged in him. He sat silently at his desk, a very small white-faced boy in his velvet jacket. When Sarah spoke to him he didn't answer, but gazed at her with a look of hostility.

'Titus, come here and answer me when I speak to you.'

Titus slipped off his chair and with as deliberate an action as his father's walked to the window, turning his back on her.

'Titus, are you disobeying me?'

The small shoulders shrugged. The action was comical and precociously adult. It was also a mask for something else. What had happened to the child?

'Did you think I wouldn't come back?' Sarah asked gently.

'I don't care!' he muttered.

'But I did come back, you see. And now you won't even speak to me. Eliza! Come and tell me what's wrong with Titus.'

Eliza came from the nursery.

'Oh, he had a nightmare.'

'But you were sleeping with him?'

'No. You said I was to, but the mistress wouldn't allow it.'

'I don't care,' said Titus again, loudly. 'I wasn't frightened.'

Sarah lifted the little boy into her arms. He resisted stiffly.

'You said you would come back and you didn't.'

'But I've come now, Titus darling. I couldn't yesterday because I have a sore foot. Look, it has a bandage on it.'

'Does it hurt?'

'It hurt a great deal at first. I fell down some stairs which was very foolish. Your papa was cross with me.'

'Lawks, Miss Mildmay!' murmured Eliza, staring. 'Was you and his lordship——'

'That's enough, Eliza. I came back as soon as I was able. Now what's this about the bad dreams, Titus. Tell me.'

'The light—went out,' the child whispered. Suddenly his hostility melted and he flung his arms round Sarah's neck holding her in a desperate embrace.

'And you thought it was the mouse?' Sarah encouraged.

'It was someone crying. I heard them.'

'That's what he said,' Eliza put in. 'There's someone crying, he said. Gave me the shivers. That was the second night. The first night he said someone had been walking in his room and leaning over him. I didn't take much notice. I said he'd been dreaming. Or perhaps the old lady—I mean, his grandmother—had come in like she does.'

'And did you hear anything, Eliza?' Sarah asked calmly. 'This crying, for instance.'

'I didn't until Titus called me, and then I thought I did. A sort of wild cry.' Eliza shivered involuntarily, her round rosy face a little pale.

'What time was this?'

'Lawks, I don't know. In the small hours. It was ever so

126

creepy.'

'Was it a windy night?'

'I didn't notice. Yes, I did,' Eliza amended excitedly, 'because the curtain was blowing, and the night light had gone out. Don't tell the mistress, Miss Mildmay, but we was that scared I took Titus into my bed.'

'That seems to be the most sensible thing you did do, Eliza. I expect the wind was rattling a loose shutter or a drain pipe.'

Eliza nodded in nervous agreement.

'I expect so, miss. It just seems scary in the middle of the night. I don't think I could have stayed here if you hadn't come back.'

'I can't stop Titus having nightmares,' Sarah said. 'But I don't think he'll have any more. Will you, my darling? Tonight you shall have hot milk after you've gone to bed, and you'll sleep so soundly you won't hear a thing.'

'Will you be here?' the child whispered.

'Of course I'll be here. And Papa's home, too. I think he has a present for you.'

You will go back to Mallow because of Titus! It had been difficult to make herself meekly obey that autocratic voice. Especially after the episode of the diamond necklace last evening, when she had wanted to burst out with the truth, to declare that she had far more right to the family diamonds than ever Amalie would have. And again this morning in the train, when, in unavoidable intimacy with Blane in the small smoky compartment, he had decided to ask her a series of searching questions about her family and her childhood. It had seemed as if he were turning the tables on her, becoming the investigator himself. But if he had suspicions of her he hid them beneath this lazy inquisitiveness and never again allowed his anger to show. She flattered herself that she had emerged from the ordeal of the questionnaire as successfully as he had emerged from the courtroom a month ago. He learned only that she had had the education and upbringing of a girl of the upper classes, until her father had died leaving little provision for his widow and family. She had even begun to enjoy herself, chattering innocently about seaside holidays, and happy nursery days, until she was afraid her secret amusement must have made her eyes twinkle too much. For he gazed at her with the most uninhibited interest. It was only when he said critically,

'But you've left out all the ruffled bits of your life, Miss Mildmay. Surely it's not all a calm stream? Or is life like that for well-born young ladies?' that she realised he knew exactly what she was doing and was laughing at her.

'I'm not well-born,' she said shortly. 'And I hardly think you would call my present status a particularly halcyon one.'

'It will end,' he murmured. 'It will end.'

Sarah had a fervent wish that it could end at that moment, for she had the uneasy feeling that in this cat and mouse game, he was the much superior cat. She would like to have stepped out of the train at Yarby and said haughtily, 'Now I am returning at once to London.'

For she had a sudden intense apprehension as to what would happen in the next few weeks. She was getting too involved. Ambrose surely had never expected her to get emotionally involved like this.

But now she was back, and watching the tremulous happiness in Titus's sensitive face she knew that she had to stay here until the end. Whatever the end might be . . .

She would have preferred to have made her injury an excuse for not going down to dinner that night. But she had not seen Blane and Amalie since that moment of their greeting, and she had a feverish unhappy desire to observe their manner at dinner. Would any comment be made on the failure of the mysterious Sammie to materialise, and would she get a clue as to why Amalie had sent for Blane to return? Most of all, would Amalie have lost that pinched look and appear happy at last?

As she was dressing Lady Malvina came in in her unceremonious way. She was elaborately dressed, and wore pearls, obviously the ones Blane had brought home, for she kept fingering them with satisfaction.

'Well, Miss Mildmay, we thought you'd run off. If governesses ever do run off. I suppose the poor things are driven to it sometimes.'

'Perhaps you've heard of my unfortunate accident, Lady

Malvina.'

'Oh, yes, I heard of it. And between you and me, my daughter-in-law doesn't think a lot of it.'

'I didn't try to fall, Lady Malvina.'

'Well, I believe she thinks you did.' Lady Malvina gave her deep malicious chuckle. 'Have you never met a jealous woman, Miss Mildmay?'

'But she's not jealous of me!' Sarah gasped.

'She's the sort who's jealous of everybody and everything. Have you never looked at your face in the mirror, girl? If you'd like my opinion, you're a great deal prettier than that foreign-looking creature. Heigh ho! I suppose I shouldn't talk like this. But I confess I have little in common with my son's wife. Why she must take to her bed like a sick cat when her husband's away for a couple of nights, I don't know.'

'Did she do that, Lady Malvina?'

'Apart from playing the grand lady at a tea party, yes. Someone told her my nephew Ambrose had gone to the West Indies, and that seemed to alarm her.'

Sarah spoke carefully. 'Why should it do that?'

'I haven't the least idea. After all, my son is my son, and Ambrose can't disprove flesh and blood.' Lady Malvina's voice had grown loud and belligerent. 'I might have known he wouldn't be a good loser. Blane says he'll fall in love with a Spanish beauty and stay in Trinidad. But my son forgets all men aren't hot-blooded like him. For my part, I can't see Ambrose falling in love with anybody.'

'Perhaps you don't know your nephew very well, Lady Malvina. Oh, dear! Now I've torn my dress.'

In her anger at not being able to defend Ambrose more openly, Sarah had snatched at her dinner gown and caught it in the wardrobe door. There was only a small rent, but it was serious, for she had only one other dinner gown, and no prospect of getting more.

'Don't worry, my dear. We have a sewing woman now. A Mrs Stone. She'll mend that for you in a moment. You'll find her upstairs in Bella's room.'

'The haunted room!'

Lady Malvina waved her fan.

'My dear, I'm sure the room isn't haunted. It's merely a foolish reference that stuck. And unless the other servants have told Mrs Stone, she doesn't know the room's history. She's a harmless creature. Looks half starved, poor thing. Run up and have a word with her. By the way, the boy missed you, Miss Mildmay. He was exceedingly naughty.'

'He had nightmares again,' said Sarah flatly. 'He said someone walked about his room. I don't suppose you did that, Lady Malvina?'

'After he was asleep? Good gracious, no. I suppose he heard that woman walking about overhead.'

'He said someone blew out his light. But that might have been the wind.'

Lady Malvina's eyes seemed to protrude more than usual. The tip of her tongue flicked over her lips.

'That's absurd. Who would go into his room at night? Who would have designs on a child?'

'Are you suggesting someone may have designs on Titus?' Sarah gasped.

The old lady made an impatient sound.

'I'm suggesting no such thing. What an idea! The only person who would stand to benefit from Titus's absence would be Ambrose, and he's in the West Indies.' She paused. 'What are we talking about, Miss Mildmay?'

'I don't know,' Sarah confessed. But it was impossible not to be unaware of Lady Malvina's uneasiness. 'Lady Malvina——'

'Yes, my dear. Speak up.'

'You are sure——' Looking into the suddenly forlorn old face, Sarah could say no more. She found she didn't want Lady Malvina to put her uncertainty into words. For some complex reason she didn't want the words spoken.

'You are sure this woman will sew my dress?' she asked hurriedly. 'I'll go up to her now.'

'Yes, you'd better hurry. The gong will be going shortly. Well, it will be nice to have someone at the dinner table this evening. We'll have a cheerful time. No more glooms.'

Sarah limped up the stairs, and tapped at Mrs Stone's door. A rather sulky voice bade her come in. The woman sitting at the table spread with sewing materials was exactly as Lady Malvina had described her, thin and nondescript, though had she been a little plumper her face would have had a certain rather common prettiness. It did have, however, a strange air of anticipation, as if she had expected her visitor to be someone else.

'Mrs Stone? I'm Miss Mildmay. Lady Malvina said you would be kind enough to do this small piece of sewing for me. See, I tore my gown. It caught on the wardrobe handle.'

'All right. Put it down. When do you want it?'

'For dinner this evening, if possible. In half an hour?'

The woman's pale lively eyes slid over Sarah with a rather unpleasant knowing look.

'So you're the young lady who got delayed in London,' she said. Her voice was conversational. It was only her expression that had the hint of insolence.

Sarah ignored the remark, and said haughtily,

'Will you bring the dress to my room when you've finished? I still find the stairs very difficult.'

'Very well. If you want it so quick, I'd better start it.'

Sarah had no desire to linger. The woman was an unlikeable type, and it was not wise to talk too much to the servants. But something made her pause and say, 'I hope you enjoy being here, Mrs Stone.'

'It's well enough. But I don't intend to stay long. Between you and me, I don't care for her ladyship.'

'Then what brought you here?' Sarah was interested against her will. She could imagine how patronising and dictatorial Amalie had been. This woman was not without wits. She must have decided at once that Amalie was no more a lady than she was.

'Have to keep myself since I lost my husband,' the woman replied laconically. 'I heard there were new folks at Mallow, so I came. But I shan't stay long. Just time enough to put a bit by.'

Eliza, giving Titus his bath in the tub by the nursery fire, had her brief comment to make about the new employee.

'She's a bit above herself, that one. You want to hear Betsey on Mrs la-di-dah Stone. She won't last long.'

'What will happen to her?' Titus asked interestedly.

'I expect she'll go the way she came, on her two feet.'

'That will be enough, Eliza,' said Sarah. 'It's time Titus was in bed.'

She waited the half hour for Mrs Stone to return her dress, and when it didn't come sighed and contemplated another painful climb up the stairs to the third floor. There was only fifteen minutes left before dinner. One might have guessed the woman wouldn't keep her word.

When she knocked at the door this time there was no answer. After waiting a moment she opened it and looked in. The lamp was burning on the table, and her dress was spread out, the needle and cotton still in it. But there was no sign of Mrs Stone.

How exasperating! Where was the woman? She must have have gone down to the kitchen to gossip. Or perhaps Amalie had rung for her. Anyway, there was no time to wait. She would have to finish the sewing herself. It seemed to be nearly done.

But it was not done particularly neatly. Sarah looked in some astonishment at the cobbled stitches. She wasn't brilliant at needlework herself, but she would have considered that kind of stitching quite clumsy and inferior.

Either Mrs Stone was a hoax and would be quickly found out, which was probably why she indicated she would not be staying long, or she had not considered the governess's work worth bothering about.

Exclaiming impatiently, Sarah swiftly finished the task herself and hurried away. She scarcely need bother to say thank you.

Late as she was going down, Amalie and Blane were later. Lady Malvina grumbled loudly at their unpunctuality.

'I want my dinner. This is very thoughtless. I thought we were all going to be gay and cheerful tonight. But I get bad-tempered if I have to wait for my food. Oh, here's Blane at last. And just about time, my boy. Where's Amalie?'

'Amalie isn't coming down. She isn't feeling well.'

Lady Malvina gave an exclamation of disgust.

'Again! What's wrong with the woman? Whatever made you marry a delicate wife?'

'She isn't delicate, Mamma. She got caught in the rain out riding this afternoon. I think she has a chill. Well, what are we waiting for?'

His face was frowning and impatient. He hadn't given Sarah even a glance. However he might defend his wife, it was clear that he was upset about something. Amalie's chill was an excuse. They must have quarrelled again, and he was making no effort to conceal his own bad temper. This was the man she had caught a glimpse of in London, consumed with dark silent anger, a formidable enemy.

Lady Malvina pouted over her soup.

'Well, I did think we'd have a little gaiety tonight. This house is like a tomb.'

'Be thankful you're in it at all, Mamma,' Blane answered curtly.

His hair, Sarah noticed, was shining in the lamplight. It had recently been wet and the moisture still clung. Either he had just bathed or just come in out of the rain. But he had not said that he, too, had been riding. He had indicated that Amalie had been alone.

'Well, Miss Mildmay, where's your appetite? You haven't caught a chill, too?'

Sarah winced at Lady Malvina's raucous voice. She bent her head over her soup, but not before Blane's moody glance had caught her.

'Toothache again, Miss Mildmay?'

The sarcasm brought the colour to her cheeks. But she answered composedly,

'Only a little remaining tenderness, Lord Mallow.'

'Then take your time. No one's hurrying you.'

That remark might have meant anything. One might have imagined him impatiently solicitous of her trifling ailments. But the letter from Aunt Adelaide the next day proved otherwise.

13

My dear Sarah,

Why did that fellow calling himself Lord Mallow come snooping here to enquire into your testimonials? He got nothing from me, I assure you. I suggested it was a little late in the day to make these enquiries since he had already employed you, and I understood that you had been with the family for several weeks. He made no explanations—he would not—he is much too sure of himself. He merely sat in my drawing-room and smiled at me with I must say a rather devastating but quite untrustworthy *charm, and admitted that you seemed to be an excellent governess, if a little unorthodox. Had you been unorthodox while in my employ? I admit that I enjoyed myself enormously inventing two daughters now at school in Paris who owed a great deal to your charming influence. I emphasised that his son could not be more fortunate in having you with him, and that if he were wise he would see that you remained until the boy is old enough to go to school. He agreed with all this. Indeed, he agreed that you were charming, if unpredictable. Then he took his departure, having discovered nothing he did not know already.*

I am telling you this so as to warn you that I fear he has his suspicions about you. He cannot know about you and Ambrose, but I would not trust him one inch. What he determines to discover, he will. I fear he is more than a match for most people. But I am confident Ambrose will cleverly bring him down, for he, after all, has the trained legal mind, and this man is nothing but a bluffer.

Have you yet heard from Ambrose? Do write to me as soon as possible. I hope receiving this letter from me does not arouse suspicions, but it is a risk I have to take, in order to warn you. I tremble for you, my dearest Sarah, but I know you will be equal to this situation. Do not, however, take unnecessary risks. Come home the moment you feel there may be danger.

Your devoted aunt.

Aunt Adelaide was letting her sense of the melodramatic run away with her. What possible danger could there be except that of being found out and summarily dismissed?

So Blane had been growing suspicious of her. She hoped she would be able to go on perplexing him for longer than he perplexed her.

She had read the letter in the privacy of her bedroom, but now Eliza had Titus ready for his morning lessons. Eliza was full of important information herself.

'Miss Mildmay, that woman has gone!'

Sarah stopped smiling. 'What woman, Eliza?'

'That woman for the sewing. Mrs Stone. Betsey hasn't been told, but the room's empty and all Mrs Stone's things gone. She must have just gone off in the night. Betsey says the mistress should count the silver.'

For a moment Sarah had an involuntary picture of the room as she had seen it last night, with her green dress spread, half-finished on the table, and the lamp burning. But Mrs Stone hadn't gone then because her things were still there, the shabby carpet bag and her shawl and a few toilet things. She had noticed. She had an observant eye.

'Betsey says in one way she doesn't blame her,' Eliza was going on garrulously. 'Putting her in that room. She might have got feared and run off.'

'We won't discuss it now,' Sarah said sharply. 'And don't gossip, Eliza.'

But later Amalie came to the schoolroom. She still didn't look well, her face pale and dark marks beneath her eyes. But when Sarah said politely,

'I hope you're feeling better, Lady Mallow,' she answered that she was perfectly recovered. The chill had not developed.

'The hot whisky and milk my husband prescribed for me cured it. He's very good at remedies, as no doubt you discovered, Miss Mildmay, when you injured your ankle.'

135

'Mrs Robbins cared for me,' Sarah answered coolly. She didn't mean to revive that uncomfortable memory of Blane's attentiveness.

'I got wet through,' Amalie went on. 'I rode too far, and the rain came on.'

'I'm glad to hear you felt well enough to go riding, Lady Mallow. Lady Malvina said you'd been poorly.'

'I get nervous headaches at times. After all, we all have our weaknesses, don't we. I trust your toothache is quite cured. Mamma was concerned for you. You went off looking so miserable.'

'I hope not to have a recurrence,' Sarah answered composedly. 'Perhaps you'd care to see, Lady Mallow, how well Titus is progressing with his letters.'

'Is he, the lamb? Come and show Mamma, Titus.'

It was the first time Amalie had come to the schoolroom. Her effect on Titus was to make him nervous and silent. She pouted when he edged away from her embrace, but in a moment said gaily, 'Little boys don't like to be fussed over, do they? I'll just sit here quietly and watch. Now, Titus, say the letters.'

She was over-dressed as usual, wearing a fine woollen shawl over a silk gown that was trimmed with a great deal of black velvet. She sat on the low chair by the fire, silent for a little while as she had promised, but with one foot tapping up and down, and a far-off look in her eyes. She must have suddenly had the desire for company. Blane was probably outdoors and she was finding the day lonely and tedious. It was to be expected that she would soon tire of the country unless she constantly filled the house with people. Also, the grey weather must depress her after the blue skies of the Caribbean. Sarah had a sudden feeling of pity. Amalie had not been friendly. Indeed, she had been over-bearing and haughty, and latterly suspicious and jealous. But the woman sitting by the smoky fire just looked rather young and forlorn.

'You no doubt miss the sunshine, Lady Mallow.'

Amalie hugged her arms about herself.

'I hate this grey weather! I hate it! And the sound of the sea in the night. Or is it the wind?' She got up to stand looking out of the window. 'My husband doesn't understand,' she added in a voice so low that Sarah scarcely heard.

'But doesn't he himself hanker for the Caribbean again?'

'Oh, yes, he does. He says he'll go. What he doesn't understand is how I would feel about being left.' She flung round. 'Can't this place be gayer? Why shouldn't it be gayer? We must have parties. Musical evenings, dancing. I enjoy playing and singing. I like to dance, too. That's what we'll do.' She lifted her skirts and twirled in a waltz. 'Like that. Don't you think Mamma should dance, Titus? And I promise you can come down for half an hour to watch.'

Her face was thin and bright with a kind of desperate gaiety.

'We'll give the ball my husband suggested. Why shouldn't we? We can afford it, and we have plenty of servants. Oh, by the way,' she dropped her skirts and looked more sedate, 'that wretched creature I engaged for sewing has gone already. Things are appalling, Miss Mildmay, when one only has to speak sharply to a servant and notice is given. I had to speak to Mrs Stone about her very indifferent work.'

'I noticed she sewed very badly,' Sarah said.

'Oh, you did? I'm glad you saw that, too. She'd lied to me, of course. She said she was an expert needlewoman. But even then I'd have given her another chance if she hadn't taken offence. She just packed her bag and went.'

'I thought she needed money.'

'I paid her a week's wages in advance. My belief is, and my husband shares it, that she'd go to the nearest public house. It will teach me not to engage staff out of kindness again.' Amalie's eyes went to Titus. 'But this isn't a subject for the schoolroom. And I'm interrupting lessons. What a pity, Miss Mildmay, that if we give a ball your ankle will scarcely be well enough for dancing.'

Amalie had recovered her poise. Whatever strange mood had possessed her, the short rather explosive conversation had eased it. Now she was behaving true to her narrow and jealous nature again, making sly comments at Sarah's expense. The trouble obviously was between herself and her husband, and she was consumed with frustration and bewilderment. Why did Blane

137

behave so badly to her? His lordly indifference suggested he was punishing her for something. Well, perhaps she would find someone at her ball with whom to flirt. That would please her, easing her pique and restoring her morale.

Sarah didn't give much thought to the strange woman who had so briefly occupied Bella's room. But later in the day some need for action to ease her own sense of frustration took her up to the now-empty room.

The lamp still stood on the table, but all the sewing materials had vanished. In the fading light it was a gloomy little room with its low ceiling and dark-coloured walls. Perhaps it had depressed the woman. Perhaps Betsey or one of the other servants had maliciously told her its history. It wasn't a room that had depressed Blane, locked in there as a boy, for he didn't even remember the event. But a woman was more sensitive to atmosphere. Sarah admitted to herself that she wouldn't like to stay there long. Her eyes went to the ceiling where the hook for the hanging lamp had once been. That had been removed long ago, but her eyes did catch something that startled her. The object looked like a black cat curled on the top of the wardrobe. What was it?

Sarah stood on a chair to look. Then gingerly put out her hand to retrieve the object. It was a black straw bonnet, with ribbons twisted to string. There didn't seem much doubt that it was Mrs Stone's bonnet.

But all her other belongings had gone. Why on earth should she hurry off leaving her bonnet? It wasn't even likely that she had had an alternative one to wear.

Sarah looked at the bonnet in her hand. The chilly distaste the room gave her seemed to centre now in this limp inanimate object dangling from her fingers. She had an overwhelming impulse to drop it and run.

But panic was unreasonable and foolish. This required investigating. At last she had something positive to do.

She went downstairs to the drawing-room where she knew she would find Amalie. Without ceremony she went in, flourishing the distasteful object.

The timing was fortuitous, for not only Amalie but Blane and

Lady Malvina were there, finishing their tea.

'Miss Mildmay?' said Amalie questioningly.

Sarah pretended a naïve surprise.

'Look what I found in Mrs Stone's room. Her bonnet, surely. Why should she leave without it? I keep thinking of her in this cold wind with nothing to cover her head, poor little creature.'

'Poor little creature!' That was Amalie on her feet, her face blazing with anger. 'No wonder she didn't take her disgusting old bonnet. Miss Mildmay, throw it on the fire. This minute. I order you to.'

'What on earth is all this?' demanded Lady Malvina. 'Amalie, are you out of your head? Burning a servant's possessions! Surely the woman wasn't that bad.'

'Bad!' Amalie exclaimed. 'She only helped herself to some pieces of jewellery and other things out of my room, including that new bonnet you bought for me, Blane. My nicest one, the blue velvet with roses. I only discovered the things missing this morning. It was too late to pursue the woman, so I decided to say nothing about it. It's unpleasant having thieving people in the house, and I don't want the servants upset. But you've forced me to tell the truth, Miss Mildmay. So throw that wretched thing on the fire.'

Then, not waiting for Sarah to do this, Amalie snatched it out of her hand and tossed it on to the flames. In a moment it had flared up and become unrecognisable. It was gone as completely as the faded little woman who had so briefly occupied the room in the top storey.

'If the woman's a thief the police should be informed,' Lady Malvina declared. 'What a fortunate thing I was wearing my pearls last evening. But if anything else is missing from my room I haven't noticed. Nor has Bessie.'

'You're not her size, Mamma,' Amalie said briefly. 'Now forget this, as I intend to. It was unpleasant, but it's over and a lesson to me. I shall make the most extensive enquiries before engaging anyone else. People are just not to be trusted.' She rubbed her hands hard, as if rubbing off the contact with the shabby straw bonnet. 'Miss Mildmay, isn't it time you brought Titus down?'

'Before Miss Mildmay goes,' drawled Blane from his deep chair by the fire, 'perhaps she will tell us just how she came to discover that unprepossessing article of headgear.' The top of his head was just visible. He hadn't turned to look at her. His voice was bland and seemingly only mildly interested. 'Just what were you doing in Mrs Stone's room, Miss Mildmay?'

If he had looked at her in his usual way, inquisitively and aggressively, she would have responded to the challenge. But she found this mildness, this almost disembodied voice, peculiarly demoralising.

Amalie's and Lady Malvina's instant suspicion was nothing to the effect Blane was having on her.

'She was doing some sewing for you, wasn't she, Miss Mildmay?' Lady Malvina prompted helpfully.

'Yes, she was. But that was last evening.' The dark head in the armchair hadn't moved. Sarah took a deep breath and decided on attack. 'If Lord Mallow really wishes to know what I was doing in Mrs Stone's room, I was testing a theory.'

She expected him to leap up and face her, throwing accusing questions at her. But his behaviour was no longer predictable.

'What theory, Miss Mildmay? That Mrs Stone was secreted in the wardrobe or behind the panelling?'

'Blane!' exclaimed Amalie breathlessly.

'Nothing so melodramatic, Lord Mallow. Merely that the servants gossip about that room, and Eliza thought Mrs Stone might have left because she was nervous.'

Now Blane had turned and was regarding her with lazily narrowed eyes.

'And what were your own reactions, Miss Mildmay? Did you sit up there in the dark and get pleasantly spooky?'

Spooky, yes. But not pleasantly. Sarah thought of the thin querulous face bent over her work last evening, and later of the lamp burning in an empty room. Mrs Stone must have come back for her possessions (excepting the black bonnet), but she had not seen her again. It was almost as if the poor common little creature with her inability to sew neatly had been a ghost.

'I did find it rather uncanny,' she said evenly. 'But perhaps women are more susceptible to these influences. I believe you weren't affected in that way, Lord Mallow.'

'In what way? I didn't sit up there in the dark, I assure you.'

'But I thought——' Sarah contrived to look embarrassed and foolish. 'Am I under a misapprehension? I thought that once your cousin locked you in that particular room.'

'Ambrose did, Blane. Don't you remember?' Lady Malvina was jogging his memory again, anxiously. 'You came out utterly furious, and saying you would kill him. Such a violent child you were.'

'Oh, yes, Ambrose insisted he did that, didn't he? But I'd forgotten the incident. So the uncanny, as Miss Mildmay points out, obviously left me unaffected. Perhaps it wouldn't have done had I been acquainted with the room's fair victim. And I don't mean Mrs Stone,' he added, twinkling outrageously.

'Blane, how can you joke?' stormed Amalie.

'Joke? But I find Miss Mildmay's adventure into the supernatural diverting. And a little surprising. I thought you were much more of a realist, Miss Mildmay.'

'I can't believe that woman was frightened away by a ghost,' Lady Malvina said emphatically.

'Nor can any of us,' murmured Blane. 'Not even Miss Mildmay.'

'This conversation is ridiculous!' Amalie's voice was high and thin, as if her own nerves were stretched beyond endurance. 'I've told you all the woman left because she couldn't sew. She was also a thief. And if Miss Mildmay is going to behave in this extraordinary way, I'm sure she's not a suitable person to be in charge of Titus.'

'Never mind Miss Mildmay,' put in Lady Malvina impatiently. 'What I can't understand is why you haven't informed the police, if the woman's a thief.'

Amalie sank into a chair. She looked exhausted and on the point of collapse. She closed her eyes.

'The woman isn't worth the fuss. I only want to forget her.'

14

'BLANE, there's no necessity to go. I settled the matter. Don't you believe me?'

'I believe you, but do you really think that will be the end of it?'

There was a momentary silence. Then Amalie said in a low voice, 'I do. That will be the end of it.' She began to laugh breathlessly. 'Perhaps I make myself believe it because I can't bear you to go away again.'

'Amalie! You know I don't like possessive women.'

'Oh! What are you made of?' The extreme exasperation and anger in Amalie's voice was painful to hear.

Sarah had begun to dread going down to dinner. She was no longer eager to eavesdrop. The zest had gone out of this adventure. As strangers, impostors, usurpers, they deserved all the harm she could do them. But whatever else they might be, they were not strangers any longer. They were real people. Even Amalie.

Foolishly, she hadn't visualised this happening, and neither, she was sure, had Ambrose, or he would not have expected so much of her. She was beginning to detest her position. Perhaps if she were to get a letter from Ambrose her ambition and her desire to see a wrong put right would return. But the time had already seemed so long, and so many things had got spoilt. The thought of wearing the Mallow diamonds, for instance, or of boisterous greedy and affable Lady Malvina being deprived of her home, or Titus being thrust back into insecurity, were difficult to contemplate.

Nevertheless, this accidentally overheard conversation revived her intense curiosity. Blane's reference to going somewhere must have meant that he still wanted to track down the mysterious Sammie. But Amalie disagreed.

Lady Malvina was coming down the stairs, her enormously wide skirts making a great rustling.

'You're still very lame, Miss Mildmay. I hope you haven't been on that foot too much.'

Sarah, caught lingering outside the drawing-room door, blessed the old lady for her genial obtuseness.

'I think perhaps I have walked a little too much, Lady Malvina.'

She waited for Lady Malvina to precede her into the room, and the conversation within ceased. Amalie was holding her hands out to the fire as if she were chilly in spite of the flush in her cheeks. Blane was pouring sherry. He looked up and said,

'Miss Mildmay climbs too many stairs. How can she expect her ankle to get well?'

'Miss Mildmay is good for the child,' Lady Malvina declared, with her happy irrelevance. 'He's getting almost as adventurous as you were, Blane. That's a very miserable glass of sherry, if I may say so. Fill it up. Well, Amalie, I'm glad to see you keep better health when your husband is home. But you've had some fresh air today. I saw you down by the lake.'

'The lake? Oh, yes. It must be a charming spot in summer, but in winter—B-r-r-r! However, one must walk somewhere.'

'Are you bored with the ancestral home already?' Blane enquired softly.

'No, but I think we should have more gaiety. We do nothing. We've been to church three times, and had people in to tea, and had a great deal of fuss and inconvenience with decorators, and that's the sum total of our exciting country life! I've been thinking about that ball you suggested, Blane. Haven't I, Miss Mildmay? Mamma, when's the best time to hold a ball in this desolate spot?'

'In the winter, of course,' said Lady Malvina. Her face brightened. 'I must say that's a splendid idea. We can all wear our finery. Miss Mildmay, I hope you have brought a ball gown.'

'I'm afraid——' Sarah began. She was impatient with Lady Malvina's stupidity in imagining that a governess, naturally poor since she had to be a governess, should possess a ball gown. Then she noticed Blane's eyes on her throat and knew that he was remembering the diamonds he had hung there.

Moreover, he was wickedly intending her to read his thoughts. Her assumed embarrassment became real. 'I will be more than content to watch, Lady Malvina. I fear my foot——'

Amalie was tapping her own foot. Her anger was scarcely concealed.

'Mamma, let's talk about more practical aspects. Whom we should invite, for instance, the catering, the orchestra. Of course, Miss Mildmay, we will expect you to bring Titus down for half an hour.'

I cannot, cannot, cannot stand this kind of treatment any longer, Sarah wrote that night. *Or my own sickly behaviour, bowing meekly, smiling, hiding my dignity, my pride, my very soul. I didn't come here to be a doormat! And why should I look dowdy while Amalie dresses like a duchess? Oh, Ambrose, I am sorry, but this has been too much to ask of me. It's all too humiliating. Though how can I forsake Titus now he has grown dependent on me? What am I to do?*

It seemed that her uncertain mind was to be made up for her.

Out riding with Soames the next day, Titus had a fall. It wasn't a severe one, but Soames sensibly carried the child into his cottage which was near at hand, and left his wife to tend him while he hurried up to the big house.

Blane had gone for a day's hunting, and Amalie was not to be found.

'Her ladyship will be down at the lake, most likely,' Soames said to Sarah in his knowing way. 'She goes there most afternoons. Perhaps you'd come, miss, and see to the young master. He's not badly hurt, only dazed like.'

'Of course.' Sarah hastened into outdoor things and followed Soames. But as they went across the park her gaze kept going towards the distant steely shine of water beyond the leafless trees. Was that really the only place Amalie cared to walk?

'There's a summer house there,' Soames said, as if reading her thoughts. 'It's shelter against the wind. It's a pity the mistress doesn't take more to riding.'

'She does ride,' Sarah said quickly.

'Not that she cares for it. She's too nervous.'

'Better than sitting in a summer house in midwinter,' Sarah burst out, forgetting to whom she was speaking.

'That's what I thought, miss.'

Soames gave her his sideways glance, and she was sorry she had spoken. This man was not to be trusted.

Titus had recovered a good deal though he still looked shaken and white.

'Dandy threw me,' he said importantly. 'But I'll ride again tomorrow, won't I, Soames?'

'To be sure you will, Master Titus. You see, miss, he's just like his father was.'

Sarah looked about the cosy firelit room. A well-furnished room for a groom's cottage, she thought.

Mrs Soames, a small woman with watchful eyes like her husband's, noticed the glance.

'Do you like our home, miss? I try to keep it nice. It must seem small to you after being up at the big house.'

'You have some nice things, Mrs Soames.'

'My husband had a small legacy from his lordship. I said we'd put it into the home.'

'From the late Lord Mallow,' Soames specified pointedly.

'That was fortunate for you,' Sarah murmured. (But bribery might pay even better than faithful service. Bribery might have bought the carpet and the carefully polished table and chairs.) 'Come, Titus, we must go. Can you walk, or am I to carry you?'

'He can ride on my back,' said Soames. 'Won't be the first time I've carried the heir to Mallow. So to speak.'

'Why so to speak?' Sarah asked bluntly.

Soames gave his ingratiating laugh.

'Just a manner of speaking, miss. Don't mean nothing. The little lad's the dead spit of his father. I could think the years had rolled back.'

Titus seemed to have quite recovered from his fall, and ate his supper as usual, and even romped a little with Lady Malvina. But by that time Amalie had heard the news, and came hurrying into the nursery. She snatched the child from Lady Malvina exclaiming, 'Are you sure he isn't hurt? Titus, my love, Mamma's darling, are you all right? Did you get a horrid fright?'

Titus immediately burst into tears.

Lady Malvina gathered up her skirts and waddled to the door.

'Well, of all the foolish behaviour, Amalie! Miss Mildmay and I had the boy perfectly calm and happy, and now you're scaring the life out of him.'

'Miss Mildmay and you! Of course you know best! You're both so wise. Especially Miss Mildmay! Then why did she allow this to happen to Titus?'

Amalie's outburst was all the more startling because it was unprovoked. Sarah had said nothing, and even Lady Malvina's rebuke had been amiable enough. But her high tense voice had frightened Titus into crying harder. It convinced her that he was seriously hurt.

'Don't cry, my lamb. You must go to bed at once. The idea of not putting you straight to bed when you're sick. Really, Miss Mildmay. I thought you'd have had more sense. But perhaps good sense wasn't part of your programme today.'

'I don't know what you mean, Lady Mallow. But I assure you Titus isn't hurt. He was merely a little dazed. Soames said so, too. He's been kept quiet since, and had his supper. Eliza was just about to put him to bed.'

'So you take this all on yourself!' Amalie's face was darkly flushed, her eyes glittering. 'You decide not to send for a doctor, not to have me told. Who's son is he, may I ask?'

Sarah bit back her swiftly rising anger. She forced herself to speak calmly.

'Perhaps we could discuss this after Titus is in bed, Lady Mallow.'

Amalie sprang up with the sobbing child in her arms.

'And I'll put him there myself. Eliza! Where's Eliza? Have you got bottles in the bed? Then get some at once. And some-one must go for the doctor. I won't rest until a doctor has seen him. Mamma, could you send Soames, or one of the servants?'

'Really, I think you've gone crazy!' Lady Malvina exclaimed. 'All that fuss. My son had falls enough, and simply got up and remounted. What do you want to turn the child into, a molly-coddle?'

She turned and swept out of the room. Titus, much distracted by now, was still sobbing, but there was obviously nothing Sarah could do about it. She went to her own room to wait Amalie's expected summons.

It came before long. There was a sharp knock at her door, and then Amalie came in. Her cheeks still had their high flush and the almost feverish brightness was in her eyes.

'Miss Mildmay, I'd like to speak to you.'

'Yes, Lady Mallow.'

'I want to know how Titus came to fall from his horse, and why, when he had had a nasty fall, you showed so little concern.'

'So little concern!' Sarah repeated, astonished.

'Don't deny it. You were letting him romp in that mad way with my mother-in-law as if nothing had happened. And that, after concussion!'

'But he hasn't concussion! There are no symptoms.'

'There are symptoms. Titus is very distressed and feverish. Do you mean to say you didn't notice? Yet when you have an aching tooth or a twisted ankle there's fuss enough made!'

'Are you accusing me, Lady Mallow, of being careless of my duties?'

'More than careless. How did Titus come to fall?'

'I wasn't with him, I've told you. Soames was with him.'

'You're sure? You're sure you weren't crossing the park and startled Dandy?'

'Just what are you suggesting?' Sarah whispered.

'I'm not suggesting anything except your attitude towards your duties. I'm trying to get to the bottom of the matter. For instance, Titus's nightmares. He never suffered from them before he came here—with you. He never complained of people walking in his room at night.'

'But that happened while I was in London!'

'And couldn't you have arranged to be away to leave the child

147

unprotected? How did it happen you were so interested in Mrs Stone, for instance? Even my husband noticed that. You were the one to find her bonnet, to display interest as to her departure. Is she a colleague of yours? You both got into this household in the same way, you remember, by simply arriving and asking for employment. I find it all exceedingly strange.'

'And I,' said Sarah icily, her chin high, 'find your attitude incomprehensible. You're not only suggesting that I might want to harm your child, but that I may also be a thief. I fear, Lady Mallow, this is where we say goodbye. I shall pack at once, and leave this evening.'

'That would be satisfactory,' Amalie said in a tight voice.

'Your accusations are scarcely worth defending.'

'Perhaps you can't defend them, Miss Mildmay. Perhaps I'm not so easily taken in as my husband by a pretty face.'

Sarah was rapidly folding gowns and gathering up her toilet things. She permitted herself to pause for a moment and give Amalie a searching glance. She didn't speak. She merely let her eyes wander with deliberate slowness from Amalie's thin face to her meagre bosom, down her fussy silk dress to her feet. Then she went on with her task. The green silk dress, the black lace shawl that Aunt Adelaide had given her, the evening slippers, the warm petticoats Lady Malvina had advised. Would she have to trudge the ten miles to Yarby, as apparently Mrs Stone had had to do? Was she letting Ambrose down too badly? Did her desire to escape from this intolerable family include him, too? She didn't know. She only knew she must go at once.

'Do I leave on foot?' she asked at last.

'Isn't that the way you came?'

'I came by cab, as you very well know. And I think my references were all that were necessary since Lord Mallow personally looked into them when last in London.'

Amalie's eyes flickered. For the first time uncertainty came into her face.

'Why did he do that?'

'I haven't the least idea. Unless a governess with a toothache requires references when a perfectly healthy one doesn't.'

Amalie turned to leave the room. At the door she said

abruptly, 'I'll give orders that Soames shall drive you to Yarby. I hope you will be ready within half an hour.'

That, Sarah reflected, would allow her to get away before Blane returned. It was possible he might make a fuss, which was a happening she wanted to avoid as much as Amalie did.

'I'll be ready, Lady Mallow. And I hope——'

'Yes?'

The words had escaped Sarah involuntarily. She had a poignant thought of Titus waking in the morning and looking for her, of the hurt and betrayal in his face. For the second time she had failed him. It was not easy or pleasant to do that to a child.

'I hope Titus will be well and happy.'

The tightness had come back into Amalie's face.

'That need be no concern of yours, Miss Mildmay.'

15

SOMEONE was hammering on the door. Sarah had not been asleep. Her light put out, and sunk deep in the downy bed at the George Inn, she had been lost in a miasma of grief and exhaustion. Ambrose and Mallow Hall were lost forever. She had voluntarily given them up. But Ambrose's image was still difficult to recall. At the moment the worst thing to contemplate was Titus's discovery of her desertion. He was only a baby and she had failed him. He wouldn't trust her a second time.

But there wasn't going to be a second time. Even Soames had known that as he carried her baggage into the George and then stood a moment watching her, his face full of unwanted sympathy.

'If you don't mind my saying so, miss, I'm sorry you have to leave.'

No explanation had been made to Soames as to her sudden departure. Why did he assume that she had had to leave?

'You didn't ought to have been scared away as easy as Mrs Stone.'

'Scared away!'

' 'Tain't everyone who'd get on with her ladyship.'

If he thought sympathy and sly hints would induce her to confide in him, he was mistaken.

'Goodbye, Soames. Thank you for driving me here.'

'I'll keep an eye on Master Titus, miss.'

Yes, and on everyone else, Sarah thought, turning away without another word. She was glad to have Tom Mercer welcome her, and at once went to her room.

But now someone was knocking on the door. She had to fumble for matches to light the candle, her hand shaking foolishly. Then, a wrap hastily flung on, she went to the door holding the candle high.

'Who is it?' she called.

But she knew who it was. Instinct had told her at once. That and not weariness was the reason for her shaking hand.

The half-opened door showed her Blane standing there in the lamplight, his hair dishevelled and his clothes mud-spattered.

'What the devil do you think you're up to, running off like this when my son is ill? Get dressed and come back at once.'

Sarah gasped, but kept her temper.

'Titus isn't ill. It's only his mother who says so.'

'He may not have been two hours ago, but he is now. He has a high fever, and is asking for you incessantly.'

Sarah stepped back, making a move to shut the door. His hand on it prevented her.

'I don't believe it.'

'Am I making it up for the pleasure of inveigling you back? Why should I trouble?'

'I don't know. But Titus was well enough when I left. Soames says he didn't have a serious fall. Why don't you ask him?'

'Soames isn't a doctor.'

'Then what does the doctor say?'

'The symptoms hadn't developed so seriously when the doctor called. They came on after Titus had been told you had gone.'

'Who told him? And at this time of night, when he was upset already. Couldn't that news have waited until morning?'

Blane shrugged. 'Or perhaps you could have delayed your departure until morning.'

Sarah's eyes sparkled angrily.

'I may have no money, Lord Mallow, but I do have some pride as a human being.'

For a moment she thought he was going to throw back his head and give his irreverent shout of laughter. Instead he said quite quietly,

'I had imagined that was something a lady in your position was expected to quell. A difficult and unfair imposition, I grant you. But my wife is waiting to apologise to you, so I hope you'll be equally tolerant. Now I'll wait downstairs while you dress. Be as quick about it as you can.'

'I'm no longer in your employ, so I won't be ordered about like this.'

'I'm not ordering you, Miss Mildmay. I'm merely stating the position. If you can forsake a sick child, then you must. If it comes to that, I'm not in the habit of pleading, either. So let's not waste any more time.'

He turned to go. He was full of assurance. He knew very well that shortly she would join him downstairs, and meekly return with him to the house she had renounced.

Then if she were to go back, she decided, this time she wouldn't weaken. She would see the thing through. And win. And if this story of Titus's illness was exaggerated or untrue, she would have no more sentiment.

Blane had driven in alone to get her. As she stepped outside, muffled in her cloak, he said briskly,

'Get up in front. It will be company for me.'

'It's a cold night. I'd prefer to ride inside.'

She found it impossible to adopt her previous submissive manner. That phase was over. Blane could make of it what he would.

'It won't be as cold as that. Come along. Up you go.'

Because Tom Mercer was watching inquisitively, she had to obey. But she didn't intend to pass the ten-mile drive by making small talk. She sat hunched in silence. The wind from the sea was very cold. It rustled the dead grass in the flat fields, and caught the manes of the horses, tossing them wildly. The moon was a blanched colour, almost as pale as the road that curved into the distance. Sarah was overcome with a feeling of desolation. This was the setting for an eerie play. The characters, already assembled, were about to make their entrance for the final dramatic act. How she knew it was the final act, she could not say. But something was about to happen. And she wished she were not to be there.

'Cold?' enquired Blane.

She hadn't realised she had shuddered.

'Sit closer to me so that I can keep the wind off you.'

Sarah didn't reply. Neither did she move.

'Who are you, Miss Mildmay?'

That did elicit an indignant reply.

'You know very well who I am, Lord Mallow. You've investigated my references yourself.'

'Unsatisfactorily. I discovered nothing personal.'

'What has that to do with it?'

'You've puzzled me from the beginning. You're obviously too well-bred to pursue a *cause célèbre* for the mere sensation. Yet you came to my house, deliberately, to ask for a position.'

'I needed work.'

'But with your references that shouldn't have been difficult. Unless, of course, you're too attractive. That's a consideration, isn't it, where the husband may be susceptible and the wife, let us say, indifferently featured.'

'You're being preposterous, Lord Mallow.'

'And you, Miss Mildmay, are an impostor.'

Sarah turned sharply to look at him, and he began laughing.

'You think me one, and I think you one. Isn't that so?'

'Many more people than I have speculated about you, Lord Mallow. But you're being extremely unjust to me. Do you think I would be a governess from choice?' Bitterness came into her voice. 'It's hardly a cheerful prospect, for the rest of one's life. With, as you say, susceptible husbands and jealous wives. Could you imagine my voluntarily choosing such an existence? I have two sisters who are both unhappily doomed to the same life. Does that convince you?'

'What are their names?'

'Amelia and Charlotte. Why do you ask?'

'Because they seem more real to me when I know their names.'

'You thought I was inventing them!'

He ignored her protest.

'Are they as pretty as you?'

Sarah stiffened. She was now very angry and disturbed. Apart from leaping from the carriage, she couldn't escape his nearness. But his familiarity was not to be endured.

'Lord Mallow, I'm coming back to Mallow Hall because Titus is ill. Or so you tell me. For no other reason. But as soon as he's well I intend to prepare him for my departure. In the meantime I'd be grateful if there were no more of these cross-examinations.'

'So you do mean to leave us. The novelty of the situation has worn off?'

'You may put it how you like.'

'You've decided I'm not an impostor after all, and so I no longer interest you?'

The carriage lights danced crazily over the hedgerows, but it was only moonlight that touched his face and glinted in his eyes. She could scarcely see his features, certainly not his expression. But her heart was beating wildly.

'Answer me, Miss Mildmay.'

She was utterly incapable of dealing with this situation. Ambrose would have been ashamed of her. Why couldn't she match Blane with coolness and wit, instead of suddenly finding her lips trembling so much that she couldn't speak.

'What is *your* name, Miss Mildmay?'

She leaned forward.

'Can't we go a little faster? If Titus is so ill——'

Blane took the whip and lightly flicked it on the horses' rumps. They increased their pace, and the carriage rocked. Sarah clutched for something to support her. Blane's hand firmly on her arm steadied her.

'Sarah!' he said softly.

He was merely telling her that he already knew her name. But did he need to speak it like a caress?

Lady Malvina was in the nursery with Titus rocked gently in her capacious lap.

'He's just fallen asleep,' she whispered. 'The fever seems a little less.'

Her raddled pouched old face lit with pleasure at the sight of Sarah.

'That was most generous of you to come back, Miss Mildmay.'

Sarah knelt beside Titus.

'I didn't know he was ill. I would never have left.'

'Fevers come on children suddenly. And his mother broke the

news that you had gone rather callously. Thank heaven Blane caught you before you left for London.' Lady Malvina looked again at Sarah. 'Are you all right yourself, Miss Mildmay? You haven't caught a chill, being out so late? You look flushed.'

'I'm cold,' said Sarah, and it was true that she was shivering. She hadn't been able to stop for some time.

'Ask Eliza to heat some milk. We'll all have some. Titus, too, perhaps, now that you're back. With a little port in it. It will do us good.'

At that moment Titus stirred and opened his eyes. They widened as they fell on Sarah.

'Mamma said you went away,' he said accusingly.

'Only for a few hours. That wasn't long, was it?'

'Yes, it was. I was sick. I cried for you.' The little boy lifted his arms, and Sarah took him into hers. There was no sulking this time. He was too happy to see her.

'You will stay now?' he said in his clear voice.

'Yes. I'll stay.'

Titus gave a satisfied murmur. His eyes went past her.

'Papa, Miss Mildmay is back. She's going to stay now.'

Sarah hadn't known Blane had come in. She saw him standing there, tall and silent. There was no mocking or triumphant gleam in his eyes. The moonlight must have made her imagine it earlier. He merely looked tired, and rather sad.

'That's splendid, my boy.' He turned to his mother. 'Where's Amalie?'

'How does the boy seem to you, Miss Mildmay?'

Titus was dozing again. Sarah felt the hot limp body in her arms.

'I'll put him into bed. I think he should be better in the morning. Children recover from fevers quickly.'

'Blane, tell Amalie not to come in again,' said Lady Malvina. 'She upsets the boy.'

'I can't forbid her to see her own son.'

'Under the circumstances you can. She upset him badly.'

'Amalie's a very difficult woman,' Lady Malvina said to Sarah when Titus, tucked into his own bed, seemed to be sleeping more soundly, and Blane had gone.

'There was an enormous row after you had gone,' she added with relish. 'Blane was mad at her. Really mad. He said you must be brought back at once, and if you weren't he would go back to sea and leave her to all this grandeur. She could then behave as she liked. Oh, it was a fine quarrel, I can tell you. The worst of it is, my son doesn't make idle boasts. I learnt that long ago. And I don't believe he makes a fig for Mallow. He never did. He only wants it for his son.'

'I believe he's quite ruthless,' Sarah said.

'You mean in treating his wife this way? But she's a poor stick. I can never think why he married her.'

'He humiliates her. And because of me, a servant.'

'I hardly think he regards you as a servant, Miss Mildmay,' the old lady murmured slyly.

Titus stirred and muttered in his sleep. Sarah felt his hot forehead. At least that the child was ill had not been a lie.

'I find his behaviour intolerable.'

'His behaviour has always been intolerable. But the heart is there, my dear.'

'Do you really believe that, Lady Malvina?'

'Now I do. Once, I admit, I worried a great deal. So did my husband. Blane wasn't a vicious boy, you understand. Just uncontrollable. But now he's changed. He's basically good, one sees. It's a great relief to me.'

'Always assuming,' said Sarah, 'that we're speaking of the same person.'

The old lady gave her a swift wary glance. Then she began to shake with silent laughter.

'Now that's a bee to have in your bonnet, Miss Mildmay. And with Titus here, a replica of my own son at that age. Features can't lie, can they? And I'll warrant by the look on your face that my son's manners haven't changed either. Was the drive from Yarby too long?'

When Sarah didn't answer she went on, 'It's unfortunate, but this kind of difficulty is often the lot of the woman in your position. My advice is to try to regard it as a compliment.'

'A compliment!'

'My dear, don't be a hypocrite. You must enjoy masculine

156

admiration as well as the next woman.'

'Why doesn't he behave more kindly to his wife?' Sarah demanded heatedly. 'Why does he make her so unhappy? I don't blame her for being jealous. Why does he keep his door locked?'

Realising she had said more than she intended to, Sarah clapped her hand to her mouth. But not before a lewd secret look had come into Lady Malvina's face.

'So you've discovered that, Miss Mildmay. I wonder how.'

'It was accidental——'

'Oh, no doubt. I won't enquire into your strange curiosity about my son. I believe your injured ankle that kept you in London was accidental, too. My dear, you have the most exquisite colour when you're angry. I like a young woman with spirit. So you just stay here and keep my grandson happy, and we'll say no more.'

She swept out of the room, giving Sarah no opportunity to reply. Indeed, there was no reply to be made. Lady Malvina was not her enemy. She was a coarse kind old woman with a streak of shrewd worldliness.

A little later Blane came back to see how Titus was.

'He's sleeping soundly, and the fever seems a little less,' Sarah reported.

'That's splendid. Then you'd better get some sleep, Miss Mildmay.'

His voice was polite and formal. There was no trace of the intimacy it had had on the drive from Yarby. That had belonged to the windy darkness and the emptiness of the winter countryside. It had been a dream.

'Thank you, I will,' Sarah said, equally formal. 'I hope Lady Mallow is able to rest.'

'She is now. I persuaded her to take a sedative. I'll bid you goodnight, Miss Mildmay. Don't hesitate to send for me if the boy seems worse in the night.'

'The night's almost over, Lord Mallow.'

'So it is. And you must be exhausted. Get some sleep.'

Sarah left her door open so as to hear the slightest sound from Titus's room. She meant to sleep only lightly, but fatigue overcame her, and she had to struggle from a sound sleep when she heard the sound at her window. It was the sound of the curtains being pulled back. Pale chilly early-morning light came in, and Amalie in a flowing négligé, with her dark hair hanging on her shoulders, stood there.

'Good morning, Miss Mildmay,' she said amicably. 'It's getting light. Look, you can see the lake quite clearly now the trees are bare.'

Sarah started up. 'Titus——'

'Titus seems much better, I'm happy to say. He's still asleep. I'm sorry he was so upset last evening. My husband said I was to tell you so.'

'He's a very nervous little boy.'

'So you all tell me. I know nothing about children, even my own.'

Standing there in the dim light she seemed forlorn and helpless, almost ghostlike.

'I think you know I'd prefer not to be here, Lady Mallow.'

'I understand. I believe I behaved badly to you. I act on impulse. I'm glad you consented to come back. My husband says I can't go on like this, engaging and then dismissing servants without real cause. He didn't object to Mrs Stone's departure, but with you he didn't feel the cause was real enough.' Amalie gave a brief laugh. 'My husband is a very domineering man. I give you a warning, Miss Mildmay. If you haven't a submissive nature yourself, don't marry a domineering man.'

She turned to go, then, as if drawn against her will, went back to the window.

'I didn't realise you got such a view from here. I believe your room is more pleasantly situated than mine. You can see almost the whole of the lake. In the summer we must have picnics down there. That is,' she came closer to the bed, 'if you're still with us.'

Her voice was perfectly friendly and amicable. It came as a distinct shock to see the hate glittering in her eyes.

16

BUT surely the early-morning light must have been deceptive. Sarah must have imagined that look of hate. For in the days that followed Amalie seemed friendly enough. She spent a lot of time sitting with Titus who was recovering from the illness which the doctor diagnosed as a sharp chill combined with the after-effects of his fall. She also busied herself with sending out invitations for the ball, and arranging the numerous details concerning that. Her manner to Sarah, whenever they chanced to be alone, was almost ingratiating.

'Miss Mildmay, you're looking pale. You should get more fresh air and exercise. You must come walking with me.'

'Thank you, Lady Mallow. When Titus is better.'

'He's better now. Another day or two and the doctor says he can go outdoors. It's this bitter English climate after the tropics that's caused the trouble. But all this is no reason why you should get pale, Miss Mildmay.'

Amalie's eagerness and brittle gaiety was puzzling. She was behaving with an almost embarrassing friendliness.

'What are you going to wear for the ball, Miss Mildmay? Have you a pretty gown?'

'I don't imagine I will be dancing,' Sarah answered, remembering Amalie's previous snub.

'Don't be offended at my saying this, Miss Mildmay, but is it because you haven't got a ball gown? I'd be very happy to let you wear one of mine. I should think our waists are almost identical.'

Looking at the thin eager face Sarah had a feeling of revulsion. She had preferred Amalie's haughtiness.

'Thank you, Lady Mallow, that's very kind of you. But I have a perfectly suitable gown. And I really don't imagine I will be dancing.'

Amalie looked at her as if she were not listening.

'I shall wear my diamonds,' she said.

Acceptances came in as if all the countryside had been waiting for an invitation to a ball at Mallow Hall. Amalie was flattered and happy. She imagined, no doubt, that this was a sign that she and Blane were completely accepted. Sarah had a shrewd suspicion that curiosity was bringing most of the people, and this suspicion Lady Malvina shared. But where Lady Malvina was saying aggressively, 'We'll show them that the Mallows are still alive,' Sarah was reflecting that this may prove to be the best opportunity yet to glean valuable information. And this time she would have no regrets. Blane had forced her to come back. He deserved anything that might happen.

But now she was desperate to hear from Ambrose, although she had a queer dread of what he might write. The situation was fast proving intolerable.

Only one significant thing happened before the ball, and that was the scrap of conversation she overheard between Blane and Amalie.

'You'll have to get rid of Soames. He's getting insolent.'

'Soames! Soames can't go.'

'Why not?'

'You know very well why not. One has some loyalty. He's been here since I was a boy.'

Amalie gave a derisive laugh.

'I realise that's quite a long time, but that doesn't excuse his insolence. I want him dismissed. If you won't do it, I will.'

'I don't think so, my dear. I don't think so.' Blane's voice was quite confident and quite cold.

In contrast Amalie lost her own self-control. She said in a high edgy voice, 'You're not going to behave over him the way you have over that woman, Sarah Mildmay!'

'We won't make any comparisons. Soames stays. You've had your fun at dismissing people. And my God, I hope you've been right about that.'

'Nothing's happened, has it? So I was right.'

'I can't believe it's as easy as that.'

'Oh, Blane, don't look for trouble. It doesn't happen if you don't look for it.'

'Ambrose will be back soon enough. Heaven knows what

he'll try to dig up. Sammie, most likely.'

Amalie, for no apparent reason, gave a high peal of laughter.

'Oh, forget about Sammie. And Ambrose. It's Soames I'm talking about. He's too familiar.' There was a little silence. Then Amalie added in a low voice, 'He watches me.'

'As mistress of a large house you must expect to be watched. I expect the other servants do that, too.'

'Oh, yes, including your precious Miss Mildmay. I gave in about her, for Titus's sake, but Soames means nothing to Titus. And he does watch me.' There was no mistaking now the note of apprehension in her voice. 'I don't know how much longer I can stand all this. I might even decide it isn't worth it.' Her voice rose defiantly. 'And then what will you do?'

'Get another wife,' Blane retorted drily. 'Don't put ideas in my head, my love.'

'I believe you would!' Amalie whispered. 'I believe you would.'

It was the Sunday before the day of the ball, and they were riding in the carriage to church, Titus crushed between Lady Malvina and Sarah, Amalie and Blane facing them.

Sarah suddenly exclaimed in surprise, 'Why, you've found your blue velvet bonnet, Lady Mallow. Didn't Mrs Stone take it after all?'

Her exclamation had been spontaneous. It could not have been more effective, though, had she rehearsed it for its element of surprise and drama.

All eyes went to Amalie's attractive blue bonnet with the French silk roses. Lady Malvina said wheezily, as if she were suddenly asthmatic, 'Then she must have gone without a bonnet at all. How extraordinary!'

'I didn't say it was this bonnet she took,' snapped Amalie. 'It was my other blue one.'

'I didn't know you had two.'

'Don't be foolish, Mamma. I have dozens of bonnets.'

'Then Mrs Stone must have had quite a problem in making a choice,' Blane murmured. His voice was gently ironic. But he was watching Amalie, too.

'She took my fur tippett, too. And jewellery,' Amalie said sulkily.

She had recovered. It had only been for a moment that that white look of fear had flashed into her face. Now it had left her, and settled instead in Sarah's heart. But what she was afraid of, she didn't know. She only felt that the four walls of the carriage, and the close-together faces, each with its private thoughts, were suffocating, and something from which urgently to escape.

But nothing happened until the day before the ball. Then Eliza, who was allowed a night off once a week to spend with her family in Yarby, came back bursting with a secret.

'Oh, Miss Mildmay, I've got an important message for you.'

'For me?' Sarah echoed.

'Yes. From a man arrived at the George. He said I was to hand it to you personally. It was very important, and I wasn't to tell anyone else.'

Without ceremony Sarah snatched the crumpled envelope from Eliza. This must be news from Ambrose at last.

But the writer of the large awkward script was a stranger, James Brodie, and apparently Ambrose had impressed caution on him, for the news of Ambrose was yet to come.

Dear Miss Mildmay,

On instruktions from Mr Ambrose Mallow who I last seed in Trinidad, I have a packet to deliver to you concerning matters you are deeply interested in. If you will communikate with me at the George and tell me where I can safely hand to you the said packet, it not to be trusted to the post, I will do my best to oblige.

Your obed'nt servant,
James Brodie

Where could she meet him? Sarah thought rapidly, momentarily forgetful of Eliza's burning curiosity.

'Tom Mercer said he was a sailor from the South Seas,' she said breathlessly. 'Is he really, Miss Mildmay?'

'Oh. No, not the South Seas. But he's probably a sailor.'

Could Eliza be trusted, she was wondering. She would have to take the risk, for she had no possible excuse herself to make the journey to see James Brodie.

'Eliza, this man has something for me from a—a friend. He's been asked to deliver it to me personally. How can I get a message to him?'

Eliza was not practical. But she was excessively romantic. Her eyes were large and shining.

'Oh, Miss Mildmay! Have you got a secret lover?'

'Indeed I haven't. At least——' Sarah hesitated, realising that this, of course, was what Eliza must be led to believe. And in any case, wasn't it true? Wasn't she overjoyed that there was news from Ambrose at last?

Eliza giggled conspiratorially.

'I can see you have, Miss Mildmay. Is he on adventure in the South Seas? I do declare!'

'Now, Eliza, don't get ideas. And not a word of this to anyone. The thing is, how to get in touch with Mr Brodie again.'

'Well, he sent the letter by Pa to me, knowing I worked with you at the Hall. But I won't be seeing Pa till my next night off. I know, Miss Mildmay. Johnnie Smith comes with the groceries this morning. If you'd write a message I could give it to him to take.'

'Could you really? Without anyone knowing?'

'Easy. Johnnie'll do what I say. And he'll keep his mouth shut, too, or I won't never speak to him again.'

'Is Johnnie a friend of yours?'

'Known him ever since we was kids,' Eliza said briefly. Then her eyes grew big and yearning. 'But I'd rather have a mysterious lover in the South Seas. Ooh, Miss Mildmay! Isn't it romantic!'

'Please, Eliza! Not a word, or I'd lose my job.'

'You can trust me to keep a secret. But if I'm to catch Johnnie you'd better write that message quick. I'll tell cook and the rest it's a letter to my Mum.'

Confusion and excitement kept Sarah from thinking clearly. She hastily wrote the first thing that came into her head.

If you could come to Mallow Hall tomorrow afternoon I'll be in the summer house by the lake at five o'clock. Come by the path through the woods. No one is likely to see you.

When it was too late and Eliza excitedly informed her that the message had gone, Sarah reflected that the summer house was not such an ideal place because of Amalie's habit of walking by the lake. But since it was the day of the ball, she was not likely to be out of the house. So perhaps the arrangement was fortuitous after all.

Eliza, now her willing ally, agreed to keep Titus happy, and cover up for her absence. She hoped not to be out of the house more than half an hour, and would be back in plenty of time to cope with Lady Malvina's nightly swoops on the nursery, and her garrulous chatter about the ball.

What was the news from Ambrose? Was anticipation of that the reason for the feeling not of excitement but of dread hanging over her?

It was very cold down by the lake. The summer house was empty. A few dead leaves rustled on the floor, blown by gusts of wind. The lake was steely grey and empty even of wild life. Now that the trees were bare the big house was visible, and in the deepening dusk lights sprang into the windows, the nursery, Lady Malvina's, and Amalie's all showing that the lamps had been lit and that the occupants of the rooms must be there. Only Blane's remained in darkness. He had been out riding, but was probably back by now, and warming himself at the library fire. Sarah hadn't dared to look lest she should be seen herself. She had put a shawl over her head and shoulders, and slipped out by the garden door, making a long circuit round the garden so as to keep out of sight of the windows.

But now it must be fifteen minutes past the appointed time, and no one had come. One of the windows in the summer house was broken, making it intensely cold. It passed through Sarah's mind that it was very odd Amalie should spend time down here, even if she were dreaming of the summer. But she had obviously been here very recently, for, as Sarah sat a few minutes in one of the broken wicker chairs, she saw something shining among the dust and debris of dead leaves on the floor,

164

and picked it up to find it was a small jet brooch.

But that couldn't be Amalie's. It wasn't good enough. It was unobtrusive and inexpensive. It must belong to one of the servants. Perhaps more than one person made the summer house a rendezvous.

But what a place in winter!

Sarah shivered, and drew the shawl closely about her. She was getting anxious and impatient. She couldn't be out too long. Someone would be asking for her. And it was growing darker all the time, with a white moon showing fleetingly behind racing storm clouds. The wind smelt of the sea.

Where was James Brodie? Had he lost his way? She prayed he would have the sense to invent a plausible story if he ran into Soames. Supposing he ran into Blane, and had Ambrose's letter discovered on him! But surely Blane would not have the discourtesy to search a man, even supposing him a poacher or a criminal.

The wind was stirring the surface of the lake, and the water lapped gently among the reeds. It was scarcely two yards from the door of the summer house, and filled the place with its cold smell. A swan flew over with a faint thunder of wings. The dark shadow of the woods in the distance gave no sign of an approaching figure.

She looked away from the lake to the house. The windows glowed with their gentle yellow radiance, infinitely warm and desirable. Now all of the downstairs was alight, too, as hurrying servants did last-minute tasks. But the ball seemed to Sarah like a dream, thrust into the back of her mind by the imminence of Ambrose's news. It might be more than a still slightly painful ankle that prevented her from dancing tonight.

Ah! Footsteps at last, crunching on the pebbles by the lakeside. Thank heaven, for in the gloom she would soon not be able to identify her visitor. She peered out of the window, trying to see from what direction he came and to get a glimpse of him before he saw her.

But a voice at the door of the summer house made her gasp.

'Amalie! Amalie, what *are* you doing here? I can't understand this nonsense, mooning by a lakeside in midwinter. You surely can't be waiting for somebody. Or are you? Don't tell me it's a rendezvous.'

It was Blane. Sarah stood petrified. She didn't dare to show her face. But how could she not?

'Amalie, are you in a trance?'

Blane had crossed over to her, and taken her roughly by the arm, swinging her round.

He gave an exclamation. His expression was hidden by the darkness. Sarah could see only the shine of his eyes.

'You!' he said.

He hadn't relaxed his grip on her arm. Indeed, his fingers were pressing painfully into her flesh. His face was near to hers.

'What are you doing here, Miss Mildmay? Tell me.'

Before she could speak, he went on, 'I don't want one of your clever plausible explanations. Indeed, you'd have to think hard to produce any explanation for being by the lakeside after dark. It can't be for the fresh air.' He went closer. Suddenly his voice was harsh and imperative. 'Who are you waiting for?'

Supposing James Brodie were to come at this minute! Sarah managed to gasp, 'No one, Lord Mallow.'

'I don't believe you. I don't trust you. You are, I believe, the most devious woman I have met. Come now, a simple answer.'

'I lost a brooch,' Sarah said on an inspiration. 'I thought it might have been down here.'

'You mean you came down here after dark to look for something! Without a light of any kind? Oh, come, Miss Mildmay, where's your ingenuity?'

'But I found the brooch. This is it.'

As she loosened his grip, she fumbled in her pocket and produced the modest ornament.

She had still underestimated him, for after striking a match and looking at the brooch, he dismissed it scornfully, 'I have yet to see you wearing something in that taste. Oh, no, Miss Mildmay. Think again.'

Sarah had regained her presence of mind. She was even conscious of a strange elation. Ambrose had not guessed how exhilarating it would be pitting her wits against this man's.

'I'm afraid I haven't time to invent an explanation, Lord Mallow. I must go up to Titus.'

'You're impertinent.'

'I'm sorry if you think so. Perhaps I resent your accusations.'

She made to leave the summer house. Another rendezvous would somehow have to be made with James Brodie. It was exasperating and dreadfully disappointing. Yet she was conscious of nothing but this exhilaration.

Blane stood across the doorway, barring the way.

'You're up to something. I should get rid of you. I should agree with my wife. But——'

She hadn't an inkling of his intention. His arms were about her before she could move. She was held in that same hard grip, and her head forced up so that he could find her mouth.

She couldn't have said how long the kiss lasted. She only knew that when he let her go she almost fell.

He was laughing softly.

'What a fortunate thing you lost that horrible little brooch. Otherwise this couldn't have happened. Could it?'

Even in her confusion she got his meaning. If she were in the summer house on some private affair of her own this episode must also remain private.

As if she would want to talk of it!

'Did you get it?' Eliza whispered eagerly, when at last she arrived in the nursery.

Sarah shook her head furiously. She had not meant to make Eliza her confidante, but she could not hide her distress.

'Lord Mallow found me there.'

'The master!' Eliza gaped fascinatedly.

'He wanted to know what I was doing. I said I had lost a brooch, and was looking for it. So then he came up to the house with me. I couldn't wait for Mr Brodie. Isn't it sickening?'

'How clever you thought of the brooch,' Eliza said admiringly.

Sarah fingered the piece of jet in her pocket. Strangely enough, she didn't want to tell Eliza that there had been a brooch. Something kept her silent.

'So now I haven't got the letters,' she said.

'Lor, Miss Mildmay, what a shame. You do look upset.'

'I'll have to find some reason to go into Yarby tomorrow and see Mr Brodie.'

'Couldn't you have the toothache again? I mean, not suffering as you were last time, but just pretending?'

'I don't know, Eliza. I'll have to think. I only hope Mr Brodie isn't angry at having his trip for nothing.'

'It's lucky he didn't run into the master.'

'Yes, at least that didn't happen.' Sarah tried to collect her scattered wits. 'Is Titus in bed?'

Eliza nodded. 'And asleep,' she said proudly. 'I promised him if he went to sleep quick he'd be allowed up later for the ball. So he went off as good as gold. But Lady Malvina's been looking for you.'

'Oh. What did you say?'

'I said you had a headache, and wanted to snatch a breath of air before this evening.'

Eliza learned quickly, Sarah reflected. Perhaps there was something devious in the simplest women. Even if, as Blane had said, she was the most devious. She couldn't think of him without her cheeks burning. And her arm already showed a bruise. She would have to keep her shawl on this evening. And stay on the stairs in the shadow with Titus. She had no wish to dance or to be seen. Ambrose would be so impatient with her bungling. And if he knew of Blane's behaviour he would be furious. 'He was a drunkard and a lecher.' Lady Malvina's words, under the influence of too much port, kept coming back to her. If that was a picture of Blane as a youth, he hadn't changed.

So this man must be the real Blane. It was the first time she had admitted it. She didn't know what to do. She couldn't think beyond this evening and the ordeal of the ball.

Lady Malvina came in in her unceremonious way as Sarah was dressing. She looked very splendid in her enormous crinoline of plum-coloured silk, with the ropes of pearls on her massive bosom, and her hair piled in a precarious erection of ringlets and jewelled combs.

'Well, Miss Mildmay, this is more like it, isn't it? The Mallows cutting a dash once more. How do I look?'

'Very impressive, Lady Malvina.'

'Impressive! What an excellent choice of word. I like that. I was looking for you a little while ago. Eliza said you had a headache. I hope it's better, though I must say you're looking rather flushed.'

'It's nothing, Lady Malvina.'

'H'mm. That's what I thought when I saw you coming up from the lake with my son. It was you, wasn't it, Miss Mildmay?'

Sarah could not escape the shrewd eyes.

'Why yes. Lord Mallow found me walking down there.'

'Well, don't let my daughter-in-law catch you at it.'

'Lady Malvina——'

'Don't explain, my dear. It's reassuring to find my son so little changed after all. But be careful, for Titus's sake. Let him grow a little stronger before he loses you.'

'Lady Malvina, I assure you you couldn't be more mistaken.'

The old lady had to take notice of the indignation in her voice.

'But I often see someone down at the lake. It is you sometimes, isn't it?'

'Today was the first time. And my meeting with Lord Mallow was quite accidental. Do you think I'm lying to you?'

'Oh, tush! I wouldn't put it past you, Miss Mildmay. You're a clever young woman. But in that case,' now the uneasiness was very apparent in her eyes, 'it must always be Amalie. And she's not the type to moon by lakes. Is she? Is she, Miss Mildmay? One night——'

But Lady Malvina didn't go on with what she had been about to say. Sarah, on an impulse, picked up the jet brooch and held it out.

'Other people do walk down there, because I found this. I should think it belongs to one of the servants, wouldn't you?' Lady Malvina looked at the brooch with interest.

'What a dreary little piece of jewellery! It looks familiar. Who have I seen wearing it?' She was about to say something more, but all at once a strange wary look came into her face.

169

She closed her lips firmly.

'Should I ask the servants?' Sarah enquired.

'No, I don't think I'd do that, Miss Mildmay.'

'But someone might value it.'

'They might value their good reputation more. We don't want a scandal.'

She couldn't be thinking of her son with one of the servants— as he had just been with Sarah, snatching casual kisses. No, not snatching, forcing them on her.

'You mean——' she faltered.

Lady Malvina nodded. 'I advise you to forget it, Miss Mildmay.'

Then, to put some disturbing thought out of her mind, she swooped on Sarah's jewel box and looked at its contents.

With a complete change of manner she exclaimed sincerely,

'Oh, dear, Miss Mildmay, your jewellery is very ladylike, isn't it? What a pity! And you have such a pretty neck. You'd set the diamonds off much better than Amalie will. Now don't get upset again!' A fat beringed finger was waved in Sarah's face. 'I'm merely stating a fact.'

It was after the ball had started and she had led an excited Titus, dressed in his red jacket, to a place of observation on the stairs, that a curious trick of memory made Sarah remember where she had seen that jet brooch before.

It had been pinned at the modest high neck of Mrs Stone's drab grey dress.

17

Titus was very excited. He hung over the bannisters looking at the gay scene and chattered incessantly. Standing beside him, Sarah, too, watched with interest as Amalie and Blane greeted their guests. The diamonds glittered round Amalie's neck. They gave her assurance. She looked affable and gracious, and was enjoying her moment of importance.

She had better make the most of it, poor thing, while she could, Sarah thought. For it wasn't going to last long. And what if she lost both Mallow and her husband's fidelity?

Blane, Sarah could scarcely bear to watch at all. But she must. For she wanted to observe every nuance of the greetings he was given by all these people whom he must pretend to know.

Tomkins was announcing the names so clearly that he was protected temporarily from mistakes. One would never have guessed from his demeanour that the evening was an ordeal. But was it? He was a gambler, a man who got tremendous zest from a challenge. And he had no conscience. One was sure of that now. Probably his black eyes were sparkling with mischief and pleasure.

If for one moment, thought Sarah, only one moment, she could have the satisfaction of seeing him at a loss, disturbed, defeated.

'The music's beginning,' said Titus. 'Are you going to dance, Miss Mildmay?'

'I'm going to stay here with you.'

The little boy's sensitive face held concern for her enjoyment. 'But you have your best dress on.' Then he slid his hand into hers contentedly. His eyes were shining. He had the entranced look of a child in fairyland. The only other time he wore this look was when he was with Soames and his pony. 'How many candles are there burning? Shall we have ices later? Doesn't Mamma look pretty? Can we watch the dancing, Miss Mildmay?'

'Yes, when it begins. We'll sit at the bottom of the stairs.' (When Titus had gone back to bed, she thought, she might slip secretly down to the lake just to see if James Brodie had lingered.)

'Will you stay with me all the time, Miss Mildmay?'

'Yes, my darling.'

'Won't you really dance? Won't someone ask you?'

'I shall refuse.'

But Blane would take no refusal. He had been dancing with his wife. Sarah had watched them, catching a glimpse of Amalie's uplifted face, strained and brilliant. But now she was being the gracious hostess once more, dancing with Colonel Fortescue, and Blane had shamelessly left the ballroom to talk to the governess.

He said, 'Where's Eliza? Get Eliza to stay with Titus. Come, Miss Mildmay, this is an order.'

'Do you want to make a scandal?' Sarah muttered furiously.

'No. I merely want to go on asking you questions, and it will look much more natural if we're dancing than talking out here. For instance, that wasn't your brooch you picked up in the summer house, was it? Tell me the truth.'

Something wild and reckless seized her.

'Very well. Since you insist. No, it wasn't my brooch. It was the person's you're afraid it was. Mrs Stone's.'

She had shaken him at last. She went on,

'I wonder what she was doing down in the summer house? She'd scarcely been here long enough to know such a place existed.'

'One might ask the same question of you, Miss Mildmay,' he countered. 'Since now you admit finding the brooch was incidental. So who was it you were waiting for?'

Titus was absorbed in watching the dancing, his small face pressed against the bannisters. Sarah moved away a little from him to say in a low voice, 'If you continue to persecute me in this way, Lord Mallow, I will be compelled to leave, after all.'

'I don't persecute you. I only find you so damnably secretive and mysterious.'

'Blane!'

Sarah started sharply at the sound of Amalie's voice behind them. She turned to see her face sharp and glittering with anger. 'What are you doing out here? Why aren't you dancing?'

'My love, I'm endeavouring to. Miss Mildmay——'

Amalie no longer concealed her enmity beneath a sickly friendliness.

'Miss Mildmay! A servant! When you've scarcely spoken to your guests.'

Blane bowed slightly. 'Your guests, my dear,' he said inexplicably.

'There's Soames!' Titus exclaimed, and began to wave excitedly. 'Soames, have you come to dance?'

Sarah saw Soames approaching across the hall, followed by an agitated Tomkins. The significance of his appearance in the house scarcely struck her, she was so fascinated by the change in Amalie's face. The rigid anger had given way to uncertainty and alarm. Her mouth was open, her eyes full of apprehension.

'Good evening, Master Titus,' said Soames, brushing the excited boy aside. 'I must speak to you, my lord.'

Blane had more self-control than Amalie. He allowed nothing but impatience to show in his face.

'It had better be something important.'

'What is it, Soames?' Amalie asked in a high edgy voice. A strange man had appeared in the hall, a middle-aged person with a weatherbeaten face. Soames was saying in a low voice, 'I'd send the boy away, my lord.'

The orchestra was playing a low romantic waltz, a buzz of chatter came from the ballroom. Amalie, thought Sarah, was like a coloured candy figure, beginning to wilt from being too near the heat of the candles.

'Who's that?' Blane demanded, indicating the strange man.

'He says he lost his way, my lord. He found himself down by the lake, and saw the——' Soames lowered his voice to a whisper. Sarah just caught the words, 'Under the jetty. Caught against the piles. Must have drowned herself, poor soul.'

'Who?' whispered Amalie. '*Who?*'

Sarah pushed Titus towards the ballroom door. Distracted by

the noise and brilliance, he stared in, still entranced. It seemed macabre that the music continued to play with gaiety and heartlessness.

'The sewing woman, my lady,' Soames said formally. 'At least, that must be who it is because you said she stole jewellery. And she—the body—is wearing a diamond ring.'

Involuntarily Amalie's hand went to the diamonds at her throat.

'I told you she was a thief!' she shrieked.

'Be quiet, Amalie!'

Blane took her arm. His face no longer wore a disguise. It was as Sarah had always known it would be, sombre, frowning, formidable. But he was quite calm.

'The police must be informed.' Sharply he added, 'Sarah, take Titus upstairs.'

He had spoken her name automatically, Sarah realised, as if privately he always thought of her by her first name. But Amalie didn't seem to have noticed. She looked on the point of collapse.

'Stop the music!' she cried. 'For God's sake, stop the music!'

Let there be silence for that dark bundle found floating in the steely water of the lake. The mysterious Mrs Stone whose taste had run to jet brooches and black straw bonnets, but who had finally left both behind, as well as the unfinished piece of work on her table.

Was it in that half hour, when Sarah had been waiting for her dress to be mended, that she had died? Sarah could remember every minute of that evening. Amalie had gone to bed early with a headache (had she? who had seen her in bed?) and Blane had come in with his hair shining and glossy with rain.

And afterwards someone had slipped upstairs and packed Mrs Stone's few shabby belongings, but in their haste had overlooked the black bonnet so that it had had to be burnt hastily the next day.

Were these fantastic and horrible suspicions true? Or had the dreariness of life been too much for Mrs Stone, and she had voluntarily ended it?

174

Lady Malvina came out of the ballroom, holding Titus by the hand.

'Miss Mildmay! Can't you look after——' Her bulging gaze took in the scene. 'What's wrong? What's happened?'

At the same moment the violins wailed to a stop. The last shivering note died away. The gaiety had been short-lived. This seemed to be the end of the music.

Sarah scarcely remembered getting Titus upstairs. Fortunately the child hadn't realised what was happening. He was still captivated by his brief glimpse of what seemed a candlelit fairyland.

Sarah neither heard what he was chattering about, nor noticed that Eliza had come in and was speaking to her.

The girl had to seize her arm.

'Miss Mildmay! Didn't you see him down in the hall? It's that Mr Brodie. What is it he found in the lake?'

'James Brodie!'

'Wasn't it him I heard Soames saying had found something?'

'What did he find?' Titus demanded, listening too eagerly.

'A—a black swan,' Sarah improvised desperately. Poor Mrs Stone had surely not been a swan, not even an ugly duckling. Or had she, in disguise? Everyone in this house was in some disguise or another. Except the simple honest Eliza whose face was full of pleasure that now Miss Mildmay would be able to get her love letters, after all.

The ball had ended. There had always been drama at Mallow Hall when Blane Mallow was home, and although deprived of their evening's gaiety, the guests were not entirely disappointed. For they were provided with a new terrible piece of gossip. There had been another suicide at the Hall, that of another servant. Inevitably Bella's hanging, which had happened not a day under fifty years ago, was revived, and the significant sequence of this poor creature going straight from that doomed room to her own death was discussed.

Finally the last carriage rolled away, and the ballroom with its only half-burnt candles was left to a few whispering and awestruck servants. Soames had been sent poste-haste to Yarby for the police. Long ago Amalie had shut herself in her room. Lady Malvina had showed her breeding by keeping her head entirely, bidding polite apologies and farewells, and behaving as if an accident such as this were a trifling occurrence which could happen to anyone at any time.

The stranger, James Brodie, had been asked to remain to answer the questions of the police, and also eventually to explain his presence at the lake. He was certainly guilty of trespassing, if not of something worse.

But Blane had behaved with impartial courtesy, and he had been given food in the servants' hall. It was there that Sarah contrived to have a brief conversation with him, during which she hid under her shawl the letter he handed her.

'You were late,' she whispered. 'I couldn't wait.'

'I mistook the way through the woods. I hung about hoping you might come down again. And then I saw this shape in the water. The moon caught it.'

'Why shall you say you were there?'

He had a creased, wind-burnt, devil-may-care face.

'I'll say I was looking for a bit of poaching.'

'You'll get jailed!'

'Pshaw! Not with all this excitement. And judging by the looks of the new lord he won't be unfair.'

Sarah thought that the letter felt cold through the silk of her gown, cold against her heart. She couldn't understand her dread of opening it.

'Do you know what's in this letter?'

'Not a word, miss. But something important judging by the gentleman's anxiety to get it to you.'

Sarah felt weak and as inclined to tremble as Amalie had been. As she tried to slip back upstairs unnoticed she encountered Blane coming from the library. His face was drawn into deep lines, his eyes hard and unseeing. She was afraid he would ask her what she was clutching beneath her shawl, but she need not have worried. He passed her as if she had been one of the servants. With a shock of pure horror she realised that his distress was far in excess of that to be occasioned by the suicide of a woman whom he had never seen.

Two policemen arrived just after midnight, and there was a little procession down to the lakeside. Lady Malvina's splendid façade had cracked. She begged Sarah to come to her room, where the curtains were firmly drawn against the desolate night, and as well as the lamp two branches of candlesticks were blazing. The room was very hot, and Lady Malvina, still in her ball finery, looked flushed and restless, and curiously forlorn.

'What a terrible business, Miss Mildmay. What do you think of it?'

'I don't know what to think.'

Lady Malvina glanced, wincing, over her shoulder.

'I've shut out the lake, you see. I fancy Amalie won't have such a liking for it now. She's inclined to blame herself for this tragedy.'

'What does she say?'

'Why, that the wretched creature had threatened all along to take her life. That was why Amalie took pity on her and gave her work. She was in such despair. Apparently Betsey, who saw her when she first arrived, can confirm this. Then her work was hopeless, as you know yourself, Miss Mildmay, and when Amalie told her so she got abusive. Oh dear, she was a sad character. So Amalie had no alternative but to dismiss her, although she still threatened to drown herself because she was so poor and unwanted.'

'But I thought she had stolen things. One surely doesn't bother to do that when planning to take one's life.'

'Revenge, followed by remorse,' said Lady Malvina firmly. 'The poor thing was quite unbalanced. I have proof of that myself.'

'Proof?'

'Yes. I looked out of my window one evening, and saw this figure running up from the lake, as if she were fleeing from some dreadful destiny.'

'Are you sure it was Mrs Stone?'

'Positive. She'd probably been looking at the lake and her courage failed.'

'Amalie also likes to walk by the lake.'

'This was not Amalie.'

Sarah was remembering evidence given in court as to Blane's identity in just such firm unyielding tones. Lady Malvina was too intelligent to deviate from whatever the story she had decided to tell.

'Are you sure you saw this, Lady Malvina?'

The tufted white eyebrows went up.

'And why should I invent it?'

Sarah was determined not to be intimidated by *grande dame* methods.

'It might make a convenient story to tell the police.'

'Miss Mildmay! How dare you!' Her voice was rich and resonant with indignation. 'Are you suggesting that wretched troublesome woman died in any other way?'

'I expect the police will decide that, Lady Malvina.'

'Oh, yes. They'll make wild guesses, and there'll be more scandal, and all the servants will leave. Just when we were all settling down so comfortably. Oh, I could have killed that woman myself.' Suddenly realising what she had said, Lady Malvina clapped her hand to her mouth. Her eyes were horror-stricken. She was deflated and piteous.

'Miss Mildmay, can you ring the bell for Bessie. I must have something to restore me. A little brandy.' She sank into a chair, her chins pressed into her neck. 'There's always been trouble when Blane's around,' she mumbled. 'Always.'

At last Sarah was alone in her room, and able to tear open her letter. The wind that creaked in the trees and rippled the water of the lake billowed the curtains, and made the candle flame dip and gutter. Ambrose's fine clerkly handwriting danced in a blur.

My dearest Sarah,

I am entrusting this letter to one James Brodie who is perfectly honest and reliable, but naturally knows nothing of the circumstances. I have impressed on him that he is to hand it to no one but yourself. He is sailing immediately for England, and

I am hopeful of following in a very short time.

Your letter regarding Thomas Whitehouse arrived safely and was valuable information, enabling me to finally unearth this gentleman. But unfortunately I could get nowhere with him. He has no doubt been well paid for he remained loyal to my so-called cousin, and merely repeated the story he had already told in court about the length of time he had known Blane. He is, as you will remember, an olive-skinned person, and I suspect his name has not always been Whitehouse. If I can prove that, it may well go a long way to discrediting his evidence, as it would point to a suspicious background.

Apart from T. Whitehouse, I have had some success following other clues, and have now derived some interesting information. It is not yet tangible enough proof to put on paper, but I hope it will be in a very short time, when several curious facts I have discovered here, including a new tombstone, an entry in a church register, and a woman called Samantha may tie up with discoveries of yours.

I am assured we will have a very strong case for the Court of Appeal, indeed more than that—final proof that this man and his wife are dastardly impostors. So don't lose heart, my love. If your task has been tedious and disagreeable you are about to be amply rewarded. I hope the odious child has not been too intolerable, and that, in spite of your humiliating position there at present, you have grown to love Mallow. For I promise you it will be our home.

This enervating climate does not agree with me, and I will be glad to be back to our more familiar grey skies. I do not need to add how I long to be with you again. Keep up your spirits, remain observant of every smallest detail, and be on your guard if the woman Samantha should materialise.

Your devoted Ambrose

Samantha! The name was screaming in her head. Sammie, Sammie, Sammie!

Sammie was a *woman*.

18

EARLY the next morning Mrs Stone's shabby canvas travelling bag was also fished up from the lake, and in it, as well as her few clothes, were the fur tippet and the jewels, a ruby brooch and ear-rings, and a garnet necklace that Amalie had missed.

'Remorse!' the sympathetic police sergeant said, echoing Lady Malvina. 'She must have took the things to spite you, Lady Mallow, even though she only meant to fling them in the lake. But you should have reported the theft.'

'I didn't want trouble,' Amalie whispered. 'My husband and I had already been through so much.' She raised her eyes appealingly. She looked pale and fragile. For the first time since Sarah had known her she was dressed very simply in a grey dress with a fichu of lace.

'And you employed her out of kindness, you say. Although she talked so desperate-like?'

'What could I do? What would you have done?'

'I'd have sent the baggage packing,' the sergeant said brusquely. But it was quite clear that Amalie had won his sympathy.

Everyone had to be questioned as to whether Mrs Stone had been observed at the lake that evening, but no one had seen her, and Lady Malvina's evidence as to her wild flight was for a previous evening. But significant, nevertheless.

'Out of her wits,' the sergeant commented succinctly.

It was obvious that he personally intended to waste little sympathy on the dead woman, poor insignificant wretch of no importance compared with these good people at the Hall. He was certainly not going to give any credence to the far-fetched idea that if someone had helped Mrs Stone to tumble into the lake they were likely to pack her bag with valuables and throw it in after her. There was the diamond ring on her finger, for instance. The wretched woman might have wanted to die with a small touch of grandeur, but it was more likely that she was filled with panic and remorse, being neither able to return the ring nor dispose of it without arousing suspicion.

But enquiries would have to be made as to her identity, and family, if any. The inquest would be postponed until this information was available.

The sergeant looked surprised when Sarah, at the end of her own short cross-examination, asked, 'What was Mrs Stone's first name?'

'I've never heard it, miss. But we'll find it out. Though what would you think that had to do with it?'

'Nothing, sir. It would just'—Sarah succeeded in looking confused—'make her seem more of a person.'

Betsey said that the light had burnt all night in the library, as if the master had not gone to bed. And neither had the mistress, for Polly, the kitchenmaid, going down at five o'clock, had seen her coming from the library, weeping, Polly said, her hands pressed to her face. It was terrible, as if that poor Mrs Stone might have been a loved relation. 'And she did put on all those airs,' Betsey commented significantly.

When the police had left the next morning Blane sent for Sarah to come to him in the library.

His face was bleak and forbidding. It wore the expression of a man who would brook no interference in his affairs. Sarah had glimpsed this look the night he had leant over her in London when she had fallen down the stairs. But after that he had been careful to keep it hidden. Now, apparently, he no longer thought it necessary to keep up a façade.

'Miss Mildmay, why were you meeting this man Brodie down by the lake?'

'Meeting him!'

'Come! None of that wide-eyed innocence. It doesn't suit you. You're a clever woman.'

'But I'd never seen James Brodie in my life. I haven't the slightest idea who he is. I thought he admitted he was looking for some poaching.'

'With a strange degree of honesty that I don't trust.' His hard searching eyes were on Sarah. 'So you swear you've neither seen him nor heard of him before?'

James Brodie was a stranger, wasn't he? Sarah was not lying

when she denied knowing him.

'Then what the devil *were* you doing down at the lake? My wife, it appears, has been haunting it morbidly, for fear this woman had carried out her threat. But that can't have been your reason, Miss Mildmay. You knew nothing of that. Or did you? I'm damned if I know what you're up to.'

Sarah's voice was cool with dislike.

'Then why don't you dismiss me, Lord Mallow, if you find me so unsatisfactory?'

'You know I can't do that.'

'Can't?'

'Then shall I say "won't"?'

She couldn't escape his intent disturbing gaze. She thought that if he took one step towards her she would have to run away. Or stay to be kissed again in that violent over-mastering way.

'Miss Mildmay, will you just assure me that you weren't meeting a lover?'

'A lover! Good heavens, no!'

Her spontaneous astonishment seemed to satisfy him. He relaxed and all at once looked desperately tired. And haunted. As if Mrs Stone's death were pressing on him.

He had gone to London to meet someone called Sammie in response to a badly-written letter saying, *Fancy, I thought you was dead*. But Sammie had meant to see him, not in London but here, and instead had encountered Amalie. And two days later Amalie was saying, 'That will be the end of it.'

Sarah only had to stay here preserving her secret knowledge until Ambrose returned.

Mrs Stone had died by drowning certainly enough, but not of her own accord. Amalie knew. Blane knew. Probably Soames knew, since Amalie had wanted him dismissed. Someone in this house had helped the woman to die.

Perhaps, without waiting for Ambrose, she should tell these things to the police. She should relate the burning of Mrs Stone's bonnet, and the way Blane's hair had shone with rain that night. And Amalie's morbid haunting of the lake.

But she knew she would do none of this. Not because it was

better for Ambrose to return with the strange jigsaw of suspicions pieced together and made coherent, but because just now Blane had demanded to know in his hard angry voice whether she had been waiting for a lover. And she had indignantly denied it as if she had no lover. Not even Ambrose.

The only comforting thing was that Titus was unaware of what had happened. It was carefully kept from him, although he sensed the subdued atmosphere in the house, and particularly Lady Malvina's unaccustomed quietness.

'Aren't you going to play with me, Grandmamma?'

'Not now, Titus. I'm a little tired, a little old today.'

'Did you dance too much last night?'

'Yes, my little love.' Lady Malvina pounced on the child and hugged him to her, hiding the tears that slid down her crumpled cheeks. 'We all danced too much.'

'Poor little grandmamma. Then may I sit on your lap and tell you a story?'

Lady Malvina's eyes sought Sarah's.

'How can he look so like my own son, and yet not be——'

'Not be what, Lady Malvina?'

'Blane was never gentle like this. Never thoughtful and loving. Miss Mildmay, I worship this child.'

Sarah didn't know how to answer the desperate unspoken plea in the old woman's eyes. Don't let everything end! it said. Don't let them say this isn't my grandson!

'Grandmamma! You're holding me so hard!'

Lady Malvina nuzzled her face fiercely into the boy's smooth dark head.

'I'm being an old bear again, an old grizzly. But grizzlies don't frighten you any more, do they, my pet?'

Titus leant trustfully against her.

'Not when it's you, Grandmamma. I love you.'

But that night Titus had his nightmare again. Someone was walking in his room and had blown out his light, he said. Sure enough, when Sarah reached him his light was out, but that may have been due to the candle wick guttering in the wax.

'It was Sammie,' Titus insisted, in his sleep-blurred voice.

Sarah's heart stood still.

'Who is Sammie?'

'I don't know. I heard someone say Sammie one night. Is it the mouse again, Miss Mildmay?'

'There's no mouse and no Sammie,' Sarah said firmly.

She held the trembling little boy in her arms, and thought she heard a door shut somewhere in the house. Again, that may have been the wind banging a shutter. The atmosphere was oppressive and uncanny. She almost fancied Mrs Stone, upstairs at her sewing, had left her work for a few minutes to prowl about the house.

For if she were the Samantha Ambrose had mentioned, she had come to this house for some explicit purpose.

Whatever had woken Titus had infected her with its intangible fear

She found she couldn't keep silent, waiting for Ambrose, after all. It might not be safe.

She waited until they were all at the lunch table the next day, and then said conversationally,

'I'm sorry to say that Titus had that strange nightmare again last night.'

'What nightmare?' Blane asked sharply.

'He thinks someone called Sammie comes into the room and blows out his light.'

There was no doubting that brief moment of suspended breathing. Then Lady Malvina said, 'Sammie? I've not heard this before, Miss Mildmay. Who is Sammie?'

'I haven't the least idea, Lady Malvina. But I did wonder if by any chance Mrs Stone's name was Sammie.'

'What an extraordinary idea!' Amalie said sharply. 'Whatever gives it to you, Miss Mildmay?'

'Only that the first time this happened was the night Mrs Stone was here.'

'But you've always complained about Titus's nightmares.'

If the police sergeant were to see Amalie now, Sarah thought irrelevantly, he wouldn't think of her as a fragile nervous little creature. Her face wore a look of extraordinary belligerence and animosity.

'Not this particular one, Lady Mallow. No one used to blow

out his light. And indeed it was blown out last night.'

'Surely the wind,' said Blane, speaking for the first time. 'The window was open, I imagine. Anyway, the child's much too big to require a night light. And as far as Mrs Stone goes, no one knows her first name, not even the police as yet. So how, pray, could Titus?'

'Unless she told him,' Sarah murmured.

Amalie gave an incredulous laugh. 'You mean she'd creep in there late at night and tell my son her first name! What far-fetched nonsense! Anyway, Sammie is a man's name.'

Sarah looked at her plate.

'It could be short for Samantha,' she said.

Again there was that tiny bubble of silence. Again it was broken by Lady Malvina saying practically,

'The thing to be disturbed about isn't the name of this mysterious prowler—if there is one—but that Titus is being alarmed. I don't like that at all.'

'Titus has always had nightmares!' Amalie exclaimed. 'Just as he's always been travel sick. He's a nervous delicate child. I can't think what the fuss is about. If you're nervous yourself, Miss Mildmay, you have only to say so and we'll find someone less susceptible to the wind in the night. And I quite agree with my husband that the boy is old enough not to require a night light.'

Lady Malvina looked perplexed. She had just contrived, in a slightly fuddled way, to analyse Sarah's implications.

'But Miss Mildmay, you aren't talking sense, you know. For if this Mrs Stone is by any chance called Sammie, or Samantha, it's certainly not her going into Titus's room at night. How can it be when she's dead?'

'I merely meant that it might have been her the first time, and now if Titus is disturbed he imagines it's the same person disturbing him.'

'I believe Miss Mildmay is suggesting that her ghost walks,' Amalie said drily.

Blane, who had again been silent, suddenly pushed back his chair.

'Tomorrow Titus shall return to London.'

His statement was an order. Sarah was startled, but not as startled as the other women.

'Oh dear, I shall miss the boy,' said Lady Malvina. 'Do you mean this, Blane?'

'Of course he doesn't mean it,' Amalie exclaimed. She was trying to look at her husband indulgently, and failing completely. Sarah had an odd feeling that under her calm there was both panic and hate. 'Titus can't go back to fogs and damp. He'll instantly be ill again. Besides, my love, it was you who said his fancies mustn't be pampered.' Her eyes widened. 'Surely you're not suggesting he must be sent away because of this unfortunate tragedy. Why, he knows nothing of it and isn't likely to. And, if you ask me, Miss Mildmay has made such curious suggestions that one wonders how much of the nightmare was Titus's.'

Blane looked directly at his mother. He behaved as if Amalie hadn't said a word.

'Perhaps you'd like to go with him, Mamma. He's grown fond of you, I believe.'

Lady Malvina's face softened.

'Why, of course. If you're insisting on his going. What about Miss Mildmay?'

'Miss Mildmay will stay here.'

'Blane, what are you talking about?' Amalie exclaimed. 'The woman is Titus's governess. Do we pay her to have a holiday in the country without her charge?'

Blane met his wife's anger with his hard level gaze.

'Miss Mildmay will be required at the inquest. That's why she stays.'

'Why will she be required more than Mamma?'

Blane sighed and began a patient explanation.

'Because, as I understand, you sent for Mrs Stone at five o'clock that afternoon and dismissed her, telling her she could stay until morning but that she must be out of the house by daylight. Isn't that so?'

Amalie nodded.

'Miss Mildmay says she took some sewing up to Mrs Stone at seven o'clock that evening when she was in her room. After that time no one else appears to have seen her. So if everyone is speaking the truth you can see that makes Miss Mildmay a very important witness. She was the last person to see Mrs Stone alive.'

Amalie sprang up.

'Then I shall take Titus to London myself.'

'I think not.'

'Am I a prisoner here?'

'If that's the way you want to look at it.'

Amalie was not acting any longer. Her face had gone very sallow and wore an expression of extraordinary malevolence.

'Oh, no,' she said. 'I don't need to be a prisoner anywhere. I'll show you that. What you seem to forget is that Titus is mine. And I shall do exactly as I please with him.'

Then she whirled round and left the room.

'Blane,' said Lady Malvina, after a long silence. Her voice had lost its resonance and was that of someone very old and frightened. 'Blane, what does she mean?'

'Mean?' Blane jerked himself to attentiveness. 'Oh, nothing, Mamma. That's just Amalie in a tantrum. She enjoys theatricals.'

'She wouldn't take Titus away?'

'You're taking him away, Mamma. That's what we arranged. Nothing has been altered.' Then Blane's expression changed from its harsh and moody reflectiveness to a curious tenderness. 'Do you love the boy, Mamma?'

'Oh, more than I can say.'

'And he cares for you a little?'

'A little, I think.' Lady Malvina's voice was humble.

'Then why, may I ask, are you looking so unhappy? You can have him to yourself for a few weeks in London.'

The old lady began to brighten.

'Can I really? But that would be tremendous fun. And the child needs a holiday. He's worked hard at his lessons, and he's been ill. But not for too long, Blane,' she added. 'I want him to love Mallow.'

'He's going to love Mallow. I don't know why you think he wouldn't.'

Sarah went upstairs and found Amalie in the nursery dressing Titus in his outdoor clothes, while Eliza stood nervously watching.

'Where are you taking him?' Sarah burst out.

Amalie looked up.

'I am his mother, Miss Mildmay. Had you forgotten?'

Titus's lip drooped. His acute sensitiveness had already told him that something was wrong. Sarah saw the appeal in his face. Long ago, for some reason, he must have lost trust in his mother. It had turned him into the timid little boy he had been. Sarah had hoped he had outgrown his timidity, but it was not far beneath the surface after all.

'He's been talking about a black swan on the lake,' Amalie decided to explain. 'We're merely going down to look for it.'

'No! You shan't take Titus near the lake.'

'Why, Miss Mildmay! I believe you think I pushed Mrs Stone in! Oh, dear, no! If she were pushed in—if she were—it would require someone with more than my frail strength.'

'You said it was a black swan,' whispered Titus. His eyes became dilated and his voice rose. 'You told me a lie!' He stood there, dwarfed by his tweed coat, a very small boy trying valiantly to cover his bewilderment with anger.

Amalie smiled soothingly.

'There, my lamb. Perhaps Miss Mildmay really did think she saw a black swan. Perhaps we'll see it, too. Now come.'

She took his hand, but Titus, suddenly reverting to being the child Sarah had first met, began to scream and tug away from her.

'No, I don't want to go! I won't go!'

'Darling! You're only coming for a walk with Mamma. Don't you love Mamma?'

'No, I'm not coming. I don't love you. I hate you!'

Red-faced and hysterical, Titus snatched his hand away and flew to Sarah. For the second time, at a crucial moment, he sought refuge in her arms. Bundled in his thick coat, she picked him up and faced Amalie.

'So you've succeeded in spoiling him,' Amalie said, with the quietness of extreme self-control. 'I always said you would. And you've done it deliberately. You're the most scheming woman I've ever met. You've stolen my husband and my son.'

Sarah's mouth dropped open in sheer surprise.

'Don't bother to deny it, Miss Mildmay. And don't think you've got away with it. I shall ruin you, I promise. And my husband as well. I can, you know. Much more easily than you think.' She paused, then added significantly. 'I only have to tell the police who Mrs Stone really was.'

'Then you did know her!'

Amalie laughed. 'I didn't. But Blane did. She was his wife.'

19

A LECHER and a drunkard. A bigamist also? And now a murderer? For Amalie's words had had a deadly implication. Blane could not afford to have a woman like that turning up to wreck all his plans. He would have to be as ruthless about her as he had been about everything else.

And Amalie, suspecting what he had done, haunted by fear, had walked every afternoon at the lake to see if the body appeared. . . .

Police sergeant Collins and the young constable were back that afternoon. They spent a long time down by the lake, walking up and down, testing the ground and the rickety piles of the jetty.

Sarah happened to pass the library door and saw Blane at the window staring out. He was watching the activities at the lakeside. There was the stillness of complete absorption in his figure. What did his face express? Anxiety? Fear?

But fear was one emotion she couldn't imagine in Blane Mallow's face. All the others had been there, anger, ridicule, pride and arrogance, merriment, even fleetingly tenderness. But not fear.

Sergeant Collins came in later and was shut in the library with Blane for a long time. Eliza reported this. The servants were all whispering and surmising. Sarah was trying to make up her mind whether, if the sergeant wanted to question her again, she would tell him of the brooch she had found. Not in the mud by the lakeside, where it might presumably have fallen off, but in the summer house. As if a struggle might have taken place there.

Under the pretence of an embrace . . . If Mrs Stone were really Blane's wife she might have welcomed his embrace, not suspecting its treachery. After all, he was given to kissing women in secluded places. His mother said he always had been. . . .

But the sergeant left without asking to see anyone else, and Sarah felt sick with relief. She knew she had not meant to say anything about the brooch. She also could not believe that Blane had ever kissed Mrs Stone's sour and secretive face.

And Amalie had certainly been bluffing when she had made those extraordinary statements, for she made no attempt to see the police.

She waited until they had gone, then came down to tea, wearing a simple dark merino dress and a woollen shawl. She had a strange extinguished look, as if her moment of madness in the nursery had burnt out all her anger.

'Well, that's more sensible, my dear,' said Lady Malvina. 'You look as if you've put on an extra petticoat.'

'I have. It's freezing cold. This house is like a tomb.'

She kept her eyes down as if she wanted to hide what was in them, but her voice was normal enough with its familiar peevish quality.

'Where's Titus, Miss Mildmay?'

'Eliza's giving him his tea, Lady Mallow.'

'Now it's so cold perhaps it's as well I didn't take him out.' That was as near to an apology as she would ever get. But at least she didn't sustain her anger, vindictive as it was at the time.

'We'll have to wrap up well for our journey tomorrow,' Lady Malvina said.

'Titus has a fur-lined coat somewhere,' said Amalie. 'I'll look it out presently. And Mamma, if you take him out walking in London do see he doesn't get wet feet. He catches cold so easily.'

'I'll look after him like a cherished jewel,' Lady Malvina said happily.

'Thank you, Mamma. I do trust you with him. I was over-wrought earlier today.'

Then Blane came in and without lifting her eyes Amalie said smoothly,

'Tea, my love? I hope the police didn't detain you too long. What did they want this time?'

'Merely to verify suspicions.'

'Suspicions?'

'Such as whether the woman's death was not suicide at all.'

Amalie's eyelids flew up momentarily. Then dropped again as she said calmly, 'They have to do their duty. Have they discovered anything more about the woman's identity?'

'Only that she arrived by train at Yarby. She asked the porter the way to Mallow. He remembered her very well. She told him she'd come a long way and wasn't sure whether she could manage the ten-mile walk, but would have to since she had no money.'

'And what did police sergeant Collins make of that?' Amalie asked.

'He would have been very mystified if it hadn't been for Mrs Stone's last remark.'

'Yes?'

'She said she'd had a lot of bad luck but hoped to catch some good from us.'

'Inferring that we were lucky?'

'I imagine so.'

Amalie gave a short laugh, then said with strange resignation,

'Doesn't she know you can't buy luck? Well, she does now, I imagine.'

Blane took his teacup and turned to the fire.

'The police have decided now that the woman probably fell in the lake accidentally. The path is very slippery and cut away in one place. If it was very dark and she was taking the short cut through the woods, she could easily have stumbled too near the water. That would account for her bag in the lake, too. And the ring on her finger. Apparently it's a strange fact that when a woman takes her life she usually preserves her valuables.'

Lady Malvina leaned back in her chair, sighing with relief.

'That's the first sensible thing I've heard since this dreadful business began. The whole thing was an accident, of course. That will be the coroner's verdict, Blane?'

'I should think so, Mamma. The woman seems to have been a vagrant and a sneak thief. I fear there'll be no sympathy wasted on her.'

Sarah could no longer keep silent.

'And no one will identify her?' she said in her clear voice.

Blane turned. He met her gaze levelly.

'Unless someone turns up from her past.'

'What about you, Lord Mallow?'

'Me! But I'd never set eyes on her before.'

His eyes met hers unwaveringly, and with astonishment. His answer had been quite spontaneous. But he was a devilishly clever actor. Ambrose had said so all the time.

For he must be lying. There was the letter from Sammie to prove it, the letter out of his past. *Fancy, I thought you was dead....*

But it was Sammie—Samantha—who optimistically hoped her luck would change who lay dead. Sammie, who had lost her cheap jet brooch in the summer house....

Amalie was standing up, smiling. Her expression was unreadable.

'Blane, let me congratulate you on finding Miss Mildmay. You recognised her talents when I was quite blind to them. She's so clever, isn't she? So observant. And so good for Titus. I think you ought to give her a present. What about the diamond ring Mrs Stone had. It's a very fine diamond.'

'Amalie!' Lady Malvina's voice was rough with shock. 'What a peculiarly grisly thing to suggest! Anyway you said the ring was yours.'

'Not mine. Blane's. I believe it would fit Miss Mildmay. She has slim fingers, too. Perhaps you've noticed the similarity, Blane? And governesses don't often have the opportunity to acquire valuable rings. Not if they're honest people.'

She lifted her head high. For a moment, her face defiant and shrewish, she faced her husband. Then she said lightly, 'I must look out Titus's fur coat for the morning. Will you excuse me?' and left the room.

'Blane! Blane!' Lady Malvina burst out pleadingly. 'That ring wasn't Mrs Stone's? Surely you didn't once give it to her!'

'I told you, Mamma. I'd never seen the woman in my life.'

'Then Amalie——' Lady Malvina began uncertainly.

'Go up to Titus, will you, Mamma. Stay with him until Miss

193

Mildmay comes.'

Sarah moved towards the door.

'I'll go now.'

'Stay here!' The harsh command stopped her. 'I want to talk to you.'

She turned reluctantly.

'Lord Mallow, couldn't I go to London tomorrow with Titus? If the police have decided Mrs Stone's death was an accident there's no need for me to stay.'

'What has my wife been saying to you?'

'Why, that—that——' She couldn't say the monstrous thing.

'Come, out with it!'

She should have flung the accusation in his face. He deserved it. But her heart failed.

'She told me Mrs Stone was your wife.' Now the words sounded only dreary and banal. 'She said she intended to tell the police.'

'And what did you think of this story?'

He didn't deny it, she noticed, neither did he seem surprised. She began to shiver, and checked herself, pressing her hands together hard.

'I thought perhaps for some reason she wanted to hurt you.'

'So she does,' he muttered. 'I believe she would swear that wretched woman turned up inconveniently out of my past and that I pushed her in the lake. Clumsily, like that, leaving her body to float. My God!'

The unguarded horror in his face communicated itself to Sarah.

'But, Lord Mallow, surely you don't think——' This new suspicion was also unspeakable.

'Where did you pick up that brooch?'

'In the summer house. It hadn't a very good fastening. It would—have fallen off . . .' Sarah's voice died away.

'The diamond was on her finger. It was a bribe, of course. She hadn't stolen it. I give her credit for that. But when and where was she bribed?'

'And why?' Sarah asked.

The ghost of a smile touched his lips.

194

'Amalie's right. You are observant, Miss Mildmay. Too observant. I think you're going to find out more than you will enjoy. That's what you're going to do, isn't it? Outdo the judge and jury and all by yourself prove I don't belong here.'

Somehow Sarah contrived to speak steadily. 'If you think that, why have you insisted on my staying? Why didn't you dismiss me long ago?'

'Because your little plot amused me. That was the first thing. The second was that you proved enormously good for Titus, as I knew you would. The third is simply that I've fallen in love with you.'

She couldn't move. He didn't need to take her wrist in this hard grip to hold her there.

'Why?' she whispered.

'Heavens knows. And a pretty mess you've made of all my plans.'

'You're being—preposterous, Lord Mallow.'

'Am I?'

'It's true you fall in love with every new face, as your mother says.'

'But that was Blane Mallow. You don't believe I'm that person, do you?'

Sarah's brain spun.

'I don't know what to think!'

'You've been trying to trick me into some admission ever since you've been here. You've taken pleasure in discovering any evidence you could, such as that verse on the window pane, and testing me with it. Or making Titus do so. You've spied and schemed. Not nice activities for a well-brought-up young lady.'

'Then why——'

'Why do I love you? Because we're two of a kind. And we'll see this through together. Won't we?'

He had let her go and she could have escaped had she wished. She stood rubbing her wrist and trying to think of Ambrose.

'Who *are* you?' she burst out in baffled anger.

He laughed and touched her cheek lightly with his fingers.

'My dear Miss Mildmay, I fear you're going to find out very soon. So don't run away. I've too much trouble on my hands already. And anyway, I should find you.'

Somewhere in the house a door banged. Sarah thought she heard Titus crying. With an enormous effort she pulled herself together.

'I must go to Titus.'

'Yes, go to him now. But he has to begin learning to do without you. That's why I'm sending him to London with Mamma.'

'So I've served my purpose!' Sarah flashed indignantly.

'Only that purpose—my dearest one!'

There were no complexities in his face now. Only longing. Tears sprang to Sarah's eyes. She must go before he saw them, and read something into them that was not there.

For this was all crazy, crazy! He was married to Amalie, and she was waiting for Ambrose.

And anyway, she hated and despised him.

But he should not have shown her even momentarily his vulnerable side. It was a low trick....

'Blane! Blane!'

Lady Malvina's hoarse voice reached them long before that lady had come bundling down the stairs, her face purple with breathlessness, her eyes full of alarm.

'What is it Mamma?'

'We can't find Titus. Eliza left him with his mother. She said she would stay with him while he had his tea. When Eliza came back to the nursery they were both gone.'

Blane was at the door. 'Where's Amalie?'

'I don't know. I thought she meant to look out Titus's fur-lined coat for the morning.'

'For now,' said Blane, his face like stone.

'But why would she be taking him out now in the dark? She said herself it was too cold.'

'The lake!' Sarah whispered.

Blane was ringing the bell for Tomkins.

'She must have been so quick,' Lady Malvina said. 'I went up at once. But I'm slow on the stairs. And I never saw her coming down. She must have gone the back way.'

Tomkins had come across the hall. Blane spoke curtly,

'Has Lady Mallow given any orders? Have you seen her go out?'

'No, my lord.'

'See if she's in the house, will you? Look in every room. Don't stop to knock at doors. Get Betsey and Eliza to help. And send someone for Soames.'

'Very well, my lord.' The man hesitated, puzzled.

'Titus seems to be missing. He's probably with his mother. Don't waste time, you fool.'

Blane himself, a moment later, had flung the front door open and was running down towards the lake. Sarah followed him, forgetful of the freezing wind and the flakes of snow in the air. It was such a cold night. The water would be icy. . . .

But the lake was deserted. A curved moon hung upside down in the branches of the elm on the opposite side. The water shimmered faintly. The little summer house was dark and deserted, the wind whistling through the broken window.

They were not too late, were they? The surface of the lake looked undisturbed, with no sinister bubbles or settling ripples. An owl called on an infinitely melancholy note. Blane stood a moment, a dark brooding silhouette. Then he swung round and saw Sarah.

'No, she wouldn't do it twice,' he said. 'She's not as stupid as that.'

There was no time to ponder his deadly words. He was hurrying back to the house, and Sarah had to run to keep up with him.

Tomkins was waiting to report that Soames could not be found.

'Where is he?' Blane's voice was a lash.

'No one seems to know, sir. Mrs Soames says he went out of the house just before six and a bit later she heard horses.'

'Well, isn't there a groom around?'

'Only young Jim, and we can't get any sense out of him. He's blubbering, and saying he had orders to do it.'

'To do *what*?'

'Saddle the horses, my lord.'

'He'll saddle some more before he's finished,' said Blane, and was off at a run to the stables.

Shortly he came back, riding his big chestnut hunter. He leaned down to say to Sarah and Lady Malvina, huddled shivering in the doorway, 'All I can get out of that fool of a boy is that he saddled a horse for Amalie and she rode off, with a bundle.'

'A bundle,' Lady Malvina echoed faintly.

'Soames followed,' Blane said grimly. 'God knows where they're heading for. Soames knows this country like the back of his hand.'

'Why should he be going?' Sarah asked.

'I thought I could trust him. I'd have sworn I could.'

'Lord Mallow, I'm coming with you!'

Blane looked down at her.

'Can you ride?'

'Of course I can.'

'Then hurry. We'll get another horse. What about your petticoats?'

'Never mind my petticoats.'

It was dark, and she didn't mind if they flew over her head. She rode astride like a boy. She had always done so, except when her mother or governess had been there, and forbade it, in horror. She didn't know what the dark night held, but this was action at last, and she revelled in it.

Amalie and Soames could not have got far, and there was not a lot of cover in the marshes. As soon as they were out of the wood they would show up against the skyline. Unless Soames had some secret hiding place where they could stay until morning.

'Is she trying to kidnap Titus?' Sarah shouted, galloping up to Blane.

'More likely to kill him.'

'*Kill* him! Is she mad?'

'When it comes to jealousy, yes. Hadn't you noticed? But why should you? For I hadn't myself until recently.'

The night was dark and the conventions far away.

'You shouldn't have locked your door against her,' Sarah said.

He turned to look at her. The wind streamed through his hair.

'So you knew that, too,' he said, and that was all.

20

ELIZA could not be made to stop crying. Finally Lady Malvina slapped her sharply across the face and exclaimed, 'For goodness' sake, girl, stop that noise! Nobody's blaming you. After all, you couldn't have been expected to defy your mistress.'

'Miss Mildmay did, this afternoon,' Eliza hiccupped. 'She didn't let the mistress take Master Titus out walking.'

'Miss Mildmay is another matter. She isn't a servant.'

Lady Malvina heard herself speak the words with some surprise. She wondered why she had not realised earlier that Sarah Mildmay had never behaved with the slightest servility. She might have tried to, but her serene confidence had always showed through. Then who was she? If it came to that, who was anyone? The poor drowned woman, Amalie, with her shrewishness, and her tendency to vulgar ostentation, the tall dark stranger who had just ridden off, and whom she had always known in her heart was not her son.

There was only Titus of whom she was sure, and Titus had been carried off, no one knew where. In the space of a few minutes her world had disintegrated. She was a forsaken old woman surrounded by stupidly weeping servants, and with only her pearls to show that this had not all been a dream.

Her pearls. In a daze, Lady Malvina went off to her room to make sure of them, at least. If Amalie had run off, one could be certain she had taken the Mallow diamonds, so if this was the pattern of future events, she might as well lay a firm claim to the pearls.

But sitting with the necklace in her hands, Lady Malvina realised that all that mattered was getting Titus back. She wanted the boy desperately. She thought that he was the only person she had really loved in her whole life. At first it had been fine to return to Mallow and to acquire her old importance. But jewels, clothes, the certainty of sleeping beneath her own roof for the rest of her days, didn't finally matter at all. Her grandson was all that mattered. And whatever else she admitted she had been wrong about, she would never admit that Titus was not her own flesh and blood. She knew that he was.

'Why, my lady, you're sitting in the dark,' Bessie exclaimed, coming in.

'Yes, it's dark,' said Lady Malvina, shivering. 'Dark.'

'I'll have the lamps lit in a moment, my lady.'

'What are the servants saying, Bessie?'

Bessie, stout and phlegmatic, made a scornful sound.

'They're a foolish gossiping lot, my lady.'

'I asked you what they're saying.'

'Oh, that the mistress has run off because she's afraid,' Bessie answered reluctantly.

Lady Malvina stared into the yellow lamplight that had driven the dark into the corners of the room.

'Afraid of my son? Do they think——'

'They haven't the brains to think. Shall I pour you a glass of port, my lady?'

'Just a little drop, Bessie. I feel faint.'

'And who wouldn't, my lady? But don't you worry. Master Titus will sleep in his own bed tonight, where he belongs.'

'Where he belongs ... What a comforting creature you are, Bessie. You've enjoyed being at the Hall again, haven't you?'

'Yes, indeed, my lady.'

'Then this is where we shall stay,' Lady Malvina declared firmly. 'Right or wrong. Well, fill the glass, woman, fill the glass!'

An hour had gone by, and it was quite dark when there was the sound of horses' hooves coming up the curving drive. Lady Malvina started up eagerly and unsteadily. Blane was back with Titus. The wine had given her optimism. She knew that all would now be well.

The door bell rang with a long clangour. At the head of the stairs Lady Malvina waited tensely, listening for Tomkins's relieved welcome. All the servants had been hanging about, waiting and whispering.

Lady Malvina felt the wind sweep up the stairs from the opened door. She couldn't hear the voices. They were too low. Tomkins seemed to be hesitating. Then the door shut with a heavy thud, and there were footsteps across the tiled floor. Lady Malvina went down several more steps to peer into the hall. She couldn't recognise the man who stood there in a riding cloak, and with the lamplight glinting in his fair hair.

Who was it? Someone with news? Tomkins was coming towards the stairs. Lady Malvina began to run down in a flurry.

'Who is it, Tomkins?'

Tomkins's face was impassive, as always.

'Mr Ambrose, my lady.'

'Mr Ambrose!'

What did he want here at this hour? What was he poking his nose into now? Blane had said he was in the West Indies. Alarm shot through Lady Malvina's fuddled head. What had he discovered there?

She contrived to complete the descent of the stairs with dignity. Her face was highly flushed and her elaborate curls coming slightly adrift beneath her lace cap. But her greeting was cool and haughty. She liked Ambrose's pale elegant face no more now than she had ever done.

'Well, Ambrose, this is a surprise. You haven't visited me at Mallow for a very long time.'

'No, Aunt Malvina. And I apologise for arriving so unceremoniously. But I've just returned from Trinidad. My ship docked this morning. I came down immediately.'

Lady Malvina's brows rose. 'There was a reason for such urgency?'

'There are various questions I want to ask. Is Blane in?'

'No. He's out riding.'

'Out riding!'

Lady Malvina nodded with deliberation.

'Don't look so astonished. I'm not lying.'

'But it's late. It's dark.'

'My son was always unpredictable. Don't you remember?' Lady Malvina gave her hoarse chuckle. She enjoyed baiting Ambrose, cold dry stick of a boy that he had been. His careful avoidance of trouble since the day of his birth had always contrasted unfavourably with her own son's endless predicaments. The consequence was that she had grown to detest Ambrose. She thought him sly and ambitious, and too self-contained ever to be at the mercy of his emotions.

'If you insist on waiting until Blane returns, and I warn you it might be any hour of the night, you'd better come into the library. We'll have some sustenance. It's a cold night.'

'Very cold,' said Ambrose, rubbing his hands. 'Especially after the tropics.'

'Ah, yes. And how did you find the tropics?'

'Of great interest, Lady Malvina.'

'H'mm. You'd better tell me. But first let us have some brandy. Will you pour it? We don't want the servants in. We have things to talk about.'

'We certainly have things to talk about, Aunt. What's this I hear about a woman being drowned in the lake?'

'You didn't take long to hear that!'

'Everyone at Yarby is talking of it. There seemed to be a good deal of unpleasant speculation.'

'Are they saying she was pushed in?' Lady Malvina asked bluntly. 'And serve her right if she was. She was a lying thieving creature.'

'Was her name Samantha?'

Lady Malvina stared. 'I haven't the least idea what her name was. Neither, for that matter, has the police.'

'Was she Blane's wife?'

'Good heavens, what nonsense are you talking?' Lady Malvina took a deep swallow of her drink. The brandy curled comfortingly inside her, renewing her optimism. So Ambrose had come here to bluff, had he? Since he was asking questions, he obviously hadn't yet discovered the answers.

But that sneaking pasty-faced woman Blane's wife! She had to conceal the deep shock such a suggestion gave her.

'I thought you had met Blane's wife. You surely did so at the time of the court proceedings.'

'Amalie?' said Ambrose. 'But I don't believe Amalie is his wife at all.'

Lady Malvina stared. How priggish this young man looked. Priggish and superior and detestable. She threw back her head and gave her shouts of laughter.

'Ambrose, my dear boy, the hot sun in the tropics has affected your brain. My daughter-in-law Amalie is a most devoted wife and mother.'

'I know she's the daughter of Thomas Whitehouse,' Ambrose muttered. 'I found that out. The wily old man changed his name from the Spanish some time ago. He has his ambitions. It was fine for him to have his daughter become the wife of an English lord. Naturally he wasn't going to tell more than was necessary. If the court hears that Blane's chief witness is also his father-in-law they might take a different view of the evidence.'

'But you've just said Amalie isn't Blane's wife,' Lady Malvina retorted.

A look of uncertainty crossed Ambrose's face. Lady Malvina pounced on it.

'Don't you think the court might be a little aware of your ambitions too, Ambrose? And if you can't prove these extraordinary statements it isn't going to look very well for you.'

'I've got to prove them!' Ambrose said with intensity. 'That's why I've come here. I intend to face this man you call you son and Amalie with some very suspicious facts. There's a newly-erected gravestone in the British cemetery at Port of Spain. It has on it only: *Evan St John. Aged 35 years. Died at sea.*'

'What of it?'

'You heard in court the story of one of Blane's miraculous escapes, how once he was the sole survivor when his ship sank in a hurricane. But a thing that didn't come out was that he came ashore, after floating on a spar for ten days, with a dead man.'

'And you're telling me the dead man's name was Evan St John.'

'That's what one assumes.'

'What a tragic story!' cried Lady Malvina. 'Poor Blane, in those desperate straits, and to see his last companion die.'

'You don't understand what I'm getting at,' Ambrose exclaimed impatiently.

'Oh, yes, I do, you crafty devil!' Lady Malvina was beyond politeness now. Her voice rose richly with anger and contempt.

'You're suggesting it was Blane who died, and this man came ashore to step into his shoes. He had seen the advertisements for the heir to Mallow, and concocted a plot, with the aid of his wife and son, to come and take possession.'

'Having, in those ten days at sea, in desperate straits, got all Blane's history from him,' said Ambrose, with some smugness. 'You must admit, Aunt, that it's a neat plot.'

'And this woman Samantha?'

'Or Sammie, as she was known. Blane's wife, of course. Whom I gather turned up most inconveniently to denounce this impostor. Or to share in the spoils, of course.'

Lady Malvina sat very quietly for a moment. She wanted another drink, but she was afraid her hand would tremble too much to pour it. And she wouldn't ask Ambrose to do it for her. She would be ashamed ever to ask him to do the smallest thing.

'Admit, Aunt Malvina, that you always knew this man wasn't your son. Oh, I know you hadn't seen him since he was a boy of sixteen. And I agree that this fellow has a certain similarity, he's tall and dark and has a look of wildness. But a mother must know her own son instinctively. And you didn't know this man. I swear it.'

'Ambrose, you're impertinent!'

'I see you have your pearls,' Ambrose said softly. 'That must have pleased you, when you thought they were gone forever. And you like being back at Mallow. You enjoy your return to importance. You could have been just an impoverished old lady living unnoticed in some insignificant place. But with your son home all this has changed. It was very lucky for you, wasn't it, Aunt Malvina? Even if you had to perjure yourself in court, and risk what would happen to you at the hands of these strangers.'

'You have no real evidence of all this,' Lady Malvina said hoarsely.

'No, but I shall have when I've put my story together with Sarah's.'

'Sarah's?'

'Sarah Mildmay, of course. She's clever, isn't she? And attractive, too.'

'That girl! What has she to do with this?' Lady Malvina's face crumpled into bewilderment and despair. 'When Blane hears this he'll be furious. He liked her, as I did.'

'But it isn't Blane, is it? Is it, Aunt Malvina?'

Lady Malvina saw the long handsome face before her in a haze. Was it true that her son was dead, and that this cold clever young man was the new Lord Mallow? Was she to lose everything, even Titus?

Titus!

Lady Malvina raised her sagging body. She got slowly to her feet. Her cap was askew, her hair tumbling down, her skirts crumpled and bunched, but she drew herself very erect. Her head was high, her eyes blazing with triumph.

'Come with me, Ambrose. Come and take another look at this.'

She led him into the hall, to the foot of the stairs. All the lamps were alight, and the portrait glowed in the radiant light.

'Look!' she said commandingly. 'You've seen Titus. Can you deny the likeness? Can any inscription on a tombstone or any marriage register explain that away? Can you say that boy can be anything but Blane's son?'

She pointed with her thick ringed finger. Her voice rang out magnificently. 'There's the heir to Mallow!'

Below stairs, Jim the stable boy came bursting unceremoniously into the kitchen.

'I heered the church bell tolling!' he gasped.

Everyone looked at him askance. The wind blew in the open doorway. There was no other sound but its creaking gustiness.

'You're hearing things, boy,' old Betsey said at last. 'There's no church bell.'

Jim looked round uncertainly. He was still breathless, his eyes dark lakes of fear.

Then faintly from a long way over the marshes came the dull boom. They all heard it. Just that single sound, and then silence.

'I telt you!' Jim whispered. 'Someone's dead!'

21

THEY came out of the woods into the empty marshland. Blane drew reign to listen. Apart from the wind in the rustling winter grass there was no sound.

'We can't be far behind them,' he said. 'Soames would take the short cut, but after that he'd keep to the road. Amalie can't jump ditches with a child. She doesn't even ride well.'

'Couldn't Soames be carrying Titus?'

'Perhaps. But I still can't believe it. Why, Amalie wanted me to dismiss him two weeks ago. That was meant to be a blind, no doubt. She must be bribing him pretty heavily.'

'What with?' Sarah asked drily.

'Heaven knows. The Mallow diamonds, perhaps. If Soames is fool enough.'

The horses fidgeted. The moon, coming from behind a dark streamer of cloud, showed an horizon empty of everything but wind-bent trees, a far-off farmhouse, its tawny roof blackened by night, and at the end of the curving rutted road the church tower. Not so many years ago smugglers had struggled over the marshes to lonely churches such as this one, to deposit their booty, presumably under the protection of heaven. Now the churches looked lonely and forsaken, standing a little apart from small villages or alone in the fields, with a muddy track to be negotiated by the congregation on Sundays.

'There's not a sound,' said Sarah hopelessly.

'I think they must be on the way to Yarby. Soames will have friends there. And to think the wretch lied for me at the trial.'

'Lied?' said Sarah sharply.

She caught his sideways glance, reckless and fatalistic.

'You knew it all the time. But I'm done with lying now. Come, we're wasting time.'

But just as they set forth again a deep reverberant sound boomed over the countryside.

'What's that?' Sarah exclaimed.

'The church bell!'

'Is it tolling? Is someone dead?'

Blane spurred his horse.

'Come on,' he shouted. 'The church, of course. Why didn't I think?'

The bell didn't ring again. There had been just that deep solitary boom to sound the alarm.

Was Amalie frantically calling for help? Or Soames? Or was it some trick concocted by both of them?

The horses galloped down the muddy track. The gate that led into the field dotted with sleeping sheep was standing open. Someone had come in a very short time ago, and in a hurry.

Then Sarah saw the horses wandering saddled but un-tethered, and Blane leapt off his and ran up the slope to the church door. Sarah followed, holding up her petticoats, her breath coming in gasps.

The door was open into the midnight darkness of the church.

Blane stood in the doorway. He put out an arm to bar Sarah, and whispered to her to be quiet.

For someone was talking. It was Soames. His uncultured country voice was strangely soft and persuasive.

'It's no use hiding up there, my lady. Bring the lad down. I'll take him safe home. I'll say I found him wandering in the woods.'

There was a little silence. Then Amalie's voice, taut and full of furious anger, came from somewhere above them.

'You're like all the rest, Soames. You only care about Titus. No one cares about me. It's Titus, Titus, Titus! What if I tell you he isn't Titus, that he's George? And that I'd never heard that other horrible name in my life?'

'He's Titus now, my lady. That can't be altered.'

Soames's voice was still quiet and persuasive, with its familiar touch of servility. He sounded as if he had all the patience in the world.

'You only want to think so, you and your precious Mallow. What did you want to follow me for? I was only taking the boy away. Why should you think I want to harm him? Anyway he's my son, and I can do what I like with him. I can even jump

208

off the tower if I pleasse. And if you try to come up here'—there was rising hysteria in her voice—'I will.'

'Don't talk daft, my lady. Come down now. I promise I'll never tell a word of what I know.'

'You're only bluffing, Soames! You don't know anything!'

Soames's voice went on patiently and calmly, as if he were relating a story.

'I'll say I never saw you in the summer house, my lady. With the woman, Mrs Stone. No, nor I never heard a word of what you said to her, telling her she could have the ring—worth five hundred pounds, you said it was—if she went away and said nothing about being the master's wife. And I'll say I never heard Mrs Stone laughing, crafty-like, and saying now she had the ring on her finger what was to stop her from having the master as well. And Titus, too. At least, she said she'd get Titus and ruin your plot. So then you said you'd arrange for the master to meet her in the summer house the next night when he got back from London. And that she might be sorry she hadn't met him there as she'd written saying she would, because here there was the lake, and sometimes people got drowned accidentally. Oh, yes, I'll forget I saw her running back like a wild thing through the garden.'

'What else—have you concocted, Soames?'

'Not concocted, my lady. I'm only saying the things I won't tell if you send Master Titus down safe now. Such as the master being with me in the stables the next night at the time when you'd promised he'd be in the summer house to meet the woman. So it must have been someone else met her there. Someone else who went back to the house alone, slipping in by the garden door. But I won't say none of that if you bring Master Titus down now, my lady. My lips is shut forever.'

'She slipped!' Amalie screamed. 'She slipped in the mud. I'm telling you the truth! I couldn't go for help. It would have been too late.'

Again there was the brief silence, as if the voices were lost, as if none of these terrible words had been said. Then, as footsteps began to grope on the stairs, Amalie's voice, high and furious, echoed through the dark church.

'Don't come another step, Soames! I warn you! I'm deadly serious. I'll jump with Titus. I'm right at the window.'

She must have moved sharply in the darkness for suddenly the bell gave a muted boom.

There was a gasping scream, and Amalie's voice came involuntarily.

'It's dark! I can't see where I am!'

Sarah gripped Blane's arm in an agony.

'Why doesn't Titus make a sound?'

'He's probably asleep. I suspect Amalie put some of her own sleeping draught in his milk. Eliza said she left him with his mother to finish his tea. Amalie couldn't risk him screaming. Listen!'

But again it was silent, and they might have been alone in the dark building.

Blane pressed her arm and whispered, 'Stay there. I'm going to Soames.'

Quiet as his approach down the aisle was, Amalie heard it, for she suddenly gasped,

'Who's that? You've been lying, Soames. You've got someone there who's heard all you said.'

Blane abandoned his caution, and shouted in the deep ringing voice with which, not long ago, he had read the lesson from the pulpit. The voice, thought Sarah painfully, of a hypocrite, a liar, a thief and an adulterer.

'Amalie, don't move, or the bell will strike you. Wait until I bring a light.'

'You! I've had enough of you! Don't you dare come near me!'

'Don't move!'

'For you! You'd better think again this time. I'm no longer your chattel who's not expected to have feelings. I have feelings, all right, and now they're all hate. I'll kill Titus rather than let him go back to you. I'll ruin your plans. You did all this for Titus, indeed! You never cared a fig for Titus.'

Sarah could hear Blane's swift footsteps. It was as if he could see in the dark, not tripping on the flagstones that covered older tragedies, older bones.

'Soames and I are coming for Titus now, Amalie. Just keep quite still and you'll be safe.'

'You won't get him!' Amalie's voice was a harsh whisper. 'He belongs to me.'

'He belongs to his grandmother and to Mallow Hall. And to Soames, who loves him.'

'I'll expose you! I'll tell everyone in England who you are. You'll be jailed. For years. I hope for ever.'

'Do what you like about me, Amalie! But let us get Titus safely down.'

'Sammie would have killed him. She was going to kidnap him one night. I stopped her. But I'm his mother, and I have a right to take him away if I like. And to do exactly what I like with him. If hurting him is what hurts you most, my *dearest* love, I'll do it with pleasure. He's here on the floor asleep. He won't know a thing.'

'Don't you *dare*!' Sarah couldn't help herself. She was stumbling down the aisle, bruising herself against the high pews that she couldn't see in the darkness. 'You monstrous woman, don't you dare!'

'Ah! The clever Miss Mildmay, too! I might have known. Then this is the end. I've finished with you all. I'm going to jump with Titus.'

'Amalie!'

She gave a high hysterical laugh. 'You might have started pleading sooner, Blane. As I had to do with you. But I won't listen any more than you did. I'm going to——'

The sentence was never finished. For suddenly the great bell boomed deafeningly, and the fragments of a scream—or was that imagined, just a drift of sound out of the church's past centuries?—were lost in the echoing sound. It seemed as if there would never be complete silence again. The decreasing circles of sound went humming on and on.

'Blane!' whispered Sarah, groping for the rickety wooden stairs.

Someone struck a match. The frail light shone for the merest moment on Soames, hanging exhaustedly to the bell rope. Then it flickered out, and that deadly little picture, too, might have been imagined.

Blane sprang up the stairs, stumbling and blundering.

After a long time, his footsteps began to descend slowly and heavily.

'I've got Titus,' he said tiredly. 'He's quite unhurt. Are you there, Sarah? Can you take him? He's still asleep.'

It was Soames then who struck matches and for a moment his long narrow face hung over the sleeping child.

'He's all right, I tell you, Soames. He was lying on the floor—as you assumed.'

That was all. In that moment Sarah knew the glimpse of Soames still holding the bell rope, and the last terrible echoes dying away, was something that would be pushed into the back of all their memories. It would never be spoken of.

As Sarah took the sleeping child there was a bustle at the front door, and alarmed voices.

'What's going on here? We heard the bell? Is there trouble?'

It was the vicar and his wife who had hurried across the field in some perturbation. The vicar carried a carriage lamp, and the scene was at last lit up, Soames with his face shining pallidly, Sarah dishevelled and shocked, and Titus wrapped in his warm coat asleep with his head on her shoulder. Blane's face had its carven look, his eyes hollowed, his nose too long and large.

He spoke in a remote voice, 'I'm afraid there's been an accident. My wife was in the belfry. In the dark she must have stumbled against the bell. It swung back—as you heard.'

'Good God! We must get help. The poor lady! Is she badly hurt?'

'I'm afraid it's too late.'

'Oh, my dear boy!'

'I'm sorry, vicar. She was always highly emotional and unpredictable. That poor woman accidentally drowned preyed on her mind. She seems to have had a brainstorm. We followed her—but too late.'

The vicar bowed his head.

'She came to my church for comfort.'

'It was a beautiful church, vicar.'

'It *is* a beautiful church. It understands death as well as life.'

Blane lifted his haggard eyes.

'And the little lad is safe,' said the vicar's wife comfortingly. She took Sarah's arm. 'My husband will know what to do here. We'll take the boy across to the house. What a good thing he's sleeping. He'll never know anything of this.'

Those comforting words were still in Sarah's head as later they rode wearily home. They had resisted efforts to have them stay at the vicarage all night. His mother would be desperately anxious, Blane said. She was dearly devoted to her grandson.

Soames carried Titus on the saddle in front of him, tenderly and possessively. Nobody spoke much, until Soames turned to say,

'This will blow over, sir.' It was significant that he no longer called Blane 'my lord'. 'It'll cause talk, but there's always been talk about Mallow when the master's home.'

'You have the master in your arms,' Blane said briefly.

For a moment, in the moonlight, the two men's eyes met. Then Soames nodded.

'You can trust me, sir.'

'I know it, Soames. I apologise for ever thinking otherwise. You'd have died for that boy, wouldn't you?'

'As I would have for his father and his grandfather.'

'Then make a man of him. Lady Malvina will help you. Now ride on. I want to talk to Miss Mildmay.'

Yet he didn't speak at once, and when he did it was to say,

'I'm going away as soon as Amalie's funeral is over. I'll never come back again.'

'You're—giving up?'

'No, I've merely done what I set out to do.'

'You mean to get Mallow for your son?'

'Not my son. Blane Mallow's son.'

'So you never were Blane!'

'No. I'm merely the younger son of another English family who also set out to make his life at sea. I'm also a wanderer. But

213

I'm not Blane Mallow. Any more than you were Lady Mallow with the diamonds round your neck.'

Had he read her thoughts then? Of course he had. He was far more subtle and clever even than she had guessed.

'Blane was my friend,' he went on. 'We'd sailed together many times. He once saved my life. When I couldn't save his, after our ship went down in a cyclone, I promised him to do all I could for his son. "Get Mallow for him," he said. And I promised. It was his last moment of consciousness, and I didn't know myself that I would ever reach land alive. But I promised.'

'And did that mean you had to impersonate him?' Sarah flashed.

'It did, because I discovered that what should have been perfectly simple wasn't simple at all. You see Titus—and I can trust you, Sarah—is certainly Blane's son, but he's not legitimate.'

Sarah stared. 'Then Blane really was married to that awful woman, Mrs Stone!'

'To Sammie. Samantha. Whatever her last name was. Yes, Blane was married to her. But she'd left him years ago, deserted him, or he her, I'm not sure which, and he genuinely thought her dead when he married Amalie. However, she wasn't. They heard of her some time later, but hoped there'd be no trouble. Amalie had her marriage certificate and her baby. She didn't expect trouble because Blane was still the ne'er-do-well sailor Sammie had left. And Sammie knew nothing of the Mallow inheritance. The newspaper advertisements hadn't reached her at that time—at least, that's what we know now. Then she'd disappeared again, and perhaps really was dead.'

'Why couldn't Amalie have brought Titus home and made the claim by herself?' Sarah demanded.

'She hadn't the courage. She knew her marriage was bigamous. She needed support. It was she who noticed how much I resembled Blane, and since we'd lately spent ten days floating on a spar in the Caribbean I'd heard every detail Blane could remember of his childhood, some related in delirium. You might have called it lucky for me. One way and another, I was pretty well equipped to make the attempt. It was easy enough to acquire a scar beneath my ear. In fact, I had one already that only needed a little improving on. It fooled the doctors.'

'And you enjoyed doing all this!'

At her accusing tone he gave his amused smile.

'I enjoy a challenge as much as you do, Sarah.'

'You didn't happen to think that you were depriving Blane's cousin Ambrose of his inheritance?'

'Ambrose could look after himself. Titus was only a child.'

'So you had it all your own way. Lady Malvina was so delighted to have her son home that she shut her eyes to trouble, and Soames had this obsession about Titus, the true heir, and willingly committed perjury. They simply carried you through. What about the other man, Thomas Whitehouse?'

Blane grinned. 'Amalie's father, with his English name. Faithful Thomas. He liked his daughter being a lady. He was quite prepared to swear he had always known me as Blane Mallow.'

'You're incorrigible!' Sarah exclaimed. 'You did have it all your own way.'

'No. You're wrong. It was far from that. You forget Amalie. And I completely underestimated her.'

Sarah looked at the bleak outline of his face.

'She fell in love with you.'

'Passionately. Embarrassingly. She drove me into every corner. She was shameless. She hadn't had an English upbringing, of course. She hadn't your courtesy or self-discipline, or the modesty of an English woman. I confess I'd never expected to have to rely on locked doors. The plan had been that I was to stay here long enough to establish Titus and her, and then go back to sea, and this time get completely lost. But Amalie began to make scenes. She refused to entertain the thought of my leaving.'

Blane shrugged wearily.

'Then you came, and I, I confess, lost my head. I saw you standing in the hall looking furious with everybody because

215

Titus was unhappy. You'd had the intelligence to see that at once. I liked the way you so firmly took his side. I liked the way you looked. You were so full of spirit and indignation and tenderness. I recognised you at once. You were the kind of woman I had always looked for. So there it was. Your arrival was unconventional, everything about your behaviour was suspicious, but so was my situation, Amalie's, everyone's in that house. I overlooked what your coming would do to Amalie, who was already jealous and difficult. I simply recognised that here in this queer business was something for me. So I determined you were to stay.'

Sarah's voice was unsteady.

'And it was worse than you had expected?'

'Oh, much worse. You know that yourself. But it's all over now.' He took a backward glance at the church tower dissolving into the night sky. 'But I never meant to bring her to this.'

'She was the kind to destroy herself.'

'Or others. Yes. You're right.' After a little while he added, 'I'll leave when the funeral's over. It will be perfectly easy. Everyone will think I have a broken heart. Titus will be all right. His grandmother will bring him up. She'll always know him as Blane's son. You and Soames, and Thomas Whitehouse, who would never betray his grandson, and I are the only living people to know the truth.'

'How are you so sure I'm to be trusted?' Sarah asked in a low voice.

'I have no doubt of it.'

'Where shall you go?'

'Who knows? The Caribbean, the South Seas. I'm a wanderer. I should have gone crazy with boredom, leading this kind of life for too long.'

They were riding up the long curving drive, the house standing pale and elegant across the meadow.

'It's a beautiful place,' Sarah said wistfully.

His voice was sharp with surprise. 'Don't tell me you had ambitions, too!'

'Let's call them dreams.'

She slid off her horse at the door. She could scarcely stand for weariness.

Blane said again sharply, 'What is this, Sarah? Had you some claim to this place?'

The great door was flung open before Sarah could answer. Lady Malvina stood there, swaying slightly, her arms outstretched.

'Blane, have you brought him back? Where's my grandson?'

'He's here, Mamma. Soames has him. He's perfectly safe.'

'Oh, thank God! Thank God! Ambrose and I heard the horses.'

'Ambrose!' exclaimeed Sarah.

Even before she saw Ambrose's lean self-possessed figure in the background she was aware of Blane's inquisitive eyes on her. His face was hard with suspicion.

Ambrose came forward quickly to greet her. He obviously intended to make no secret now of their relationship.

'My dear Sarah!' He took her hand and kissed it tenderly.

'You two appear to be old friends,' Blane's voice came with detached interest. 'Or should I say, more than friends?'

'Miss Mildmay! What is this Ambrose has been telling me?' Lady Malvina demanded. 'How long have you known each other?'

Ambrose answered for her. 'Sarah is my fiancée.'

Sarah withdrew her hand.

'We can talk later. At present Titus must be got to bed. Fortunately he's been asleep almost all the time. He knows nothing.'

'Nothing of what?' The fear was naked in Lady Malvina's eyes. 'Ambrose has beeen driving me mad with questions, and now you make these strange statements. Where's Amalie?'

'Lord Mallow will tell you, Lady Malvina.'

Sarah went to take Titus from Soames. She caught the look of cunning triumph in the man's eyes. He had stared at Ambrose with defiance and dislike. So that was another thing that had been in his mind. He had not wanted Ambrose to be master here. Their dislike had been mutual.

'Blane, what is this?' Lady Malvina was insisting.

'Amalie has had an accident, Mamma.'

The bleak words told her everything.

'Not dead?'

'I fear so.'

Lady Malvina clutched her throat. 'Do you want to tell me how?'

'Not now, Mamma. It was the result of her brainstorm.'

'It was more than a brainstorm, running off with Titus like that. I believe she was quite mad. Thank heaven Titus is safe. Blane, my poor boy! You look quite exhausted.'

'I'm all right, Mamma. Shall we talk about this in the morning?'

'No,' interposed Ambrose. 'It must be talked of now. You can't make these extraordinary statements and not explain them. What has happened to Amalie? How did she have this brainstorm? Sarah, give that child to Betsey. She's perfectly able to put him to bed.'

Sarah obeyed, handing the child to the elderly servant. Titus stirred for the first time. His heavy eyes lifted. 'Grandmamma?' Then he was asleep again.

'The little love,' said Lady Malvina unsteadily. 'Now come into the library and we'll have this out once and for all. But Ambrose, I ask you to have some delicacy, if you're capable of it. Remember that Blane has just lost his wife.'

'If she was his wife.'

'Oh, I know you have this fantastic story about Samantha and tombstones and suchlike, but we really can't believe them at this hour of night.'

'Sarah must know the truth by now,' Ambrose said pointedly. 'You've been putting two and two together, haven't you, my dearest? Tell me what opinion you have formed. Is this man Blane Mallow? Was Amalie his wife? Is that boy just carried upstairs his son? Come, you don't need to be afraid any longer to tell what you know. I'm here to protect you. We're simply fighting for our rights.'

Blane had not spoken. He stood negligently leaning against the mantelpiece. His gleaming eyes were fixed on Sarah. His expression told her nothing. She looked from him to Ambrose. She had thought she loved Ambrose, she reflected in astonishment. He was so handsome, so elegant and cultured, so sure of himself. He had represented a kind of life she had thought immensely desirable.

But she had not realised he was so cold. His eyes were the colour of the lake water.

'Ambrose went to the West Indies to discover all these things,' Lady Malvina said. 'But he seems to have failed. He has no proof of anything. And he a barrister, too, with a trained legal mind. But Miss Mildmay, is it really true that you're his fiancée? How could you be so deceitful?'

Sarah didn't enjoy meeting the hurt old eyes. Suddenly Blane answered for her.

'The Mallow diamonds suited her very well. And I grant you, she loves this house. Everyone has ambitions, Mamma. Why shouldn't Miss Mildmay?'

He was mocking her. He was accepting the challenge. He was an adventurer. He lied with amazing ease and versatility. He had tried to secure the Mallow inheritance for a bastard. He had no sympathy for Ambrose's rights. But her decision as to how she would act in this situation had been made when she had seen Ambrose standing in the hall. Or had it been made weeks ago?

'I haven't found out anything of account, Ambrose. To the best of my knowledge this man is Blane Mallow, and Titus is his son. As far as I know, Mrs Stone was a dishonest vagrant, and Amalie was Blane's wife. Both of these women are tragically dead, so now I fear we'll never know if anything is different from what we imagine.'

Ambrose's gaze was narrowing in disbelief, and a frightening cold anger. Sarah had seen that expression only once before, just before he had sailed for the West Indies. She hoped fervently never to see it again. It was as if she were waking from a dream.

'So I must release you from your promise to me, Ambrose. You must marry an heiress, as I advised you at the beginning. You'll soon forget me, I assure you.'

She didn't add that she realised now she had never loved him. Poor Ambrose, one must spare him that final humiliation.

She turned to Lady Malvina to say sincerely, 'I apologise for my deception to you, Lady Malvina. I thought at the time that I was justified, but I realise now that I was not. I also apologise to you, Lord Mallow.'

The man at the fireplace didn't move.

'I shall arrange to leave tomorrow morning. Titus will be very happy with his grandmother, and perhaps a tutor could be arranged for him shortly. He's getting too big for a governess.'

She withdrew a step. 'So may I say goodnight, and goodbye?'

'Sarah!' Ambrose protested, in a frozen voice.

'Leave her,' said Blane.

'But, Blane, must Miss Mildmay go like this?' Lady Malvina said peevishly. 'I admit she's been very deceitful and secretive, but Titus loves her. And so, I believe, do I.' The old lady sank into her chair, her affectionate blurred gaze on Sarah. 'Heavens, I'm tired. Let's forget this and go to bed. Tomorrow we can go on as usual.'

'Not as usual, Mamma. I'm sorry. I'm afraid Sarah must go.'

'You call her Sarah!' Ambrose burst out. 'You always were a mannerless cad!'

'Thank you, Ambrose. So at last you credit me with a past.' He turned to Sarah. 'I shall take you to London myself. After all, everyone must agree, especially you, Ambrose, that this is no place for impostors.'

'Sarah! Will you go with him? What would your family say? Your cousin at Balmoral?'

Cousin Laura, thought Sarah, was not likely to bother herself too much about a penniless relative's exploits. But her sisters, Amelia and Charlotte, with their dull existences, were going to be deeply envious. And Aunt Adelaide was going to say drily that as usual Sarah had done the unexpected, which was hardly the way to get a husband.

'Some day, Lord Mallow,' she said, her eyes downcast to hide their leaping joy, 'I hope you will meet my cousin Laura. When she is free from her duties with the Queen. But I myself don't intend to take another imprisoning situation. I haven't the disposition for this kind of life. I think I will travel. So I will be happy,' she lifted her eyes to his shatteringly bright gaze, 'to begin my journey with you.'

THE MILLIONAIRE'S DAUGHTER

DOROTHY EDEN

The unforgettable nineteenth-century love story of a beautiful American heiress.

Christabel Spencer's life had been carefully planned before she was even born. For her father had decided his daughter should have everything. And as New York's newest millionaire, Harry Spencer believed that money could buy it for her.

And Chrissie was as beautiful as she was rich. Surely this combination would be irresistible to an eligible English aristocrat. But Chrissie knew she could not live without love – and she would find it at any cost . . .

'Quite the best novel Dorothy Eden has written yet . . . It is good reading, and vastly entertaining.'
Publishers Weekly

CORONET BOOKS

THE HOUSE ON HAY HILL

DOROTHY EDEN

Mistress of the light touch Spinner of the heart's dreams Compelling storyteller

Dorothy Eden has shown in her novels that she possesses an extraordinary insight into the secret ways of the human heart. These stories, collected together for the first time in book form, prove again that no-one knows its passions, betrayals and jealousies better than she. *Love* is her theme; while the title story also sees her on top form as mistress of suspense . . .

'Miss Eden is a most accomplished storyteller'
Homes and Gardens

'From the first page of all her books Dorothy Eden never fails to intrigue'
Books and Bookmen

CORONET BOOKS

ALSO BY DOROTHY EDEN
IN CORONET BOOKS

All these books are available at your local bookshop or newsagent, or can be ordered direct from the publisher. Just tick the titles you want and fill in the form below.

Prices and availability subject to change without notice.

CORONET BOOKS, P.O. Box 11, Falmouth, Cornwall.

Please send cheque or postal order, and allow the following for postage and packing:

U.K. — One book 19p plus 9p per copy for each additional book ordered, up to a maximum of 73p.

B.F.P.O. and EIRE — 19p for the first book plus 9p per copy for the next 6 books, thereafter 3p per book.

OTHER OVERSEAS CUSTOMERS — 20p for the first book and 10p per copy for each additional book.

Name...

Address..

....